HALO®
BATTLE BORN:
MERIDIAN
DIVIDE

HALO®

BATTLE BORN:

MERIDIAN DIVIDE

CASSANDRA ROSE CLARKE

SCHOLASTIC INC.

© 2019 Microsoft Corporation. All Rights Reserved. Microsoft, Halo, the Halo logo, and 343 Industries are trademarks of the Microsoft group of companies.

All rights reserved. Published by Scholastic Inc., *Publishers since 1920*. SCHOLASTIC and associated logos are trademarks and/or registered trademarks of Scholastic Inc.

The publisher does not have any control over and does not assume any responsibility for author or third-party websites or their content.

This book is a work of fiction. Names, characters, places, and incidents are either the product of the author's imagination or are used fictitiously, and any resemblance to actual persons, living or dead, business establishments, events, or locales is entirely coincidental.

Library of Congress Cataloging-in-Publication Data available

ISBN 978-1-338-28099-9

10 9 8 7 6 5 4 3 2 1   19 20 21 22 23

Printed in the U.S.A.   23

First printing 2019

Cover illustration by Antonio Javier Caparo

Book design by Betsy Peterschmidt

CHAPTER ONE

VICTOR

An explosion rippled across the field, sending up waves of black smoke. Victor slammed into the ground, fingers curling around his rifle.

"What happened?" Evie's voice crackled in his ear. "The map just lit up!"

"Orvo saw me," Victor muttered, hunched down low in the tall golden grasses. The motion sensor display in his HUD monocle blinked rapidly. Saskia was approaching.

Victor scrambled to his feet and ran along the wall of fire, coughing against the smoke. He ducked his head down, hoping the flames would be enough to keep him hidden from the watchful digital eye of Orvo, the AI that currently had them trapped here in the shadow of Hestia V, the planet they were orbiting.

"Victor, what are you doing?" Evie said. "Saskia's headed toward *you*. That was the plan."

"Yeah, but the field is burning!" He slowed to a jog, crouching down beneath the black clouds of smoke pouring off the smoldering grasses. He could just make out Saskia through the haze, a slim figure barreling toward him with a battle rifle slung over her shoulder.

"I see her," he said to Evie. Then he took a deep breath and launched himself over the low-burning fire, feet pounding as he moved to intersect with Saskia.

"He can see us!" he bellowed, cupping his hands around his mouth. "Turn around!"

Saskia faltered, lifted her rifle. Heat rolled across the prairie in waves, thick and choking.

"Turn back!" he shouted, just as another swell of heat exploded out of the dirt behind him. He lost his footing and plunged forward. Saskia caught him in one smooth movement, dragging him toward the outcropping of rocks they'd been using as a shelter.

"Victor!" Evie shrieked. "Tell me you're okay."

"I'm fine," Victor muttered. "We're getting the hell out of here."

"You were able to get ahold of Evie?" Saskia asked, glancing at him out of the corner of her eye as they tore through the waist-high grasses.

"Yeah. She has no idea where she is either."

Saskia groaned, shaking her head. The shelter loomed up in the distance, the rocks a faint promise of safety. And failure.

Victor really thought his plan would have worked. Keep low in the grasses, get to the comm station down by the creek so Evie could send him the map. But Orvo had spotted him anyway.

At least Saskia wasn't pulling any kind of I-told-you-so. Dorian probably would, though.

They darted through the gap in the rocks and into their makeshift shelter, where Dorian was crouched over a comm pad that emitted a glowing terrain map of the prairie.

"Knew it wouldn't work," he said without glancing up from the map.

Victor rolled his eyes.

"I'm thinking he's got a camera—here." Dorian enlarged the holo and pointed with one finger. The map gleamed with thatched white lines. The fire. "Both times the flames went up, you were in this area." He circled with his finger.

"So we try again," Victor said. "And avoid it."

Saskia glanced at him. "There could be more cameras."

Dorian tilted his head, shrugging a little. "Maybe. We know we've got a clear path here"—he traced his finger along the map, cutting straight through the flames—"but out here? No idea." He waved his hand around wildly. "And we still aren't sure how far it is to Evie."

Victor slumped back, arms crossed over his chest, thoughts whirring. Saskia crouched down beside Dorian and frowned at the map. All Evie knew was that she was trapped in some kind of structure—no windows, the door barred. While the three of them had been trying to figure out the best way to evade Orvo, she had been hacking away furiously on the computer ONI had left in the room for her. It was the one tether between her and the rest of the group—at least, it had become one, once Victor managed to scrounge up the comm pad Dorian was currently using to create their map.

Two days ago, the four of them had learned they would be playing Capture the Flag. It was a huge surprise when it turned out Evie was the flag.

Orvo is toying with us, Victor thought. Everything seemed easy on the surface—a simple game, Evie locked up with her biggest strength. But the game had split them up, and Evie hadn't been able to highlight her location, no matter how deep she went into the base's systems.

Victor crawled forward, studying the map. *Simple on the surface.* Just like their path across the prairie. He should have known better.

Dorian sighed and tapped the comm, shrinking the map down. Dust from the rocks flitted around in its wake.

"Now what?" he asked. "Clearly, charging across the prairie isn't going to work."

Evie's biggest strength, Victor thought. *Simple on the surface.*

"The comm pad," he blurted. "The answer's on there."

Dorian rolled his eyes.

"No," Victor said. "Listen." He glanced over at Saskia, and she nodded at him, eyes bright with encouragement. He felt a little flutter of his old crush and threw her a big grin. Then he turned back to Dorian. "Everything keeps seeming like it's going to be easy, right, but there's some twist. They tell us we're playing Capture the Flag—well, we've done that before, no big deal, right? Except—"

"Except they split us up," Saskia said.

"And gave Evie a computer. Like, straight up *gave* her one. But it hasn't been any help, other than us talking to each other."

"What are you getting at?" Dorian said.

Victor pointed at the comm. "They're forcing us to play *against* our strengths. Orvo knows what we're going to do, and created a puzzle that challenges those instincts."

He sat back, triumphant. Dorian just blinked at him.

"So what does that have to do with the comm pad?" he asked.

Victor sighed. "Don't you get it? Saskia knows the weapons, you're the terrain guy, I'm—" He gestured, hoping one of them would say it for him. He was the one willing to blaze across the prairie—to do whatever it took to get the mission done. Ever since Meridian, he'd gotten braver.

"The muscle?" Saskia said uncertainly.

"Whatever. None of us are *hackers*, really, the way Evie is. So that's where the answer is." He nodded at the comm pad.

"It makes sense," Saskia said carefully. "It seems like something Orvo would do."

It seemed like something ONI would do too. None of the training Victor and the rest of them had received on the UNSC military base had been straightforward. Not from the moment they arrived. But it had been useful. Victor couldn't deny that.

"Well, get Evie on your HUD," Dorian said. "Have her walk us through it."

Victor wondered if getting in touch with Evie had been part of Orvo's plan. Hard to say.

"Evie?" he said into the microphone. The HUD on his monocle flickered, and then Evie's voice came through, striated with static.

"What happened?" she asked. "Is everyone okay?"

"We're all fine," Victor confirmed, switching on the speaker so all three of them could hear her responses. "We think the key to finding you is in this comm pad we scrounged up. The thing is, we're going to have to go in and look around, and you're—"

"Stuck in a tin can." She laughed. "Seems about right. What are you thinking it's going to be?"

Victor glanced at the others.

"The map," Dorian said suddenly. "We both have one, right?"

"Yeah," added Victor. "And Evie was able to see the explosions live."

"Bring it up," Evie said. "I'm doing the same on my end."

The map materialized in the air above them. The fires still lit up white hot on the holo, crisscrossing the terrain.

"Tell me what you see," Evie said. "Let's make sure it's the same."

Dorian's eyes flicked across the map. "We've got the fires. The prairie. Basically what we can see if we look out past the rocks."

"Are the rocks marked? I can see them on mine."

"Yes," Saskia said, pointing at a bright dot in the bottom of the corner of the holo.

But Dorian shook his head. "That's not the rocks; that's our location. I could track you running across the field earlier. Is that what you're seeing, Evie?"

"No," she said, and Victor felt a jolt in his chest. *We're getting somewhere.* "This is stationary. I can't actually see where you guys are." The line went quiet.

"What other differences are there?" Saskia said. "Our map doesn't have much of anything on it. Just stuff we've already discovered."

"Except for the rocks," Dorian said.

Simple on the surface, Victor thought. But maybe things could be complicated on the surface too.

"She's under us," he blurted out. "Her map isn't marking the rocks; it's marking her *location*—"

Gunfire tore across their sanctuary—dirt and chunks of stone exploding into the air. Victor shouted and dove for cover, scrambling toward the edge. He could hear Saskia gasping behind him and Dorian cursing. Victor heaved himself out from between the rocks and helped pull Saskia out after him. The air was still thick with ash and smoke.

"Well, I think you might be onto something." Dorian emerged from cover, his face streaked with dirt. "How did we not see those guns in there?"

"They came out of the rocks," Saskia said. "The rocks must have been decoys. Artificial."

Victor groaned. Already he could hear Orvo's condescending debrief: *You children shouldn't be so* trusting.

Evie's voice spilled through the speaker. "—come in. Victor? Dorian?"

"We're here." Victor stared at the rocks.

"I heard gunfire," she said. "Not over the headset. From—outside."

Immediately, the guns started blazing again, light and dust exploding from the outcropping.

Saskia reached over and grabbed Victor's helmet and then stomped on the receiver with her heavy booted foot.

"What the hell!" Victor sputtered.

"That's how Orvo is listening in," she said. "Or maybe just pro-grammed the guns to react to key words. Either way, no more field helmet."

"I'm going to get *charged* for that thing," Victor ground out.

"Sorry." She didn't sound sorry, though. "The turrets on the fence back in Brume-sur-Mer had been like that. Programmed to react to certain sounds."

"Fine!" Victor said, throwing his hands in the air. "But how do we know there aren't any sensors down there? You said yourself the rocks were probably fake."

"Because Orvo didn't want us to be able to talk with Evie," Dorian said. "Of course there are sensors down there: They've been monitor-ing us the whole time. But this was about us bending the rules."

The gunfire stopped. Victor's ears rang in the silence.

Dorian leaned over the rocks. "Isn't that right, Orvo? You didn't want us doing anything you hadn't planned?"

No answer save for the crackle of fires in the distance.

Saskia knelt at the rocks. "We need to figure out how to get to Evie," she said.

Nothing happened—no gunfire, no *actual* fire, nothing.

She glanced at Victor over her shoulder. "Told you." She smiled.

Victor shrugged. "Fair enough."

"So now what?" Dorian asked. "We scoured the rocks earlier. There was no sign of an entrance."

"Maybe it's not in the rocks themselves," Saskia said. "We didn't look closely enough at the surrounding land."

Dorian considered this, shrugged.

"Fan out," Victor said. "See what we can find. And be careful. I imagine Orvo isn't going to let us get to Evie that easily."

The other two nodded. Saskia pulled her pistol out of its holster and moved north. Dorian went west. And Victor went east. The prairies were still burning to the south. He only hoped the entrance wasn't hidden under the flames.

Victor pushed through the waist-high grasses, hitting at them with the butt of his rifle so that he could see the strip of dry dirt beneath. Hot, smoky wind blew up from the fires, and Victor wiped the sweat from his forehead. Hestia V floated pale in the sky. On the other side of it was Meridian, Victor's home. On the other side of Hestia V was the Covenant.

Victor shook the thoughts away; he had to focus on finding the entrance and getting to Evie. Doing well in their training here on Tuomi Base was the only way he was getting back to Meridian, to Brume-sur-Mer.

Suddenly, plasma fire ripped across the prairie. Victor jerked around, rifle raised and ready, aimed in the direction of the sound. North.

Saskia was firing her pistol into a hulking rumble of machinery, its curved, insect-like lines familiar and terrifying. For a moment, Victor was seized with a wild panic—the Covenant had found them.

But then Saskia called out, "It's guarding the entrance! A little help?"

The entrance. ONI must have reconfigured a Covenant Locust— one of their automated, weapon-mounted walkers—for training. Victor raced forward, slicing through the grass. Dorian was headed toward them as well, a dark speck in the distance.

Saskia's pistol clicked, and she tossed it aside. Pulling her rifle around on its strap, she fired it at the turret, already charging up with a pale pink light.

Victor fired off a round from his rifle, not that it did any good. Plasma sliced through the air and ignited the grasses with a plume of smoke. Saskia vanished behind the fire.

"Saskia!" Victor shouted, pumping his legs harder. The turret on the Locust tilted toward him, and he lifted his gun and fired off three shots before the plasma beam shimmered hotly through the air. He dove to the ground, rolling through the grasses.

There was a hole, big enough that the Locust must have crawled out of it. But there were stairs too.

His heart surged. They'd found it. But knowing Orvo, they were going to have to take out this Locust before they would safely be able to enter the structure. Good thing it was something they'd done before.

"Victor." It was Saskia, emerging from the grass. Dirt smudged her face. "Where's Dorian?"

"I saw him—"

An explosion rang out, fire and plasma erupting over the prairie. Victor slammed into the ground, his ears ringing. Everything sounded fuzzy and far away. But the Locust had toppled, three of its four armored legs now nothing but black chunks. The Locust's cannon housing had been neutralized, and it now hung at an angle, its muzzle pointed into the ground.

On the other side of the smoke was Dorian, holding up his assault rifle and grinning.

"Got it!" he called.

Victor rolled his eyes. Saskia laughed, crawling shakily to her feet. "You learned that from me."

Dorian grinned. "Right into the ventilation shaft," he said.

"We're not there yet," Victor said, trudging over to where Dorian stood. Black ash flaked off the remains of the machine and trailed through the air, stinging Victor's eyes. He refilled the magazine on his rifle and then edged toward the hole in the ground. Metal stairs gleamed, shining and out of place among the smoke and the grass. Victor watched them warily.

"You know Orvo has something else planned for us," Saskia said in a low voice.

Victor nodded. "I'll be the scout."

The three of them moved forward. Victor pressed one foot lightly on the top stair, then followed with the rest of his weight. Nothing happened. He moved down, gun up and ready, descending into the gleaming underground room. Lights blinked in the walls: cameras. Orvo wanted them to know they were being watched.

"Clear!" Victor yelled out when he touched down at the base of the stairs. He swept his gaze around. The walls were smooth. No sign of a door. He thought of the wall that had surrounded Saskia's house back in Brume-sur-Mer, the way the gate had materialized with her touch.

"I think it's the same tech as your parents' home defense system," he said when she and Dorian had made it in. "Door hidden in the wall."

Saskia frowned. "If it's like the defense system at my house, then you have to know where the door is in order to access it. And I'm sure there's a code."

Once again, they needed Evie's hacking skills. He sighed. "Too bad you stomped on my HUD."

Saskia gave him a sideways look. "Even if we had it, I bet those things wouldn't have let us get down here." She jerked her chin at the wall. "You can actually see the guns here."

"She's right," Dorian said, and she was. Dark circles ringed around the top of the walls, peering down at them. Muzzles.

"I bet we can still get to Evie, though." And with that, Dorian marched up to the far wall, the one, Victor realized, that was closest to the rock outcropping. Then he lifted his gun and banged the butt hard against the wall.

"Evie!" he shouted. "You hear us?"

Silence. Then:

A faint tapping. Two slow taps, three quick, over and over again in an unmistakable pattern.

Saskia shouldered her gun and moved up to the wall, leaning close, eyes half-closed, listening. She pressed one hand against the wall, slid it along. Then, abruptly, a holographic keypad materialized.

"Found it!" she said.

"What's the code?" Victor said.

The tapping was still echoing from inside the wall. Two slow taps, three quick.

Saskia pressed the two, then the three. Nothing. She tried again. Still nothing.

"Dammit," Dorian muttered.

The tapping stopped. The silence buzzed in Victor's ears.

Then it picked up again. The same tempo, all quick: one-two-three-four-five. A pause. One-two-three-four-five.

Saskia's face lit up. "Got it," she whispered, pressing the *five* key.

Immediately, the keypad vanished and a doorway slid open, revealing a narrow room and, at its center, Evie, already leaping to her feet and rushing toward them.

"I can't believe that worked!" she cried. "They had me playing these dumb puzzles, and the answers were always two, three, five." She laughed and threw her arm around Saskia in a quick friendly squeeze.

"Congratulations." Orvo's deep, sonorous voice echoed through the room. "You have successfully completed the exercise. Completion time nine point seven hours. Please report to Commander Pereira immediately for debriefing."

All four of them groaned. "We don't even get to clean up?" Dorian yelled.

"No," Orvo said, almost cheerfully. "She wants to speak with you while the exercise is still fresh in your minds."

"Never ends around here," Dorian said, but he headed toward the stairs, just like the rest of them.

CHAPTER TWO

EVIE

vie lay down on her bunk with her comm pad. She had a couple of messages waiting—one from her dad, through the civilian channel, and another from her mom, through one of the UNSC channels. It was still strange getting messages from her mom like that, as if they were both part of the military now.

You are, she thought. *Technically.* Which was an even stranger thought.

Evie opened her father's message first. The holographic image of him waved at her, grinning. "Hate that I can only leave a recording," he said, and Evie smiled a little at that. It was true too that it stung, knowing that she hadn't been able to speak to both of her parents directly in nine weeks, ever since they arrived at the base. Not that she'd have been able to, even if instant communication across the galaxy were possible. Her training just kept her so busy.

Her father went on, telling her about settling in at the new colony the Brume-sur-Mer survivors had been sent to after Evie, Dorian, Saskia, and Victor, along with a Spartan super-soldier named Owen, had flown them off Meridian. It was on the other side of the Outer

Colonies, a few weeks away. Too far for her to visit. She had only seen his new apartment—he kept calling it *their* new apartment, but she couldn't think of it that way at all—through his messages. UNSC had provided the apartment and all its furnishings, a thank-you for the work Evie and the others had done. He was going to be teaching at the colony's local university once the next semester started up. Sometimes, Evie wished she were with him, getting ready to start her own classes at the colony school. But she also knew if she hadn't teamed up with the others when the Covenant invaded, there was a good chance no one would have made it to the colony. And that was why she was still here, dodging practice gunfire and letting herself get locked up in a tiny metal room.

Because the Covenant were still on Meridian, still searching for Forerunner artifacts. And when they got what they came for, they would glass the entire world.

She couldn't let that happen. None of them could.

Her father finished off his message with an *I love you* and an *I'm proud of you*; then it flickered away, replaced by the face of her mother, hair pulled back regulation-style, the collar of her UNSC uniform just peeking into the frame. Her expression was serious, her eyes worried.

"I got your last message." She leaned closer, her holographic face looming in the space above Evie's bed. "It really sounds like they're pushing you through that training fast, huh?"

Evie's chest knotted up. *They are?* She had only told her mother the barest details in the last message, assuming that if she went into too much detail they'd be censored anyway, since her mother likely didn't have the clearance to hear about Evie's assignments.

"I know they've sweetened the deal for you," her mother went on, "all those scholarships and such. But just—be careful. Okay? I don't want to lose you before they have a chance to pay out."

Evie smiled a little at her mother's worries, but her expression told Evie she wasn't joking. Evie watched the rest of the message with a dull ache in her chest, and when it was over, she left the hologram running, empty light swelling in the air above her bed. Their training was scheduled for ten weeks, the same as UNSC basic, but there was just so much to learn, it almost did feel like they were rushing. Dorian had even commented on it a few days ago, before they were informed they'd be playing Capture the Flag.

"You think everyone in UNSC had to learn as much as us?" he'd asked. They'd been eating in the mess hall, the two of them separated from the UNSC soldiers who were at the base to help establish a foothold against the Covenant occupation of Meridian. It was loud and bright and noisy, and Evie had felt small and unwelcome, especially without Victor and Saskia, who had been helping Commander Pereira at the time. None of them ever interacted with the base's usual population, recruits brought in from the ranks to monitor the fighting on Meridian.

Technically all four of them were doing the same thing, but their situation had always been different. They had been high school students who became soldiers when the Covenant invaded Brume-sur-Mer and started drilling in the center of the town, chasing after an ancient Forerunner artifact. Even with her head full of protocols and regulations and prioritized directives, Evie still didn't feel like a soldier most of the time.

Back at the mess hall, she had shrugged off Dorian's question, even if she did agree with him, to an extent. But she also thought that perhaps it only felt abnormal because nothing about their experiences since the invasion had been normal. Dorian had always been eager to question authority anyway. Maybe too eager.

Or maybe not. Evie stared at the hologram of her mother's serious expression, the worried lines etching out from the corners of her eyes.

Two hours later, Evie headed down to the Tuomi Base command center for weekly cleaning duty. No breaks during ONI training: Two measly hours were all she and the others got between the Capture the Flag debrief and the tedium of running a disinfectant stick over the base's old-fashioned consoles.

The lights in the building were already on when Evie arrived, each window lit up bright yellow against the falling purple twilight. Cleaning duty had been the first assignment Orvo gave Evie and Dorian when they arrived at the base. Their very first day, Commander Pereira herself had marched the four of them down to the blocky cement building set away from the base proper and handed them their cleaning supplies. Now, two months later, Evie felt like she knew the routine at the command center better than anything else she'd learned during their training.

Lights on meant one of the others had beat her to the command center, and sure enough, Dorian was already there, music pumping faintly out of the comm stations.

"Orvo's going to report you for that," Evie said from the doorway.

Dorian glanced up. The glow from the disinfectant stick stained his hands a brilliant blue.

"Pereira doesn't care," he said. "It's not like we can access anything important on these computers anyway."

Evie smiled and walked over to the rack of cleaning supplies. She'd been the one to show Dorian how to use the comm stations to patch into the music channel from the barracks; the Tuomi command center was so old it had taken her all of five minutes to do. Granted, while she'd been in the system, she'd seen that someone had gone in and patched in software updates to keep her or anyone else from retrieving data from the satellites monitoring the situation on Meridian, but Orvo had still sent a message through to inform her she was breaking rank.

That had been her first experience with the strict command structure on Tuomi Base. She still hadn't gotten entirely used to it.

"What do you want me to do?" she asked Dorian. "The usual?"

He made a grunt of affirmation, and she pulled out the sterilization mop and switched it on. She pressed it against the floor, the pressure from the cleaning light keeping it buoyed a few centimeters above the drab beige tiles. She swept it back and forth, listening to Dorian hum along to the jangly song coming out of the system.

"I'm surprised you know this one," she said.

Dorian gave a sad little laugh. "Remy was always listening to this singer," he said.

A pang of sadness stung at Evie's chest. Remy was Dorian's nephew. Another Brume-sur-Mer survivor who'd been swept off to the colony, along with Dorian's uncle Max. He'd told Evie a little about them, and Evie knew that he sent Remy a message every day, even if it was just a few minutes long.

"I feel like your nephew would have cooler taste in music than that."

Dorian laughed, more robustly this time. "I was always trying to educate him," he said. "I played him stuff like Weeping Carnage and Corroded Winter, but he just wasn't having it."

Evie grinned. "I can only imagine."

They fell back into working, not speaking, the music floating hazily around them. The command center was small and cramped and seemed to gather dust instantly, despite the officers who worked here during the day, drawing up plans for the defense of Meridian. Evie had gleaned from listening in on conversations at mealtimes that before the invasion Tuomi Base had been all but decommissioned. It had always existed for the purpose of monitoring Meridian, but in its early days, UNSC had used it to keep an eye on the insurrectionists who once sought to rise up against the local military presence and rend the colony from its ties to Earth. The base had lain abandoned for years, a barely habitable chunk of rock save for a slim belt around the equator. And that was where the base had been built.

Suddenly, the music cut out, the singers' shrill voices distorting as the sound careened away. Evie sighed. "Told you," she said. "Orvo doesn't want us messing in the comm station—"

The entrance to the command center slid open and a warrant officer stepped in, uniform crisp, insignia gleaming. For a moment, Evie forgot what to do, and she let the mop fall out of her hands. It cracked against the floor as she squeezed herself together for a salute. Beside her, Dorian was doing the same thing.

"At ease," he said after an awkward pause. Evie slumped, hand dropping to her side. All these protocols still didn't come naturally to her.

"You're both to report to room 34B immediately," the warrant officer said. "Captain Dellatorre needs to speak with you."

At the mention of Captain Dellatorre's name, Evie felt a grip of some emotion that might have been excitement and might have been panic. When Evie had first met Captain Dellatorre on board the *Sparrow*, she had introduced herself as Daniella, right before making the offer that would bring Evie and Dorian and the rest of their friends to Tuomi Base. It was here that Evie learned Daniella's rank in the Office of Naval Intelligence. Namely, that it was high.

If Captain Dellatorre wanted to speak with them, it only meant one thing: They were going back to Meridian.

The meeting room was located in the center of Tuomi Base, and as Evie sat in the plush seat, her fingers drumming nervously against the table, she was aware of the reality of the base spiraling out around her: the reinforced buildings, the monitoring equipment, the weapons, the weak atmosphere, and then the blackness of space. All those layers between her and the Covenant.

Victor was already in the meeting room, his back straight, his hands folded in front of him. He always looked like he was playing soldier these days. More than any of them, he had taken to the training at the base. Finally following in his sisters' footsteps, Evie supposed.

"Looks like they're sending us back," Evie said, her voice sharp in the room's silence.

Victor grinned, the military facade evaporating. "I hope so. I'm ready to get down there and kick some Covenant ass."

Dorian rolled his eyes.

"This is happening sooner than I thought," he said after a pause.

"We don't know exactly what's happening," Victor said. "We're just *hoping*." He grinned again, but Dorian's expression was full of foreboding.

The door opened. Evie tensed, but it was Saskia who dashed in next and took the seat across from Evie. Her skin was flushed, her hair damp with sweat; she must have been working out. Saskia tended to do that on days when Evie had messages waiting, like she could sweat away the pain of not being able to reach her own parents.

Too many times Evie had woken up to the soft glow of a comm pad, Saskia whispering into the recorder: "I don't know if you'll get this, but I just want you to know I'm okay. I'm trying." Always, Evie pretended to still be asleep as Saskia sent the message out into the colony communications systems. She never got anything in return.

At least Evie's dad would always ask about Saskia. That was something. But Evie knew it wasn't what her friend was looking for either.

"You really think they're going to send us back?" Saskia said. "Already?"

Dorian shrugged. "They've been rushing us through everything fast enough."

"We've been here almost ten weeks," Victor shot back. "That's a typical time for training. And besides, we already fought the Covenant."

The door whisked open and a pair of uniformed officers marched into the office. Victor immediately snapped to attention, and the others followed behind him.

"At ease," said Daniella—Captain Dellatorre—as she strolled in behind the officers in her slim-fitting UNSC uniform. She slid into the seat at the head of the table, tapped her comm pad, switched on the holo. Only after all this did she look up and make eye contact, glancing at each of the four in turn. When her eyes caught Evie's, Evie immediately straightened her spine.

Captain Dellatorre smiled.

"You all have done very well," she said, a gush in her voice like a teacher. It didn't suit her severe appearance, and Evie felt a shudder of dissonance that was quickly swept up by a rush of pride. Whatever doubts she had vanished. Maybe she *was* suited to military life after all. Just like her mother.

"Orvo has been giving me regular reports," Captain Dellatorre continued. "I'm extremely impressed by your teamwork, your problem-solving ability. Your fearlessness." She glanced up at Victor when she said this. "Although charging across a field armed with explosives was perhaps not the *wisest* course of action."

Victor sat up in his seat. "I didn't see any other option at the time, ma'am."

Captain Dellatorre smiled. "Fair enough. I can't question your commitment to the mission, at any rate." She leaned back in her chair, her expression serious once again. Evie clasped her hands beneath the table. Her palms were damp and hot with sweat.

"We've been monitoring the situation in Brume-sur-Mer," Captain Dellatorre said. "The Covenant are still searching, but they have to be getting close to whatever it is they're after. There isn't much space for them to cover in that area, and they've made no indication that they will be moving out of the vicinity of the town." She paused. "While the UNSC and Meridian's air and naval forces have been holding off the worst of the Covenant attacks, we can't guarantee the same opening to deploy will exist next week, or even tomorrow. We can't delay deployment any longer."

Evie knew it was coming, but hearing it out loud made her heart thrum. Three months ago, she had fought to get off Meridian. Now she was going back.

It felt like madness. But at least it wasn't a madness she would be facing alone.

"You really think we're ready?" Dorian said.

Captain Dellatorre looked at him. "I see not all of your training has stuck."

"You said it yourself," Dorian shot back. "We aren't training to be soldiers. We're going down to serve as part of a militia. So I'm not going to worry about protocol. Do you really think we're ready?"

"Come on, man," Victor muttered. "Of course we're ready."

Dorian ignored him, though. Evie knew he wanted to hear Captain Dellatorre say it. He wanted to see if she was lying.

"You've trained for almost three months," she said. "That's nearly equivalent to basic training, though *your* training was a bit more specialized than a normal boot camp. And as Mr. Gallardo has pointed out, you weren't exactly inexperienced when you came to the base."

Dorian stared at her, expressionless.

"You will be serving as part of a special task force to monitor the Covenant's interest in the Forerunner artifact underneath Brume-sur-Mer," Captain Dellatorre said. "All four of you have proven yourselves more than sufficient for the task. However"—and here she narrowed her eyes in Dorian's direction—"there might be some issues with your ability to follow orders."

Dorian said nothing. Evie knew he wasn't going to break first.

And the captain wasn't going to make him. She leaned back in the chair, her countenance smoothing over. "Luckily you'll be facing less rigidity with the Meridian militia. We don't necessarily want UNSC soldiers for this—it's better to have a team that knows the terrain." She smiled. "And that makes you all perfect for the task."

Dorian nodded once, accepting the answer. But Evie felt a flutter of fear in her stomach—was that a way of saying they weren't *really* ready, despite their training? But maybe it didn't matter. They weren't ready when the Covenant invaded twelve weeks ago, and here they were, sitting around a meeting table on Tuomi Base.

"You ship out tomorrow morning," Captain Dellatorre said, rising from her seat. "Good luck. Dismissed."

CHAPTER THREE

DORIAN

The bulkhead of the stealth transport shuttle shuddered against Dorian's back. He sat very still, staring straight ahead at the empty seats across from him. The ship was clearly designed to carry an entire platoon, but today it only carried the four of them, the heavy engines taking them away from the safety of Tuomi Base and across enemy lines into Meridian.

Evie sat to his right and Saskia to his left; both were quiet, had been quiet all morning. Evie had her doubts about all this, Dorian knew—they had talked about it a few times, in vague, circular conversations. But for all her doubts, she thought this was the right thing to do. Dorian agreed, but the real reason he was sitting on this shuttle was because he couldn't bear the thought of any more people dying. For Evie, the moral rightness was an abstract. For him—he still had nightmares about the high-pitched whine of the Drones, the cries of the people aboard Tomas's boat, the wide eyes of his friends the last time he'd seen them—

At least Remy and Uncle Max had survived. He wanted to make sure it stayed that way.

The shuttle jolted, flinging all four of them sideways against their jump seat restraints. Dorian braced himself on the seat's thinly cushioned back.

"Have we crossed over into the fighting?" Saskia asked, peering down toward the cockpit. The door was shut tight. "Already?"

"I don't know." The shuttle jerked again, then dropped suddenly. The g-forces tugged on Dorian's skull, and he choked back a swelling of vomit. Red emergency lights flashed along the floor, a line pointing toward the exit hatch. A reminder that they'd be jumping out of here soon enough.

"I'd say that's a yes!" Evie shouted as the shuttle jerked sideways again. Victor let out a whoop of excitement; Dorian had to suppress the urge to tell him to shut up. Ever since they'd escaped from Meridian he'd started buying into this military stuff completely.

"You kids are strapped in, right?" The pilot's voice pierced through the hold's communication system. "We're about to take evasive maneuvers."

And then the shuttle tilted into a free fall. The hull shook violently. *Impact*, Dorian thought, remembering the flight out of Meridian, how the ancient Insurrection ship he'd flown had jolted in his hands every time the Covenant hit them.

"We're hit," the pilot said. "Stay in place—"

Suddenly, the shuttle swooped up, forcing Dorian sideways against the seat. Another impact slammed through the hull, and the emergency lights began blinking wildly. A siren wailed up from inside the cockpit. He thought he smelled the acrid tang of burning fuel.

The cockpit door flung open and the copilot burst out, her face shining with sweat, her eyes bright with panic. For a half second, Dorian saw something burning around the shuttle's viewscreen before the cockpit door slammed shut again.

"You're deploying early."

"What?" Evie jerked herself straight up. "What do you mean?"

"The Covenant have augmented their defense lines since our last pass. There's no way we're getting through. So you're deploying early."

"How can we possibly—" Saskia started. Then her eyes went wide.

"What?" Dorian demanded. "What are you thinking?"

The copilot made her way to the far end of the shuttle, her hands bracing against the ceiling. "Drop pods," she said. "We weren't supposed to use them on this run, but we don't have any other opt—"

The shuttle careened sideways, throwing the copilot against the far wall. She caught herself like nothing had happened.

"Drop pods?" Victor said. "You mean like an SOEIV?"

"Yeah." The copilot slapped her palm against a sensor and the wall split open, revealing a dark, narrow walkway. The drop pods hung like ugly, metallic ornaments from the branches of a Christmas tree, and Dorian felt the weight of what was about to happen sink deep in his belly.

"We haven't been fully trained in this!" Evie protested. "We can't—"

"This shuttle will not survive full pass, the way these Covenant weapons are stripping through it," the copilot snapped back. "My job is to get you groundside at any cost. You need to get out now."

Fear seized Dorian's chest. He pressed his ear to the shuttle wall, listened to the engines shrieking up through the hot metal.

The copilot looked at him, her eyes dark. "I know you can hear it," she said.

Dorian closed his eyes. What he heard was not a good sound. He knew that much.

"Well?" said Evie.

"All right," the copilot said, clapping her hands together. "We don't have time to sit around debating this. The drop pods are programmed for this scenario. They'll get you down to the rendezvous coordinates. There's no other choice. We need to abandon ship, and we need to do it now."

Abandon ship. Dorian undid his buckle and stood up, blood rushing to his head. He moved forward without thinking, his heart pounding fast. The narrow hallway seemed to tighten as he crept toward it, lengthening in a dark hole that would drop them out into the black of space.

Another blast. This time Dorian felt the heat sweep up from the floor.

"Now!" the copilot screamed. "I've got to get you four out first before the crew can evacuate. Go, go!"

The others were jumping to their feet, making their way toward the drop pods. Dorian got there first. They'd done a few drop simulations while at Tuomi, a what-if scenario that Dorian never thought would actually come to pass. The drop pods were mainly operated by the UNSC's Orbital Drop Shock Troopers, soldiers who had been specially trained to deploy from high orbit. And that's what the drop pods did: jettison you from orbit through the atmosphere and down to the surface of a war-torn planet.

It was awkward clambering into the drop pod, situating his body into a casket-shaped object that would be launched out into real space, instead of virtual space.

"Face the hatch and strap in!" the copilot was shouting at Victor. "That's right. I'm going to walk you through the safety protocols—"

Another shudder. The siren wailed louder.

"—as fast as we can. Okay, hit the button on your right-hand side— that will run the systems check. Say *clear* when it's done."

Dorian watched the green light spiral through the drop pod's system, looking for flaws. Sweat dripped down his face. *It'll just be like flying that old scud-rider*, he told himself. *That thing was way more rickety.*

It also never left atmosphere.

The systems check finished. Dorian shouted, "Clear," joining a chorus of the others.

"Now we remove the safeties," the copilot called out. "First one is near your feet—"

Dorian moved by rote, pressing his thumb against one button, flipping another switch. The drop pod lit up. The shuttle siren screamed.

"We're ready!" The copilot's voice seemed far away. "Initiating countdown now."

A holographic light flicked on, right in Dorian's line of vision. *Thirty. Twenty-nine. Twenty-eight . . .*

He sucked in a deep breath of air. His heart hummed with panic. *Twenty-five. Twenty-four. Twenty-three . . .*

Everything was silent inside the drop pod except for his own panicked breathing. Silent and dark. He knew on the outside there was red light, the wail of a siren, the threat of plasma breach.

Fifteen. Fourteen. Thirteen . . .

Dorian closed his eyes. He was aware of the weight of the drop pod closing in around him, the tight squeeze of metal and ceramic and whatever else was supposed to keep him from burning alive as he fell through Meridian's atmosphere.

Five.

Four.

Dorian took one last long breath and thought about the music he had been creating the night the Covenant first attacked.

His bandmates. Xavier and Alex and Hugo. All of them had died.

Then he thought about Remy, frightened and dirty but safe as he emerged from the shelter beneath Brume-sur-Mer.

He was doing this for them.

Two.

One.

There was a breathless pause. Dorian thought the pod had malfunctioned.

Then the floor ripped out from under him.

He was falling.

It was all he was aware of, that sensation of falling. He closed his eyes against the force yanking him down toward the moon and tried not to think about the battle raging in the atmosphere around him. Even if the Covenant didn't fire on the pods specifically, one stray shot would be enough. After all, they had learned in training that was why the UNSC used these things—because it was better to lose one man than an entire team.

Dorian ground his teeth together. The temperature in the drop pod rose, a choking, enveloping heat that threatened to strangle him. He heard the shriek of ceramic as the outer layers of the pod stripped away.

Atmosphere. He'd made it to the atmosphere.

Relief swept over him as fast and sudden as the heat had. He sank back into his pod and let the memories of his brief training take over. The copilot had said the shuttle programmed their drop pods with the destination. He should land in the forest outside Brume-sur-Mer, where the shuttle had been taking them originally. Deep in the thicket of trees and underbrush, far away from the Covenant scavenging under the soil for some magical artifact.

Dorian could feel the pod slowing, the braking chutes kicking into action the way they were programmed. He let out a long, shuddering breath.

Prepare for Impact flashed in red letters in his line of vision, right where the countdown had been.

Dorian heard what he later realized was the scraping of tree branches against the side of the pod as it bounced back and forth. He fought against the dizziness in his head, the reminder that he was plummeting from the atmosphere.

Prepare for Impact flashed one more time. And then—

Impact.

Even with the restraints strapped across his chest, Dorian was flung forward into the hatch. He cursed and fumbled for the release. The hatch hissed open and exploded outward with a flash of light as he unstrapped himself and tumbled out onto the wet soft soil of the forest. His entire body ached. He lay in the damp underbrush, breathing in the smoke from the pod's entry, listening to the familiar rustle of the forest. He had gotten so used to that noise during his days fighting back against the Covenant. Hearing it now was like a jolt to his heart.

Eventually, he sat up, blinking. The pod lay discarded, the outer shell scorched black from atmosphere entry. Smoke twisted up from the charred, broken trees he had hit on his way in, shimmering in the dim sunlight. He stood up, legs shaking, trying to remember the training. There were supposed to be weapons inside those things. Supplies. Would this one be the same? The pods weren't intended for them, which meant they'd probably been intended for actual ODSTs—or Helljumpers as he'd heard them called at the base. He understood the nickname now.

That was when Dorian realized the rifle he'd been issued before deployment was still on the shuttle—in the rush to the drop pods, he must have left it strapped to the shuttle hull. Yet another reason why he wasn't cut out to be a soldier.

Dorian dragged himself over to the pod and tried to remember from the training holo how to dismantle it for the secondary weapon. He was in enemy territory; he would need to arm himself as well as he could before he went looking for the others.

His stomach twisted at the thought of them. With any SOEIV drop, there was the chance of failure, the possibility not only that they would be hit by enemy fire but that the pod would malfunction on reentry, or that it wouldn't slow enough for impact. He couldn't remember the exact percentages. But there had only been four of them. Six, if you included the two pilots.

Dorian crouched next to the pod. It was still giving off waves of heat from its reentry. That detail had been left out of the holo simulation, but there was just a latch to press—there. He fumbled around in the underbrush for a stick and then used it to pop the latch open. The outer shell of the pod slid away, revealing an MA5 rifle and a supply bag. Dorian grabbed the rifle and checked the ammo—two hundred rounds. The supply bag had a few days' worth of food rations, more ammo, a military comm pad. He shouldered it and stood up, cradling the rifle in front of his chest.

Then he started forward through the woods, keeping to the underbrush. The motions came back to him instantly. How many times had he done this in those weeks before the escape, trudging miserably damp through the rain? At least it wasn't raining now, although it would probably pick up again soon. Dorian calculated in his head—there were about another two weeks left of the rainy season. Then the storms would stop and they'd have to find some other cover to help them fight against the Covenant.

The wind gusted; Dorian caught a whiff of burning wood up ahead of him. He moved faster, ducking low-hanging vines and flat, glossy tree leaves. He wanted to call out, make it easier to find whoever it was, but he knew better. They were supposed to have landed deep in the woods, but he didn't know how deep they actually were.

He ducked around a feathery palm tree and found the smoldering wreckage of another drop pod. The hatch had been released. Dorian let out a long sigh of relief. Two definite survivors.

A branch cracked behind him; he whirled and found himself pointing his rifle at Saskia, who lifted her hands sheepishly.

"Sorry," she said. "I was trying *not* to sneak up on you."

Dorian let out a nervous laugh and lifted his gun. "You're fine. I'm glad to see you. Have you found the others?"

"Not yet. I just got out." She shook her head, her hair flying loose into her face. "That was . . . not something I ever want to do again."

"Yeah," Dorian said. "Me neither."

Saskia crouched down beside the pod and pulled her rifle out from its slot beside her seat. Figures *she* wouldn't leave it behind. "Did you notice where we landed?"

Dorian shook his head. "I was a little too worried about dying to remember to check out exact coordinates."

Saskia leaned into the pod's hatch and tapped at the holo display. "So was I," she said. "Fortunately, these things can tell us our coordinates after we've landed."

Dorian didn't remember that from the simulation, but then, Saskia always knew more things about weaponry and military material than the others did. That was what happened when your parents worked for Chalybs Defense Solutions. Their prototypes had come in handy during the escape from Meridian three months ago. Wouldn't have them now, though.

Saskia straightened up. "Good news is we landed pretty close to the original drop point. We just need to head"—she whirled around and pointed—"that way."

"Where are we exactly?" Dorian fell into step beside her.

"About five kilometers north of Brume-sur-Mer," she said. "Deep in the protected part of the forest."

Dorian snorted. "Not so protected now." Inside, though, he felt a tremor of nervousness. He'd known the area around town extremely well, thanks to the handyman work he'd done with his uncle. He'd never had any reason to go this far into the protected woodland that surrounded the town. Which left him wary. Uncertain. He liked knowing where he was.

Especially here. This close to the Covenant.

The woods were damp and thick and overgrown, and Saskia and Dorian had to stomp a path through the brush, slicing away vines with the butts of their rifles. Dorian had gotten used to the dry air at Tuomi, and the once-familiar humidity of Brume-sur-Mer choked him. It wasn't long before he was sore and sweating, as if he hadn't spent the last ten weeks undergoing accelerated UNSC training.

"I'd forgotten how much this sucks," he announced.

Saskia smiled at him. But then her smile evaporated and her expression went dark. She lifted her rifle. Dorian immediately forgot the thick air and his sore legs. He whipped his body around, peering into the brush where she looked, rifle ready.

"What'd you see?" he said as softly as he could.

She shook her head. "Something big," she breathed.

Dorian tightened the grip on his rifle and peered into the dark tangle of the forest. There—a shimmer of light. A shadow, moving toward them.

"Put your weapons down," said a familiar voice.

Dorian blinked. *"Owen?"* he said.

The figure emerged from the trees, two meters tall and enormous in Mjolnir armor, its photoreactive coating shining softly in the damp light, mirroring the tangle of vegetation around them. *That's new*, Dorian thought. Indeed, the armor in general looked different from what Dorian remembered—it must have gotten an upgrade in the last nine weeks.

The Spartan tapped the side of his helmet and his visor depolarized, and there was Owen, his young face dark with scars and a grim determination.

"You're fine," Owen said. "We have the area secured. I've already picked up Evie and Victor. Let's get you to camp."

"What about the pilots?" Dorian asked. "Didn't they make it?"

Owen looked up at the sky. "Haven't heard from them. They weren't coming here, though." He tilted his head toward the twist of vines and glossy leaves. "Let's get you situated. Welcome to the Brume-sur-Mer Militia."

CHAPTER FOUR

SASKIA

The camp was designed to blend in with the forest, syncamo tents shivering with reactive images of leaves and vines. Up close, everything looked warped, as if reality had shattered like a mirror. But Saskia knew that this kind of camouflage was meant to deter aerial surveillance. From up above, nothing would look unusual. A few years ago, her parents had been developing similar technology, trying to find a way to mask heat signatures to complement the visual disguise.

A face peered out from one of the larger tents, a man with dark skin and a few days' growth of beard. "You find the rest of them?" he asked, stepping out into the open. He wore a drab Meridian military uniform, a rifle strapped to his back.

"Yes, sir." Owen stopped, looked over at Dorian and Saskia. "This is Commander Marechal. He's overseeing the operation here in Brume-sur-Mer."

Saskia snapped to attention, and Dorian trailed behind a few beats later.

"At ease." Commander Marechal gave a half-hearted smile. "You kids know as much as ONI claims you do?"

Saskia glanced over at Dorian, unsure how to answer. Dorian frowned.

"These *kids* led over two hundred evacuees out of Covenant-occupied territory," Owen said. "Their knowledge of the terrain is unsurpassed . . . and they're not bad in a fight either."

Commander Marechal nodded, ducked back inside the tent.

"Some welcome," Dorian muttered.

"Marechal is your commander. He was one of the most decorated officers in the Meridian Special Forces," Owen said. "Be respectful."

Dorian glanced at Saskia and rolled his eyes.

Owen led them to a tent at the edge of the camp. "You'll be staying here," he said, pulling open the flap. Evie and Victor were both inside—Victor sprawled out on one of the cots, Evie staring down at a comm pad.

"Recovered the rest of the team," Owen said.

Evie glanced up and a smile broke out across her face. "Oh, thank god!" she cried, tossing the comm aside. She rushed over and threw her arms around Saskia, then Dorian. "I was really worried when I didn't see you. Victor and I landed fairly close to each other—"

"We were a bit off course," Saskia said. "I'm so glad you made it through okay."

Evie laughed. "Yeah, me too. I never thought for a second when we did that training that we'd actually wind up in one of those things."

"Yeah, me neither." Saskia smiled.

Victor ambled over to them, hands shoved in his pockets. "Yeah," he said. "I'm glad you came through okay." He wasn't exactly looking at Saskia, but she knew he was talking to her. He kicked at the floor. "I didn't think it was as bad as the simulation made it sound."

Dorian snorted.

"Get settled," Owen said. "Claim a cot, unload your supplies. I want to see all four of you at the camp center in five minutes." Then he ducked out of the tent.

Saskia took a deep breath and sank down on the cot next to Evie's. She dropped her bag and her weapon to the ground, letting herself ignore protocol as she collected her thoughts. Part of her was still shaking from the descent in the drop pod. She wasn't sure it would ever stop shaking.

"How long have you been here?" Dorian asked, slinging his own bag onto the remaining cot.

"Not long," Evie answered. "Maybe twenty minutes."

"Owen won't tell us anything," Victor said. "Said we had to wait for you two."

"I'm sure he's about to," Saskia said, staring up at the tent's green fabric fluttering overhead. The reactive camouflage flickered faintly on the other side. It was a far cry from their base of operations before. She wondered what had happened to her house. If the Covenant had rolled through and turned it to rubble.

The possibility didn't make her as sad as she thought it should.

She kicked herself up to standing and stepped out of the tent. The camp seemed quiet. Small. The mission brief she'd read had been, well ... brief, but it had said there were seventy-five soldiers. Why didn't this feel like seventy-five people?

She felt a hand on her shoulder—it was Evie, holding a hydration pack. "You should drink some water," she said quietly. "It'll help you calm down."

Saskia smiled, and the shaking seemed to subside. She took a long drink, the water sweet and cold on her throat. She hadn't realized how thirsty she'd been.

"We should head over to the briefing," Evie said, and Saskia nodded. Together they walked through the gently blowing tents, the flash of artificial flora. The chatter of human voices drifted on the wind, and the camp seemed livelier than it had when Saskia and Dorian had arrived. People moved from tent to tent, all of them with the rough expressions of soldiers.

"Look at the uniforms," Evie whispered. "Most of them are Meridian military. Very few are actually UNSC."

They stepped into a clearing in the forest, a round patch of damp ferns beneath the outstretched branches of a rain tree. About fifty people were gathered, standing in loose clumps, all of them armed.

Saskia felt suddenly very bare, having left her rifle back at the tent.

Dorian and Victor clomped up beside her and Evie. "Finally going to find out what we're here to do," Victor said.

"We know what we're here to do," Dorian answered. "Stop the Covenant from getting that artifact they want so bad."

Victor laughed. "Sure is taking them long enough, isn't it?"

Saskia frowned. It was taking a long time. Which meant they must be scouring every centimeter of Brume-sur-Mer. Which meant they had to be close to finding whatever was there.

If it *was* there. Maybe the Covenant were just shredding Brume-sur-Mer for no reason. Maybe they'd give up and glass the moon before she and the others even had a chance to fight.

Commander Marechal stepped into the clearing and jumped up on one of the arching roots of the tree. His presence immediately quieted the soldiers.

"Our remaining members have finally joined us," he said, voice soaring out through the clearing. Saskia wrapped her arms around her stomach as the crowd turned toward her, all those wary, appraising eyes.

"Look kind of young," a woman called out.

A swell of faint laughter. Commander Marechal frowned and held up one hand. "Knock it off," he said. "They're the same age most of you were when you joined up." He glanced at Owen, who was standing off to the side. "And the Spartan says they know what they're doing."

Owen nodded. "They can lead us through the terrain better than anyone."

"He keeps mentioning that," Victor said softly. "We can fight too."

Evie nudged him, hissed at him to be quiet.

"This is what we know," Commander Marechal said, and nodded at a serious-looking woman standing beside Owen, who immediately activated a holo map that shimmered in the air in front of the crowd. Saskia recognized the street layout of Brume-sur-Mer immediately, although half the map was blotted out by dark splotches—including the place where Saskia had led the survivors of the invasion out of the underground shelters a month ago.

"The Covenant is convinced there's a Forerunner artifact somewhere in this area," Commander Marechal said. "They have been drilling all over town and have not appeared to find anything yet, based on our surveillance intel. Our job is to find this artifact before they do and prevent them from reaching it."

A hand went up. Commander Marechal nodded.

"How do we know there's even an artifact here?"

Commander Marechal glanced at Owen. "You're the ONI liaison."

"We don't. Not for certain," Owen answered. "But the Covenant aren't exactly wrong about these kinds of things. They have instruments capable of locating Forerunner artifacts, and when those machines target a location, the Covenant don't stop until they find it. We've seen this play out repeatedly since the start of the war. It's out there somewhere."

Voices rose up in a mumble. Saskia kept staring at the map, looking at the places the Covenant had tried and failed to find the artifact. Downtown, of course. The high school. Several spots along the strip of public beach. She sighed.

"You will be going out in teams of four," Commander Marechal continued. "Spartan Owen will explain the details." He jumped down from the tree roots and stepped aside, Owen taking his place.

"Thank you, Commander." Owen gazed out over the soldiers. "The teams will search the places the Covenant have not been to yet. Since the artifact is likely underground, we will be using the tunnel system. That's where our latest arrivals come in."

Once again, all eyes fixed on Saskia and the others. She gave a thin smile, heat rushing up to her cheeks.

"Brume-sur-Mer has an extensive underground shelter, as well as a series of service tunnels. The Covenant are aware of it but aren't patrolling it in any way—after the escape a month ago, they did another sweep of the town, didn't find anyone, and resumed their excavation efforts. That gives us a distinct advantage." He nodded at Saskia and the others. "These four have been trained in reconnaissance and sabotage, and they know this area better than anyone here. They'll be leading our teams through the tunnel system. The rest of you will be responsible for providing tactical and combat support while we're searching for the artifact."

Victor made a strangled noise in the back of his throat. "He *knows* we can fight," he said furiously.

"Be *quiet*," Evie hissed. Saskia thought she looked relieved, though, that they were only here to serve as guides. Saskia knew she ought to be relieved too, but part of her was as disappointed as Victor. You couldn't easily distinguish yourself in the military if you were just a guide. And if she didn't do something of note, there was a chance that, when the UNSC found out about her parents' less-than-legal activities, she'd be held responsible too.

Sometimes Saskia wondered if she should have told the UNSC the things she knew about her parents' illegal weapons dealings, even though she had never been directly asked. But it was easier for her to dedicate herself to the UNSC and its mission. If the truth did come to light, and Saskia had proven her worth in the meantime, maybe the penalties wouldn't be quite so harsh.

"First reconnaissance mission leaves tonight," Owen said. "Flaherty, Rees, Zabinski, Latre: You'll be heading out with Saskia Nazari as your guide."

A spot on the map illuminated pale blue: the old tourist district, from back when the town still had tourists. Long before Saskia lived there.

"Intel says the Covenant are concentrating on this area," Owen said. "You will be heading down into the shelter to learn what you can." He nodded and the map vanished. "You leave in two hours. Dismissed."

Saskia splashed through a few centimeters of muddy water, her high-ankled boots keeping her feet dry. It was the last vestiges of the flooding, although evidence of the flood hung heavy throughout the underground shelter. Black splotches grew along the cement walls, and the air stank of mold, even through the filter she wore. Every now and then their lights swept over a filthy stuffed bear, a pile of rotting clothes, a flyer for a concert. A reminder that people had been down here before the corridors flooded.

Saskia felt a tap on her shoulder; it was Flaherty, the team leader. She gazed down at Saskia over her filter. "How much farther?" she asked, her voice distorted.

Saskia took a deep breath, glancing up at the walls. The distance markers were faded, but she could just make out a dusty *4*.

"A while," she said, pointing. "About four kilometers to the next exit. Although I'm not sure where the Covenant are drilling exactly."

Flaherty pressed her mouth into a thin line. "Which exit is it?"

"The one on Rue Coquillage," Saskia said. Was that where Dorian's band had played the night before the invasion? She knew it had been an entrance in the tourist district. But Rue Coquillage didn't sound right. "Entrance seven on the maps."

Flaherty nodded. "What's above us right now?"

"Houses," Saskia said. "Old tourist houses, so there should be service tunnels around here too, to take us off the main path." If they hadn't been destroyed. Dorian had pointed them out to her on the map even though they hadn't been marked, said people like his uncle had used them back when tourists still stayed in town. It was a way to get repairs done without being seen. Of course, the service tunnels had been sealed when the Covenant invaded. If Salome, the town's quirky AI, hadn't sealed them, they could've been used to access the shelter during the attack three months ago. But thanks to Evie's hacking skills, the tunnels were open again. She had gotten very good at working around Salome's complicated programming directives during the invasion. Three months ago, she had helped them bust out the trapped survivors . . . in her own way, at least.

Flaherty's eyebrows rose when Saskia mentioned the service tunnels. "Well, let's find one."

Saskia nodded and pushed forward through the grimy water. Her heart thudded. Why hadn't Owen sent Dorian out as the first guide? He was the one with all the knowledge of the town's layout. She hadn't even lived in the town proper.

They continued on, the only sound the splashing of water. Saskia swept her eyes over the walls, looking for the symbol Dorian had drawn for her on his comm: a stylized oval that almost looked like a closed fist. It might have been close to the old insurrectionist symbol. Decades ago, Brume-sur-Mer had been a stronghold for the colony rebels who pushed back against the UNSC's rule. But that was before humanity knew about the Covenant, and now the only thing that old symbol indicated was the location of a service tunnel.

Something flashed up ahead.

Saskia froze, lifting one fist to stop the others. She pulled her rifle around on its strap and held it tight.

Flaherty was at her side instantly, her own rifle pointed dead ahead. "I saw it too," she murmured. She gestured to the others and they fanned out in formation. "Stay with me," Flaherty told Saskia, and Saskia felt a rankle of annoyance; she had rescued two hundred people from these tunnels. She had even stopped an Elite from slaughtering them—more or less—on their way to the escape ship.

The team crept forward. Shadows slipped across the water.

Then there was the sudden burst of plasma fire, the tunnel filling with white light. Saskia flung herself up against the wall and fired into the light. Plasma bolts streaked past, exploding the wall into bursts of hot dust. She returned fire, and there was a strangled squawk and then the plasma fire stopped and the tunnel went dark again. Saskia blinked against the shadows.

"Everyone okay?" Flaherty asked.

A round of affirmations rang out. "I'm fine," Saskia said, blinking straight ahead. Her night vision slowly crawled back to her.

"Good, keep moving forward," Flaherty said. "Saskia, get behind me."

"You don't know where—"

Flaherty glared at her. "Get behind me. Look for the service tunnel entrance."

"We need to check that it's a clean kill," one of the others called out. Saskia still didn't know whose voice belonged to whom.

"It's too dark down here to risk it," Flaherty said. "It was likely just a Grunt. Stay alert and we should be fine. Now, let's move."

Saskia gripped her gun tightly as they proceeded deeper into the tunnel. She swept her eyes over the walls, desperate to find one of those service tunnel symbols—although if the Covenant were down here, they could easily have found them first. They could be excavating out of sight of ONI, and she and the rest of the team could walk straight into them.

Then she saw it, a pale smudge against the concrete. A flattened oval crossed with three diagonal lines.

"Wait," she said. "Stop." She couldn't remember the proper terminology. She broke away from the formation before anyone could answer.

"What is it?" Zabinski asked. "We shouldn't be stopping down here like this."

"It's a service tunnel," Saskia said. "Like you asked me to find." Except there was no entrance. No clear doorway. Just the symbol, barely visible beneath the encroaching mold.

Flaherty sighed. "I don't see anything, Nazari."

Suddenly, a loud, inhuman shriek tore through the tunnel, and the space filled again with blazing plasma light. A tall, avian figure raced toward them, screeching and hissing. A Jackal. It bounded through the water in wide, leaping strides. The team fired on it, but their bullets sputtered against the pale glow of its energy shield.

"Retreat!" shouted Flaherty, and Saskia immediately whirled around—only to find two more figures leaping toward them, their movements illuminated by their shields.

All of Saskia's breath left her body.

"Pull in!" Flaherty screamed, and the others fell into a tight circular formation, firing upon the approaching Jackals. Saskia froze. All she could think of was one of her parents' sales pitches she overhead once, their weapons laid out on the table in front of them as they shared the terrifying statistics on the likelihood of surviving a Covenant attack without the right weapons.

Statistics weren't on their side right now.

Plasma streaked past Saskia's head and she jerked down, her heart hammering. Then she looked over at the wall again. At the symbol. There had to be a way in. It was their only way out.

She pushed her rifle around to her back and dropped to her hands and knees. Desperate, she crawled over to the wall, feeling its surface for any kind of latch and opening. The shelters were old and low-tech; she doubted there would be any kind of holographic keypad or smart security system. But there had to be something.

Plasma fire erupted over her head. She pressed farther down into the water, hands fumbling over the wall, slick with water and mold.

Then she felt something. A faint indentation. When she pressed it, the wall groaned open, releasing a rush of muggy, musty air.

"This way!" Saskia screamed, ducking into the service tunnel. The stench of mold was worse in here, and something dark and wet peeled off the walls in thick strips. But it was clear the tunnel hadn't been opened in ages, and that could only mean it would keep them safe from the Covenant.

"Move!" Flaherty shouted. "Go, go, go!" The others poured into the tunnel. Saskia pressed up against the wall, feeling around for another activation button—there. She slammed down on it as Flaherty rushed past her. The walls shuddered toward each other.

A Jackal leapt between them, firing off its rifle. Saskia screamed and returned fire, blowing dark indentations into the metal of the door. The Jackal snarled something at her and tried to lunge forward, but it was caught by the door. It shot another round at her, half-heartedly, before ducking back out into the main tunnel.

The door slammed shut.

They were plunged into darkness.

Then there was a click and a sphere of light materialized up ahead. One of the team—Rees? Zabinski?—had activated a light.

"Good work, Nazari," Flaherty said, clapping one hand on Saskia's shoulder. She gave a wavering smile that Saskia doubted anyone saw. "Now, is there a way to jam that door before the Jackals find their way in too?"

Saskia's relief evaporated. Of course. The man with the light—it was Rees—came over to her side and held it up to the door. Saskia could just make out the screeches of the Jackals' conversation on the other side.

"I don't know," she said. "Dorian's the one who told me about the service tunnels." *Why* hadn't Owen just sent him? It made no sense.

"It was a mechanical latch," said another member of the team. *Latre*, Saskia thought with a spark. She was an engineer for the Meridian Army. "Old-rebel-style. Give me a minute." She pushed past Saskia and knelt down in front of the latch, frowning. The light bobbed over her head. The Jackals chattered outside the door.

Then Latre reached over and snapped the latch with a quick flick of her wrist. She stood up, turned to the others. Her face was hidden in shadows. "That should do it," she said. "I'll show you how once we're back at camp. Could come in handy again."

Almost immediately, a grinding sounded out from deep in the walls. Saskia froze, her heart pounding—but the door stayed put.

Latre grinned. "Told you. But that won't hold them forever. They'll try to blow their way in here next."

Flaherty looked over at Saskia. "You know how to get us out of here?"

Saskia took a deep breath. "The service tunnels were used to maintain the old tourist houses," she said.

Latre snorted. "And to smuggle Inny supplies, I imagine."

"That was fifty years ago," Flaherty snapped. "Saskia, go on."

"This should lead us to one of the houses," Saskia said. "I don't know where exactly we'll come out, though."

"So we'll need to be careful." Flaherty lifted her rifle, stock gleaming in the halo of the light.

They set off into the tunnel. Saskia walked alongside Flaherty again, hoping that Dorian was right about the service tunnels. She wondered too about what Latre had said—if the tunnels had been used by the Insurrection, they probably went all over town, probably all the way out to the woods. She felt certain there was one that led to the hangar where they'd found the old Insurrectionist ship during the rescue.

She filed this information away to take to Dorian and the others. If they had to be guides, at least they could be good ones.

CHAPTER FIVE

VICTOR

Victor couldn't believe this crap.

Why had ONI even bothered to send them to training if they were just going to be traipsing around the woods, something they had gotten extremely good at three months ago? What was the *point* of specialized training with ONI if they were just going to be glorified maps?

He pushed aside a damp fern with the barrel of his rifle and wound more deeply into the underbrush. The team marched softly behind him, their footsteps almost sounding like rainfall. He sighed and breathed in the faint toxic whiff of plasma from the Covenant installation in town.

They were deep in the woods, but they were close too. Coming at the drill site from the back. Pretty soon they'd start seeing the dilapidated old tourist houses.

He was leading the team toward 21 Rue Coquillage, where the service tunnel had expunged Saskia and her group twelve hours earlier. Their assignment was to explore the tunnels more thoroughly, see if there was any way to use them to access the drill site two blocks over.

A reconnaissance mission. Fine. They needed information before they could act. But when Victor had brought up the possibility of being involved in that action, Owen had just sighed, looked away. "Haven't you had enough of that?"

The question burned at Victor's thoughts as he swatted away vines and broken branches. Enough? His hometown was being drilled into dust and stopping it was something he was actually good at. Something he could actually *do*, something that for once in his life felt right and that made his family proud.

A flash of color appeared through the trees. Victor stopped, held up one fist. His team leader, Mousseau, stopped beside him.

"That's it?" he said. Mousseau was a great hulking mountain of a man, his voice and skin rough. He was the only one of the entire militia that came remotely close to Owen's size, but even he fell about a half meter short.

"That's it," Victor sighed.

Mousseau's dark eyes glittered. "You want to fight, kid?"

Victor just glared straight ahead, at the faded houses, at the dark smoke trailing up behind them from the drill site.

"Well, this is the first step."

"Yeah, I know," Victor snapped before he could stop himself. "Gather information, then enact a plan. But I'm not going to enact anything."

Mousseau glanced down at him. Victor's cheeks went hot. He wanted to defend himself, wanted to point out that he and the others had gotten almost three hundred people away from the Covenant and off the *moon* and there was no point in him just playing tour guide now that all of Meridian was at stake.

But Mousseau didn't say anything more about it, just gestured with one hand and called for the others, two men and a woman almost as gruff as he was. They had all served together as part of the same squadron on Caernaruan, the northernmost Meridian continent.

They walked single file down to the houses, Victor cutting a straight trail through the ferns with his rifle. Smoke twisted up toward the pale sky, dark, foamy streaks that made his stomach feel heavy.

"Keep a sharp eye out," Mousseau said behind him. "They're getting to work over there. Probably have some scouts around."

Victor gripped his rifle a little more tightly. He'd show them how well he could fight.

But they made it to 21 Rue Coquillage before any of the scouts made themselves known. When Victor saw the number *21* in faded gray lettering on the side of a big yellow house, he sighed in disappointment. Mousseau glanced over at him, smiled a little. Said nothing.

Mousseau pushed open the front door of the house, did a quick check, gestured for the others to follow him inside. The place was gutted, the floors littered with the detritus of Brume-sur-Mer kids sneaking out for the night: empty glass bottles, crumpled wrappings from the sandwich place around the corner, long since destroyed by the Covenant. Victor felt as if the air had been knocked out of him; he stood, swaying a little, remembering the time before the invasion. Saturday nights staying up, making props and miniatures for his holo-film, never being cool enough to come to parties at 21 Rue Coquillage.

But none of those cool kids were here now, were they?

He turned around and looked at the group. "The first scout team said they came out of the tunnel in the master bedroom closet. They said it looked as if there were additional service tunnels branching off from the one that led them here, and Dorian corroborated."

The team knew this already, but they indulged him. Mousseau nodded. "You heard the kid," he said. "Let's head to the tunnels."

The master bedroom was in the back of the house, a vast room with a rotting bed collapsing in the center. The closet door hung loose on its railing, and when Victor shone a flashlight inside, he saw only walls graffitied with various obscenities.

One of the other team members, Valois, chuckled and nudged at Victor. "Guess there wasn't much else to do around here, huh?"

Victor stepped into the closet, scowling. Before the invasion, he'd complained of the same thing, but hearing it from a stranger rankled him. He pointed the light at the walls, looking for the symbol that Dorian had shown him. Not that he could see anything through the graffiti.

"You sure this is the right place?" Valois asked.

Victor knelt down and ran his fingers along the wall, feeling for the indentation Saskia had described—there. Was that it? He pressed hard and the wall slid away, revealing a narrow metal stairwell.

He stood up and tossed the light at Valois, who fumbled for it and then shot Victor a dark look. Victor just grinned at him.

"All right, good job." Mousseau sounded bored. "Take it away, Gallardo."

They made their way into the service tunnel. It was narrower than the shelter tunnels, the ceilings lower. At times, Victor had to duck to keep from hitting his head. As he walked, he pictured the layout of the street overhead. He knew the neighborhood fairly well, having shot a few scenes for his holo-film here. It seemed childish to him now that he had been so into filmmaking. As if any of that had ever been important when humanity was being forced to the brink of extinction.

Still, when the corridor split off to the left, he knew it was heading toward the big falling-apart gray house on the corner of Rue Coquillage and Rue Flot. And Rue Flot was where the intel showed the Covenant dig site.

Reconnaissance for now, he told himself as he motioned for the others to follow him down the split. *Even if I'm really hoping for a fight.*

They walked single file, Victor leading the way. Their footsteps clattered against the metal walls, bounding off one another. If there were any Covenant scouts down here, they'd hear them coming.

Victor was so focused on the sound of their footsteps that he didn't notice the *other* sound at first. It was like wind moving through the tunnel, even though the air was utterly still, almost to the point of stifling. And it was getting louder.

"Do you hear that?" He stopped, turned around to Mousseau.

Mousseau nodded, frowning.

The rushing wind sound swept around them. It reminded Victor of the beach, only more steady than the roar of waves. More mechanical.

He gasped and then slapped his hand over his mouth. Suddenly, he knew where he'd heard that sound before.

"What is it?" asked Bellamy, the youngest member of the team aside from Victor.

Victor looked up at the team with a slow-creeping apprehension. "It's the drill," he said weakly. "The plasma drill."

All of them stood in the dark tunnel, listening. Then Mousseau said, "How close do you think it is?"

Victor shook his head a little. "Not on top of us." He was pretty sure, anyway. "But close. Maybe—" He pressed his hand against the wall. It was warm to the touch, a warmth that sent a chill shooting straight down his spine. "They're digging beside us," he said hoarsely.

The others erupted into frightened chatter. Half of the team wanted to go back, and the other half wanted to tear the walls down themselves.

"Quiet!" shouted Mousseau.

Everyone looked over at him. Victor pressed his ear against the wall, listening to the drill's constant roaring, trying to picture where it was positioned. This tunnel was heading toward the dilapidated gray house, which sat on a big lot, if he remembered correctly. It had always looked as if a fragment of the jungle had been dropped in the middle of the neighborhood. An overgrown garden. If the service tunnel ran under the street—and he was fairly certain it did—then the drilling was happening in the garden.

The drilling stopped.

Every member of the team froze in place. Mousseau lifted his rifle, pulled back softly on the bolt.

Then, abruptly, a new sound started up again. Quieter, much less organic, like an insect whine from a mechanical mosquito. It shifted up in pitch, squealing and shrieking. Victor thought about all the time he'd spent building models for his holo-films, the different sounds of the different tools. Higher pitched meant a smaller movement. A more refined movement.

"I think they found something," he said.

"What?" Mousseau jerked his gaze toward him. "What are you talking about?"

"Maybe they switched out the drill?" Victor said, tilting his head toward the wall. "You can hear it, right? It sounds different. They probably hit something and are trying not to damage it." The words came out faster and faster. "I bet I can get up there and see what it is."

Valois laughed. Victor ignored him. Mousseau just narrowed his eyes.

"I'm serious," Victor said. "There's this overgrown garden thing—that's where they're drilling. I know it. I used to—" He stopped himself in time from mentioning his stupid holo-films. "I used to hang out around here. If I can get up there, we can find out for sure."

Mousseau stared at him. The whine of the new drill carried on in the background. Victor didn't look away. He held eye contact. He knew he had already made a decision: He was going up there regardless of what Mousseau said.

"Valois, go with him."

Victor expected Valois to protest, but he just stepped forward. "You sure about this, kid?" he asked.

Victor bristled at that but nodded.

"All right, then." Mousseau took a deep breath. "We'll patrol down here. I'm giving you thirty minutes. You're not back by then, we're coming out for you."

Victor adjusted his rifle. "We'll be back."

"Good boy."

Valois slapped Victor on the shoulder. "I hope you know what you're doing."

He led Valois down the service tunnel, following the symbols carved into the walls to indicate the exit. It didn't take long for them to come upon a metal staircase leading up to a barred door. Victor slammed the butt of his rifle on the bar, and it shattered into dust.

Valois laughed. "Probably gonna want to be more subtle out there."

Victor glared at him. "I've done this before."

Valois raised an eyebrow. "Yeah? You got this close before?"

"Can't tell you." Victor stared at him, deadpan. "It's classified by ONI."

That shut Valois up, and Victor slid the door open. Like the entrance they had taken, it opened into a small, dark room that smelled of mildew—a closet. Victor stepped out cautiously, pushing open the doors to reveal a cavernous room littered with broken glass and rotting carpet.

Everything was lit by the purple glow spilling in through the empty window frames along with a strange, toxic heat.

Valois let out a low whistle. "They were closer than I thought."

Closer than Victor thought too, but he didn't say anything. He crouched down low and crept over to the closet window. It looked out into the garden, flat glossy leaves and huge red flowers all overgrown with weeds. And choked out with smoke from the drill.

"Stay here," Victor said. "Watch the entrance."

Valois laughed. "I was supposed to watch you."

Victor glared at him. "You know this place is gonna be crawling with scouts. We can't let them find out that the service tunnels run this close to the drill site. We're lucky they're so distracted by their work that they haven't set up patrols down there."

The expression of resignation on Valois's face gave Victor a surge of superiority.

"Fine," Valois said. "But if you get killed out there, Mousseau's gonna kill me. So don't die."

The superiority vanished. They still just thought of him as a kid.

"I won't," Victor snapped.

He hoisted himself out the window, landing softly in the mud outside. The whine from the drill sliced through the trees. Victor darted over to a towering jacaranda tree and scrambled up the thick hanging vines into the spread of branches. He moved to the edge of the canopy, grabbing at leaves to keep himself steady. This had been Evie's and Dorian's thing, getting up high, but it had worked for them.

He peered out from between the leaves and couldn't see anything aside from a swell of purple light arcing over the garden. He was going to have to get closer.

He inched toward the end of the branch, took a deep breath, and jumped. For one exhilarating moment, he was slicing through the wet, fragrant leaves. Then he grabbed on to the outstretched branch of an empress tree and swung hard, slamming into the trunk. The air fell out of him, and he hung there, arms aching.

The drill sang through the air.

Victor pulled himself up into the tree's canopy, the branches bending beneath his weight but not breaking. He pushed through the leaves at the top of the tree, making sure to keep his head covered with the purple blossoms.

Directly in front of him, crouched over the crushed remains of houses, was the Covenant's drill.

"Got you," he whispered.

He tapped the side of his helmet and zoomed in on the site. The drill was enormous, much bigger than the Locust he and the others had taken down before—it was as big as the surrounding houses, if not bigger. However, the plasma beam it emitted was wider and brighter. Victor counted five Elites on the ground, and none of them looked like they were equipped to fight. They stood in a clump, conferring together, their eyes fixed on the drill. Grunts churned around them, jumping up and down, knocking up against one another. A pack of Brutes at the edge of the scene bellowed at the Grunts with triumphant nods.

Celebrating, Victor realized with a cold slow creep of dread. *They're celebrating.*

Immediately, he zoomed in as far as his HUD would take him. The image was blurred a little at the edges, but he could still make out the beam of the drill shooting straight into the ground, ringed by the charred wreckage of the neighborhood. The light flickered and burned at his eyes.

He pushed the zoom away. So they found something enough to celebrate, but they were still drilling? He wished he could get closer, find out what they were actually drilling at.

Mousseau's voice crackled in his ear. "You on your way back? Because we're about to come get you."

Victor cursed, checked the time. He'd been out here almost twenty-five minutes. He sank down beneath the canopy. "Yeah," he said. "I'm on my way back."

"Good." A pause. The drill's whine sang out in the background. "What'd you find?"

Victor took a deep breath as he sent the feed to Mousseau. "I think they've found something," he said, staring at the patterns in the tree leaves. "I think we've got to act fast."

CHAPTER SIX

DORIAN

ere's what we know," Commander Marechal said.

They were all huddled together beneath a tent in the center of the camp. Rain battered against the fabric, distorting the camouflage patterns, and blew in sideways through the flaps. The air was hot and muggy, and Dorian could barely breathe. He actually found himself missing the dry, sweltering prairies where they had done their training.

A hologram flickered on above everyone's heads, showing the map of Brume-sur-Mer. Dorian sighed. So they didn't know much.

"The images we've managed to retrieve haven't been entirely clear," Commander Marechal said, striding back and forth in the holo light. "But combined with the reports that Beta Team and Gamma Team have brought back, they—"

Victor gave a huff of displeasure. Gamma Team had been sent in after he'd brought back the intel about the drilling site. Both Commander Marechal and Owen had refused to let him go. They'd refused to let any of them go, in fact. Owen said there was no need to endanger them; their expertise had already been put to good use.

"—show that the Covenant, using a Type-47A excavation platform, or Scarab, have uncovered an encased object about four meters below the surface. They are currently attempting to break through the encasement, as best as we can tell. Farhi?"

A short, muscled woman stood up and turned toward the crowd. Alisa Farhi. She'd been the one to run up to the site during reconnaissance, blasting Covenant soldiers left and right, just so she could stick her head over the edge of the drill hole and see what she could. At least, that was the story according to Caird and Dubois, a couple of Meridian marines from Port Moyne who used to go to the same shows Dorian did, back before the invasion.

Dorian wasn't sure he believed their story, but judging from the scowl on Victor's face, he almost certainly did. Dorian only hoped Victor wouldn't try to pull the same thing the next time they were out reconnoitering the service tunnels.

Farhi stood with her feet planted, her fists jabbed into her hips. "From what I could tell," she said, "the artifact was about half a meter by half a meter—that's including the encasement, which didn't look like any material I've ever seen before. Not Covenant, certainly not human."

A soft murmuring from the crowd. Owen held up one hand.

"It looked a bit like obsidian," she continued. "But that energy beam the Covies had pointed at it wasn't doing much. Not melting it, not shattering it. Nothing. And it was a pretty concentrated beam."

"That's good news," Mousseau said to the crowd. "Buys us some time to bring down that energy shield covering the drill site."

More murmuring.

"What I want, though," Commander Marechal said as Farhi took her seat again, "is to buy us even more time. What that means is take out their setup, then draw them away, see if we can get in and extract that thing ourselves. Get it out of their reach."

"Permission to speak, sir!" someone shouted.

Commander Marechal sighed. "Granted."

"What makes you think we can move it?" Dorian recognized the speaker; it was Corbett, one of the few UNSC marines in the group. "The Covies aren't moving it. If they can't move it, how will we?"

"The Covenant want what's inside." This from Vicente, the medic, who, Dorian had gathered, had actually been a nurse before he'd enlisted with the Meridian militia forces one year ago. "So that's what they're focusing on. That doesn't mean the encased object can't be moved."

"Sure, it's not big," Dubois called out, "but who the hell knows how heavy it is? Farhi said it herself—she didn't know what material it was made of."

"Don't bring me into this," Farhi said.

Dubois grinned flirtatiously at her, which she steadfastly ignored. Caird cackled beside him.

"Enough," said Commander Marechal. "Yes, there is concern that we won't be able to move the object. Although I'll remind you all we do have a Spartan." He nodded at Owen, who was standing off to the side, as usual. "Also, our primary purpose here is to prevent the Covenant from reaching the artifact at all. Sabotaging their excavation site will achieve that objective. So that's what we're doing."

More murmuring, but this time Commander Marechal didn't motion for anyone to quiet down, just stepped back and let them talk. Evie and Saskia both twisted around in their seats and looked at Dorian.

"What do you think it is?" Evie said. "If it's only half a meter square? I mean, that's something we could *carry*."

"If it's not heavy," Dorian said. "I mean, Dubois is right about that."

"First time he's right about something," Caird said, and she and Dorian high-fived over their chairs.

"There's no way we're going to draw them all off the site," Saskia said. "I feel the commander is planning something else. Owen too."

Dorian considered this.

"I'm sure he knows what he's doing," Victor said.

"That's not what you said when he didn't let you go with Gamma Team," Evie said.

Victor glared at her. Dorian had to smother a laugh. The last thing he needed was Victor trying to kick his ass once the briefing was over.

"I doubt any of it matters," Saskia said—glumly, Dorian thought. "You know we're just going to have to stay behind for this one."

"Seriously," Victor said.

The four of them looked at one another. Dorian had to admit that he was starting to see where Victor was coming from. Ten weeks at Tuomi Base under intense, accelerated training, and so far he hadn't done anything on Meridian but study some maps and explain the service tunnels. Wouldn't it have made more sense for him to go down himself? He was the one who had used the tunnels before the invasion. Sparingly, but he had used them.

But then Owen gave a shout, calling for attention. The voices fell silent. Everyone turned to look at him.

"As Commander Marechal mentioned, we want to act fast," he said. "So I'll be taking in an experienced team to help with the sabotage."

Victor rolled his eyes.

"Blue squadron, Green squadron—you'll be backup. You'll be keeping the Covenant off our tails."

A whoop went up from the two squadrons, their members scattered across the crowd. Caird was part of Blue squadron, and she slapped Dorian on the shoulder. "Better luck next time, kid," she said.

"You are literally one year older than me," Dorian said.

"Who's the lucky team?" yelled Rees.

Owen gave a small, stiff smile. That much was the same at least.

"Our latest arrivals," he said, "Local Team." And he gestured, pointing straight at Dorian. At all of them. Dorian blinked as the rest of the militia turned toward him. Dubois gave him a big grin and a thumbs-up, and Caird feigned surprise, to which Dorian replied, "Better luck next time, *kid*."

"Someone's salty." She laughed.

The rest of the militia wasn't in as high of spirits, though. Their expressions were stony and unreadable, and Valois, that private who was always hassling Victor, actually looked angry.

"These four successfully sabotaged a Covenant drill site before," Owen said. "They can do it again. You four"—he nodded at them—"meet me at the Command tent. The rest of you—get back to work."

Dorian thought there would be some mass protest—the militia wasn't about to put this assignment in the hands of a bunch of teenagers. Because, despite his joking around with Caird, that's what he was. That's what all four of them were. Sometimes, it was easy to forget, after everything he'd seen. After everything he'd done.

But no one said a word.

"Thank you!" Victor cried when Owen stepped into the Command tent twenty minutes later. "I knew you hadn't given up on us."

Owen gave Victor an amused look. "Let's not forget protocol."

"Oh, right." Victor straightened his spine and saluted. "Sir, permission to—"

"At ease. Granted." Owen waved one hand. He was smiling again. Was that a joke? Dorian couldn't be sure. He found the notion of Owen joking faintly alarming.

"Thank you!" Victor said again.

"It is nice to feel like we have a purpose," Saskia added shyly.

"You always had a purpose." Owen settled down at the glossy black monitor table that was serving as a command desk. Readings blinked in multicolored rows up and down the glass. "You're here because you know the terrain."

"Yeah, but we did all that training—" Victor started.

Evie swatted him on the arm. "We don't need to have that discussion again," she said. "We've got an assignment. And it's something we all know we can do."

Owen nodded. "Exactly. Thank you."

Evie shot Victor a smug look. This time, Dorian didn't bother to hide his laughter. Her gaze swept back over to him, and she gave him a wide, bright smile.

"We need to act quickly," Owen said. "We're heading out at nightfall."

This sobered Dorian fast enough. Looked like it did Evie too.

"Nightfall?" Saskia said. "That's in like an hour. Are you sure?"

"You've done this before," Owen said. "Our basic plan's going to be the same. We'll have better explosives this time around, though. No offense intended, Dorian."

Dorian shrugged.

"We'll be using skinners, specifically," Owen said.

Saskia let out a low whistle. "So this time around's also going to be more dangerous."

"Of course it is." Owen looked at Victor. "That's why you had the training."

Victor said nothing.

"What exactly are skinners?" Evie asked. "How are they more dangerous?"

"They're more volatile," Saskia said. "They can set off a lot more easily. So if we're placing them by hand—"

"Then you'll need a gentle touch," Owen finished. "But their volatility makes them more powerful, and that's what we want here. We want to make sure the drill equipment is completely demolished, and if there's a chance the skinners can get through the encasement, well, that's a bonus. Aside from the Scarab, they don't have a big array out here; they'll have to wait for backup equipment before they can continue."

"And then we can destroy that too," Victor said with a grin.

"That is the general plan, yes. Keep them distracted with that while we figure out a way to secure the artifact for ONI." Owen nodded.

Saskia frowned. "Secure the artifact? With skinners? Aren't you afraid that they'll blow it to pieces?"

"It's a concern, yes. But we're going against a Scarab. It's much bigger and much more dangerous than the Locust we took down before. And as Commander Marechal said, our primary focus is on preventing the Covenant from accessing the artifact. If we can get it to ONI intact, so much the better. But even a fragment of it could be useful."

Owen turned to the rest of the group. "But we're jumping ahead. Right now we need to focus on the plan tonight. The site is more secure than the one we blew up the first time, but that's why we've got Green and Blue out there clearing a path for us. Once they engage the Covenant in fire, we'll set the explosives, then clear out."

"Who'll get to do the honors?" Dorian asked, remembering the first explosion, how the whole world went bright as a supernova after he pressed the detonator. He had felt as if the light was shining straight through to his bones.

"You all will," Owen said. "The explosives are wired to separate detonators. Helps with stability."

Dorian nodded.

"And that's the real reason I brought you in here," Owen said, standing up, his armor gleaming in the thin lights hanging from tent poles. "I want to make sure you know how these damn things work."

He reached under the desk where he'd been sitting and pulled out a lockbox, red warning lights blinking in a ring around the rim. Dorian recognized the design from other lockboxes he'd seen at Tuomi Base. They were designed to store weapons.

Owen pressed his gloved hand into an indentation in the side of the lockbox. The lights shimmered, blinked, turned green. The lid popped open. Dorian found himself holding his breath, as if just opening the box would detonate the skinner.

"So have you used one of these before?" Victor said suddenly. It took Dorian a moment to realize he was talking to Saskia, who laughed in response.

"Are you kidding?" she said. "My parents wouldn't have kept anything this dangerous in the house. They weren't stupid, just—" She stopped.

Just criminals, Dorian thought, then immediately felt bad about it. He didn't know that for sure. But Saskia had certainly implied some things.

"That was a wise decision on their part," Owen said, pulling out a long, thin tube that glowed with a harsh frozen light against the metal of his glove. He set it down gently on the table. "Do not touch it."

No one moved. Everyone seemed to be holding their breath.

Owen reached back into the lockbox and pulled out a small black cube. "The detonators are physical," he said. "We won't be using comm pads like before. Don't want to risk the enemy hacking into them." He set the detonator beside the skinner, and they sat there like a still life.

"The detonator won't work until the skinner has been activated," Owen said. "That's the dangerous part, because if you activate incorrectly, you risk setting the explosive off prematurely."

Dorian shivered.

"We also have to ensure we detonate all of them at once to bring the shield down," Owen continued, "which means we have to ensure they are activated well before the detonation point. There is, I'm afraid, a lot that can go wrong with the skinners."

He looked up at them then. "Do you understand?"

There was a round of *yes, sir*'s. Even Dorian joined in, his voice shuddery.

"Good." Owen picked up the skinner again, pressing the tube between his palms. "Activation is simple. You just—"

He exerted a microscopic bit of pressure and something inside the tube clicked into place. The white light brightened and began to turn a pale rosy-pink and then red.

"I have to be more careful than you," he said, setting the skinner back on the table. "They're designed so that normal human strength can't shatter them. But you still need to take caution." He picked up the detonator and rotated it to reveal a flat disk of red light—the same light that was currently emanating from the explosive. "This wasn't lit up earlier. It indicates that the skinner is ready. Once we're clear, you just press in."

Dorian nodded silently. Victor and Evie both muttered another "Yes, sir."

Saskia just stared at the skinner glowing on the table.

"What are you going to do with it now?" she said. "They can't be deactivated."

Owen smiled. "Yes, that is true. Fortunately, we're about to launch a diversion, aren't we?"

A pause as they all considered this. Dorian's chest felt tight. It was the first time he'd be leaving the camp since they'd arrived here.

"Suit up," Owen said. "We're heading out in fifty minutes. Dismissed."

CHAPTER SEVEN

EVIE

Evie crouched down amid the tangle of thick forest growth on the edge of the beach. The ocean rushed before her, the tang of salt heavy on the air. It almost felt normal, like the invasion had never happened. But when she peered through the greenery, she saw the places where the sand had melted from plasma blasts, chunks of blackened glass rising like sculptures out of the familiar landscape.

Owen ran through those sculptures now, rain misting across his armor. He carried a red light in his left hand. The detonator.

"He's at the marker," said Dorian. "Move out."

The marker was one of those scorched sand sculptures, a light affixed to its surface. Evie jumped to her feet and followed Dorian as he threaded toward a nearby shelter entrance. It was weatherworn and overgrown, and the door creaked in protest when he dragged it open. But it was there, just like he'd promised.

"Remember it's going to be a ten-minute run to the service tunnel," Dorian said. "They've got this timed out so that it'll be clear of any scouts. No showing off, Victor!"

Evie glanced over her shoulder as she darted into the stairwell.

Owen was still barreling toward them, the detonator glowing red in his palm.

"Shut up, Dorian," Victor said.

Evie turned forward again and made her way down the stairs, right behind Dorian. Their footsteps clattered against the walls, and the overwhelming mustiness of rotting vegetation filled the air. Her backpack pressed heavy on her shoulders, the two skinners tucked away inside their protective cases. She tried not to think about them. Instead, she focused on the timer blinking steadily in front of her right eye. It was frozen at ten minutes.

A clank from above. Owen had made it to the shelter.

"Here it comes," Victor said breathlessly.

And then there was a sound like the sky tearing itself in half, and the ground moved, as if the tunnel were a starship jerking up out of gravity. Dust and stone showered down over the walkway. Evie was flung against the moldy tunnel wall, the dampness seeping into her clothes. Everything vibrated.

Up in the right corner of her HUD, the clock was counting down.

"Move!" Owen's voice echoed behind them. "They'll be scouring this area any moment now!"

Evie peeled herself away from the wall and started jogging. The tunnel was still shaking from the aftershocks of the explosion, and she found it difficult to keep her balance. Dust floated through the shadows, clinging to her skin.

But she kept running, following the flat, dark lump of Dorian's backpack up ahead. Two minutes until their scheduled arrival. She only hoped the explosion and the two diversionary squads would clear out the drilling space enough for them to get the job done.

They wove through the tunnels, still and quiet now that they were farther away from the explosion. The grating was slick with moss and knots of tangled grasses that had been washed into the tunnel during the flooding a month ago. At least there was no sign of the Covenant.

Five minutes left. Dorian veered sharply to the right, taking them into a narrow service tunnel that was supposed to connect with the tunnels Victor and Saskia had explored the day before.

Over the metallic clamor of their footsteps, Evie thought she heard voices. She slowed, reaching for her pistol. Victor slammed into her.

"What are you doing?" he said.

"I hear something—"

"It's coming from the surface," Owen said, bringing up the rear. "They're fighting overhead. I can hear better than you. Keep moving."

Evie nodded, took off again. He was right, she realized. The faint strains of gunfire and screaming drifted down through the tunnel ceiling.

Two minutes left.

"We're almost there!" Dorian called out.

"Looks like a dead end!" Victor called back—Dorian was leading them straight into a wall.

"It's not a damned dead end," Dorian grumbled, and as if to prove it, he picked up his pace, barreling straight toward the wall, his arms stretched out in front of him.

He slammed into it and it swung open, revealing another narrow tunnel.

"See?" he shouted as he slowed, leading them inside. A doorway loomed up ahead. "This is it. Victor, you should recognize this place."

Thirty seconds left.

"Yeah," Victor said begrudgingly. "I do. But we aren't there yet. We still have to get to the drill site."

"He's right," Owen said. "Keep moving."

And they did, scurrying single file down the tunnel. When they arrived at the exit, Dorian stopped and turned around. Evie thought his face looked pale.

0:00 blinked the countdown on her HUD.

"You know what you're supposed to do," Owen said, and Evie turned around, along with Victor and Saskia. He stood a few paces away, holding his gun at his chest. "I'm going out there first. Let's hope Green and Blue cleared it out for us. But be prepared if they didn't."

Evie glanced sideways at Victor, but after all his complaining, he only responded with an expression of grim determination.

"Let's get this done as quickly as possible," Owen said. "Dorian."

There was a long pause, a moment of inhaled breath. Then Dorian pushed open the entrance door.

Muggy heat wafted into the tunnel. Owen nudged himself to the front of the line, ducking out into the closet first. Dorian went next. Then Saskia. Evie. Victor brought up the rear. They stepped into a moldering old bedroom, weapons raised and trained on what was ahead. Clouds of smoke drifted up near the ceiling, and Evie caught the scent of expelled plasma. But the world was quiet. No rifle blasts, no harsh squawking of the Covenant language.

Owen crawled out the open window, disappearing into the growth outside. The others followed, moving in tandem, the way they had during training. The rain had stopped, and the sun peered out from behind the gray clouds, turning the world to steam. Evie wiped the sweat from her forehead and followed behind Saskia as they wove through the tangled, overgrown path. A garden, she remembered. This had been a garden, gone to seed when the tourists left Brume-sur-Mer for wealthier destinations.

"They've shut off the drill," Victor whispered into her ear. "I can't hear it."

She nodded. That should be a good sign, then. Took all their minimal resources to deal with the more immediate threat of the two squads. Still, she gripped the handle on her pistol so tight her knuckles bleached, and she kept sweeping her gaze over the greenery, looking for a rustle of movement, a flash of Covenant armor.

Nothing.

The plasma scent grew stronger. It reminded Evie of melted metal, of chemicals burning in the science lab at school. She caught sight of something big and silver and glittering through the web of flowering bushes, and her breath caught.

"Get down!" Owen roared just as a white plasma bolt blasted overhead.

Evie hit the ground hard, rolling immediately into the bushes, scanning the garden to find the source of the shot. Owen's rifle fire shredded the leaves. More plasma bolts scorched through the garden, leaving charred vegetation in their wake. Evie spotted a flash of pale light, and finally she saw it: a Jackal, firing off its plasma rifle from behind an energy shield. She pushed herself up to sitting and fired off a round of shots from her pistol, trying to aim in from the side.

She must have been successful; the Jackal howled and whipped its body toward her, the plasma bolts streaking through the trees. She dove back down and crawled more deeply into the vegetation. Where were the others?

A blast from a rifle. Saskia, shooting from Evie's left. The Jackal shrieked and whirled around again, firing rapidly in Saskia's direction. But its movement gave Evie a clear shot of its armored back. She aimed her pistol at the narrow wedge of flesh beneath its quills. She took a deep breath. Fired.

The Jackal dropped forward, dark blood splattering over the leaves.

Evie slunk back, let out a long breath of relief.

"No time to rest!" Owen yelled. "Someone's going to hear that. Keep moving!"

Evie pushed herself up from the ground, her clothes and backpack streaked with mud. The others emerged too, stepping out cautiously from the growth.

"Nice shooting," Saskia said.

Evie smiled. Three months ago, Saskia had shot a Jackal to save Evie's life. "Just returning the favor."

They rushed forward, hacking through the damp growth, clearing a path until suddenly there was no more growth at all, but rather a vast sunken clearing, the earth scorched black, a huge four-legged structure stretching up toward the sky. Not a structure, Evie reminded herself—it was a Scarab, a massive vehicle that had left a path of destruction as it crawled through the old neighborhood. Now it squatted above the dig site, a stationary energy shield shimmering around the entire city block, preventing any entrance.

"Commander didn't mention this in his briefing," Owen said quietly. "But it is strange to see a Scarab used like this. They normally level cities, with that cannon turned on buildings and streets. We need to go unnoticed for this plan to work."

It was bigger than the Locust they had taken out last time. More fortified. But there were ventilation shafts—weak spots. The right amount of firepower could take it down.

Once they got through the shield.

"The skinners should be powerful enough to overload the energy field," Owen said. "Then the chain reaction should knock out the Scarab as well. But we're going to have to use all of them. Hurry. There are probably other scouts in the area."

Evie and the others scattered, running around the perimeter of the drill. Evie could feel the heat from the energy shield, a different heat from the air's thick swelter. It was more mechanical. Less human.

She pulled her backpack around front, her hands shaking. Lifted the first of the explosives out, unlocked its case, nestled it into the ground next to the shield. She started to do the same with the second one. Eight skinners going off at once. It had to work.

Plasma fire exploded from somewhere off to her left; she yelped and dropped the second explosive, and the whole world went still. But it didn't set off. Evie breathed a long sigh of relief and hunched down lower. She could hear Owen returning fire. She reached over, activated both of the explosives. Then she grabbed her pistol and ran back toward the old tourist house. Someone was up ahead of her—Dorian. He fired into the trees just as a green plasma bolt streaked past Evie's head.

"Watch out!" he called. "Grunts!"

She still couldn't see them, but she fired in the direction the plasma bolt had come. Something squawked in anger. More plasma fire, setting the tree leaves to smolder. Then Owen came crashing through the greenery, laying down a hailstorm of bullets. Saskia and Victor were right behind him.

"Get inside!" Victor shouted. "There's more of them coming! We've got to blow the bombs now!"

Evie nodded and scrambled through the empty window. Dorian was leaning up against the tunnel entrance, breathing heavily, his hair soaked with sweat. He had pulled out the detonator. "We shouldn't go underground," he said. "Not with all those explosives going off at once."

"Will we be safe here?" Evie asked.

"We should," Saskia said, crawling through the window. "We placed them so that the blasts are shaped inward toward the shield. But—"

Plasma burned through the wood of the house, centimeters from her head. Saskia shrieked and dove inside. Victor whipped around, firing into the garden.

"Get inside!" Dorian bellowed. "So we can set these things off!"

"What about Owen?" Saskia said. She already held the detonator loosely in her hand, her eyes wide. Victor swung himself up through the window, firing his rifle over his shoulder.

"He's on his way," he said.

And then there he was, a gleaming streak of metal against the greenery.

"Blow it to hell!" he ordered through his helmet's comm. "Now!"

Evie looked up at Dorian. At Saskia. At Victor. Their detonators glowed red.

"Now!" Owen shouted again.

Evie closed her eyes and pressed her thumb into the indentation. She heard the sound of exactly one of her inhaled breaths.

Then the roaring came. A wave of furnace heat. Owen dove through the window of the house as the walls trembled and cracked. The ground lurched, and Evie flew into the closet, landing hard on the floor. The ground groaned beneath her. The floorboards cracked.

"Those tunnels are caving in," Dorian whispered.

No, she realized, with a shout—it was just her ears ringing hard from the explosion.

Evie got shakily to her feet. She flung open the door to the service tunnel. The steps were still there, everything coated in dust. But the ceiling was lower. The metal was dented, distorted.

"Did we get it?" Victor asked. He sounded a million kilometers away.

"Waiting on visual confirmation," Owen said.

"Is it safe to go down there?" Evie asked, nodding at the tunnel entrance.

"Do we have a choice?" Dorian asked.

"Surveillance team said we got it," Owen said. "The Scarab's been taken out."

Relief flushed through Evie, and exhilaration overpowered her exhaustion. But then she smelled smoke, heard a roar like the ocean that she thought was her damaged eardrums but was really, she realized, a fire. Distantly, there came a strange, alien wail. An alarm system, its inhuman baying calling the Covenant to action.

"Take the tunnels," Owen said. "It's worth the risk. We're going to run headfirst into the Covenant if we take the surface streets."

Evie didn't doubt that. She glanced at Dorian. A flicker of panic passed between them.

"Let's go," he said, heading down the stairs. A plume of dust swallowed him, and Evie took a deep breath before stepping into it. Even with the helmet, her eyes immediately stung with tears, and she blinked rapidly, focusing her gaze not on the thick white dust in front of her but on the readings on HUD, on Dorian's bio-signs. With her damaged hearing and the heavy dust, the readings were the only sound pulling into the tunnels. The rest of the world felt muffled and claustrophobic.

Then a low, sharp screech cut through the silence. The dust billowed, clearing briefly, and Evie saw Dorian crouching up ahead, a large sheet of metal from the tunnel's ceiling dangling at an angle above him.

"We've got to hurry!" His voice came through on the helmet's comm system. "This whole thing could collapse."

The dust was closing in around him again. Evie dove forward, the particles burning the back of her throat, the inside of her nose. "Saskia?" she said into her comm. "Victor? Are you okay? Owen?"

"I'm fine," Saskia said.

"I'm clear," Victor said. "Keep moving. The dust is starting to settle. I've got a visual."

"Clear," said Owen. "And Victor's right. Keep moving."

Evie crept forward through the slow-falling dust. It settled in jagged, unnatural shapes—the distorted metal that had once lined the tunnel keeping it secure. The ceiling dropped dangerously low, metal hanging in shredded stalactites that reflected the light from Evie's helmet back into her eyes. Evie wound through them, her gaze on Dorian's back.

A crash behind her; a scream on her comm. Evie and Dorian both froze, and Evie whirled around into another blinding cloud of dust.

"Saskia," Dorian said, rushing up beside her. "Saskia, are you okay?"

"The ceiling dropped," Owen said over the comm. "Dorian, Evie, keep moving. Saskia—"

"I'm clear. A piece of the ceiling almost hit me. I'm fine. Keep going."

The dust was clearing again, and Evie saw Saskia pulling herself up. A shard of metal jammed out of the ground beside her.

"We're almost there," Dorian said, grabbing at Evie's hand. "Come on."

They moved on, the tunnel groaning and shrieking around them. The walls shifted centimeter by centimeter, kicking up new showers of debris and dust—so much dust, thick and choking like smoke.

"There," Dorian said. "We're almost there."

Evie could barely see anything in front of her. Dorian was little more than a dark blur moving across the shadows of the tunnel. Her helmet light could barely penetrate the dust. Or maybe it was so coated it was useless.

Dorian let out a shout. There was the horrifying screech of metal against metal. But it wasn't the ceiling collapsing. It was the exit, grinding open, revealing a wash of lemony sunlight and clear, clean air.

Evie bounded forward, back into the surface world.

CHAPTER EIGHT

SASKIA

Saskia sat on the cot in their tent, her fingers wrapped loosely around a hydration pack of stale-tasting water. Three hours since the explosion and her ears were still ringing.

At least they'd been successful, the reports said. The skinners had burrowed the entire dig site deep into the ground, wedging it between the tunnel systems. Of course, now the whole camp was on high alert. The Covenant would be gunning for them big-time. So far, they hadn't come this far out into the forest, though, thanks to Owen's explosion out on the beach. They were focusing their search on the water, not the woods.

Still, when she and the others made it back to the camp, a team was already patrolling the perimeter, and the nonessential tents and structures had been dismantled to shrink their coverage area. Seeing that had solidified to Saskia what they had accomplished. Would the Covenant rebuild? Of course, they had before. But it was so *satisfying* knowing that her actions would set them back. It was the sort of reassurance she needed, the whole reason she had agreed to come back and fight: She wanted ONI to know she wasn't like her parents.

In the week since coming back to Brume-sur-Mer, she hadn't had much time to really think about her parents. No one was getting messages from their family anymore, and it was easy to let herself get swept up in the routine of life with the militia. But when she had these quiet moments between ops, she would find herself wondering, yet again, what her parents were doing. Where they had wound up after leaving Brume-sur-Mer before the invasion. If they were still working with Chalybs Defense Solutions. If they had tried to find her. If she would even want to see them if they had.

Saskia drained the last of her water and tossed the hydration pack onto her cot. She was the only person in the tent aside from Victor, who was sprawled across his own cot, sleeping soundly. Evie and Dorian had gone to look at the reports themselves. Dorian wanted to find out what happened to the rest of the tunnels. The trip had been terrifying, all that unsettled dust, the steel walls bowing inward from the force of the explosion.

Saskia drifted to the tent's entrance and peered out at the camp. Everything shimmered as the tents reflected the faint misting drizzle. No one was out—they'd been told to stay inside unless absolutely necessary, but Saskia didn't want to be in that tent anymore, the air damp and stifling. She wanted to talk to someone, to not think about her parents anymore, and their months-long silence. It was strange how less lonely she had felt during the invasion, huddled up inside her parents' house not knowing yet that they had abandoned her. Here, surrounded by grizzled soldiers, part of her felt lost.

She slipped out and cut across the clearing, heading toward Owen's tent. Maybe Dorian and Evie needed another set of eyes as they looked over the reports and the city maps. Evie had also mentioned something about trying to get in contact with Salome as a way of finding out the extent of the tunnel damage.

The flap to Owen's tent hung open, and Saskia ducked in without announcing herself. She was startled, then, to find it empty except for Owen himself, who was sitting behind his desk, reading over a data pad. His brow was furrowed with something that almost looked like concern, although the expression vanished as soon as he glanced up at her.

"Oh," Saskia breathed, stumbling backward. "I'm sorry, I was looking for Dorian and Evie."

Owen set the data pad down. "I sent them off to help patrol," he said. "Yellow squadron needed them out in the woods more than I needed them here looking at maps."

Saskia's heart thudded. "Do you want me to go out there too? I've spent a lot of time in that terrain."

But Owen shook his head. "We don't want the group to be too big. Ideally I would have only sent Dorian, but I don't like putting the four of you in danger without backup."

"Are we in danger?" Saskia slid into the chair across from Owen's desk. "I thought the Covenant were focusing on the ocean—"

"They are," Owen said. "That's what the aerial reports are telling us." He tapped the data pad. "The UNSC has remotely piloted drones patrolling the shoreline, looking for UNSC watercraft. But that doesn't mean the Covenant won't send a team out to scour the woods."

Saskia shivered. "Do you think we did too much, blowing the whole thing up like that? They'll know we're here now."

"They knew we were here already," Owen said. "They were just more focused on unearthing the artifact. And they're still focused on it." He shook his head. "We slowed them down, but we didn't stop them."

Saskia shifted in her seat. The data pad lay angled between them, and she wondered what information he'd been reading on it. She knew better, after her training, than to ask, and that was frustrating. Another way things had been easier when it was just the five of them.

"Why do they want it so badly?" she asked. "I mean, I know it's part of their religion, but just—" She shrugged. "We've destroyed their excavation equipment *twice*, and they keep going after it."

Owen frowned. "That information is classified," he said.

Of course it is, Saskia thought.

"Even I barely know the details," he continued. "It's ONI's purview."

ONI. Saskia thought of Captain Dellatorre, laying out promise after promise to entice them into returning back to Meridian.

"ONI really doesn't want them to have it either," she said. "And it's not just because ONI doesn't want to see Meridian glassed, like us."

Owen stared at her, blank-faced. "Of course ONI doesn't want to see Meridian glassed."

"That's not why they sent us back here, though." She looked down at her lap, her thoughts still on her parents. She wondered if she could say something to him, if he would understand. The others didn't, not really.

"It's fine, you can say it," she continued. "I understand people have . . . multiple reasons for doing things. My parents—" She stopped. Would Owen run to ONI with the intel that her parents were traitors? She decided to risk it. "They weren't good people. But they weren't bad people either. You know?"

"I can't afford to think that way," Owen said after a time. "Not during a war like this."

"I'm not saying ONI is bad," Saskia said quickly, although part of her did wonder how they could send all four of them back to the place they had barely escaped from. "I'm just saying people are complicated."

Owen sighed and leaned back in his chair, his gaze fixed on the ceiling. For half a second, Saskia saw in him a regular person, a man not much older than her. He had told her once that he had been a war orphan, that ONI had found him on Jericho VII after the glassing. Which meant that all the million rumors about the Spartans—they were genetically engineered, they were grown in vats, they were elaborate AI, not even human at all—weren't exactly true.

Which meant that at one point, Owen had been like her.

"Your training," she said, before she could stop herself. "What was it like?"

Owen jerked his gaze back to her, and Saskia shrunk down in her chair, cheeks burning. "I was just wondering," she mumbled. "The training they put us through, it wasn't exactly what I expected."

Owen's stare was piercing. "I don't imagine it was anything like the training I went through."

"Of course not," she said quietly. "I just—did ONI ever send you back?"

Owen frowned. "Send me back where?"

Saskia regretted ever asking the question, but she still wanted the answer. She wasn't *exactly* an orphan, but it felt that way sometimes. And ONI had sent her back to the place where it had happened.

"To Jericho VII," she said.

Owen took a deep breath. "I see."

Saskia shook her head. "Look, if you don't want to answer—"

"I can answer. Yes, once. There was some rumored Covenant activity." He said it so flatly, as if the world were any other.

"Was it hard?"

Owen studied her. "No," he finally said. "Anything that would have made that hard was—trained out of me."

The way he said *trained* made Saskia shiver.

"I told you," he said. "I lost my family, and ONI gave me a new one. They did that through the training, but also through—" He stopped.

"Let me guess," Saskia said, smiling a little. "Classified."

"Let's just say that I'm not the same Owen I would be if I had grown up on Jericho VII with my parents."

"You mean the augmentations?" Saskia asked. "That's what people say about the Spartans. Or one of the things. One of the less . . . fantastical things."

"Yes, they enhanced me to be what I am today." He shrugged. "And then they made me part of a new family," Owen said. "But that's—"

"Above my clearance, right? You must have been young, though." The reality of it gnawed at Saskia's insides. A child plucked out of one hell and then dropped into another. Procedures and injections and *enhancements*.

Not good people. But not bad people either. ONI did what they had to, and now Spartan Owen existed. Someone to fight the Covenant. Someone who couldn't stop what happened on Jericho VII but *could* stop the same thing from happening on Meridian.

"Thanks," Saskia said, standing up. She wasn't sure what exactly she was thanking him for, but it seemed the right thing to say.

"You're welcome," Owen said, as if he understood better than she did.

Saskia smiled. Then she slipped back out into the muggy air. She needed to make herself useful.

That night, Saskia dreamed about her parents. They wore ONI uniforms as they showed their weapons to shadow-faced men in dark suits. "For our latest prototype," her father said, smiling too big, "we're going to make our daughter part of the *family.*" And then they were in an operating room, bright lights and steel walls, her father leaning over her with a massive, dripping needle. Saskia's mother was screaming, her voice modulated and strange, like an electronic alarm.

Saskia gasped awake with her mother's strange scream echoing in her ears. No, not a scream at all. An actual alarm. The perimeter warning.

"They found us!" Victor hissed, right next to her ear. "Saskia! Get your rifle!"

The dream dissipated, replaced by a sudden and very real terror. She flung herself out of bed, scrabbling through her trunk for her clothes, her hands shaking as she reached for the strap of her gun. The others were doing the same, a strain of panic shooting through the tent.

"We don't know that for sure," Evie said. "Just that the alarm went off."

"What else could it mean?" Victor shot back.

"Could be a drill. We're deep enough in the woods for it," Dorian said. "We need to stay calm. Let's not assume the entire Covenant army is out there waiting for us." Somehow he'd managed to get dressed the fastest; he was already shoving ammunition into his rifle.

"He's right," Evie said. "There's no reason to panic."

"There's also no reason to not be prepared," Saskia added.

"Thank you!" Victor said, hefting his pack. "At least one of you is reasonable."

Saskia checked her ammunition and slung her rifle over her shoulder; she followed Dorian and Evie out of the tent. They weren't the only ones either. The rest of the militia was already swarming into the pathways, dozens of soldiers adjusting their weapons and hollering questions at one another:

"What the hell is going on?"

"We under attack?"

"Where's the Spartan?"

And all the while, the siren wailed, shattering the muffled silence of the surrounding forest.

"You four!" It was Commander Marechal. "Get back to your tent. We don't want you in harm's way."

"Are you kidding me?" Victor yelled back. "We're the ones that blew the Scarab sky-high—"

A Banshee came streaking over the forest canopy, its weapon pods blazing, incinerating a row of tents. Saskia zigzagged sideways, plunging out of the clearing and into the cover of the woods. Evie was right beside her, eyes wide. "Now what?" she cried.

Another blast from the Banshee's plasma cannon. There was an immolation of white-hot light and then a wall of blue-tinted flame. Saskia and Evie crouched down beside each other among the ferns. More of the militia had followed them into the forest, and Saskia scanned each face, looking for Dorian and Victor.

Another explosion, another wave of heat. Evie pulled on Saskia's arm. "They're not pursuing us; they're only focusing on the campsite right now," she said. "We've got to get deeper into the woods before they come after the survivors."

Saskia nodded, although she peered through the smoke. "Where are the others?" she asked.

"They were right behind us," Evie said. "I know they got out. We've got to go now!"

Saskia shouldered her gun and followed Evie into the thick tangle of trees. The rest of the militia was doing the same. Saskia wondered how they were going to regroup after this. All their communication equipment was burning up into the thick black smoke choking out the air.

"Saskia!"

She whirled around; it was Dorian, plunging through the over-growth, mud smudged across his forehead. "And Evie," he added. "Thank god."

"Keep moving, kids!" Dubois pushed past them. It was strange seeing him without Caird at his side, although him calling them kids rankled—he was only two years older, and from Port Moyne. Not that much different from the four of them. "We don't know what they're going to do once they're done with the camp."

"Where are we even going?" Dorian asked.

"The emergency coordinates," Dubois said. "Get going!"

Saskia's mind went blank.

"Don't tell me you don't remember them," Dubois said, shaking his head.

"Of course we do," Dorian snapped, and immediately they came back, a string of numbers that were utterly useless to her in that moment. She'd left her data pad behind.

Fortunately, Dubois had a map up on his data pad, and he led Evie, Saskia, and Dorian through the thick forest. Eventually Saskia couldn't even smell the smoke of the burning camp anymore, and the greenery of the forest seemed denser, more overgrown. They must have been deep into the protected part of the forest, much farther than she or the others had ever gone during the initial invasion.

"Where do you think we're going?" Evie asked, shoving aside a fan of palm leaves with the stock of her rifle.

"The backup coordinates," Dorian said. Dubois let out a strangled laugh.

Evie rolled her eyes. "Yes, but *where*?" She frowned. "I hope Victor knows where to go."

"I'm sure he does," Dubois said, his eyes on the data pad. "Kid's the real deal."

"Yeah, I wouldn't worry about him," Dorian said. "But where are we going exactly?" He craned his neck to peer at Dubois's map, and Dubois tilted it toward him.

"Probably the middle of nowhere," Saskia said.

"Probably where we should have been in the first place." Dorian swatted at a dangling tree branch, sending it flying.

"We *were* in the middle of nowhere," Evie mumbled. "They still found us."

The four of them went silent at that. Saskia trudged through the greenery, wiping away the raindrops that splattered across her face. She should have expected this when they blew up the Scarab, and probably Owen had. It had been easier for them to hide before, when it was just the five of them, tucked away in a house that looked abandoned. But an entire military camp? No matter how well they tucked themselves away in the woods, no matter how high-tech their syncamo tents were, they were never going to stay hidden for long.

The hum of voices cut through Saskia's thoughts. She stumbled to a stop and glanced over at the others. "You hear that?"

"Sounds human to me," Dorian said.

Dubois nodded. "I bet it's the new camp."

They pushed forward toward the voices. It was definitely the militia; Saskia could hear people speaking frantically in lowered voices, demanding reports, looking for missing comrades.

She hoped Victor was one of those voices.

She was the first to push through the vines and step into a small cleared space that had been carved out beneath the tree canopy. Most of the militia was there, regrouping with their weapons. Commander Marechal stood in the center, staring intently at his data pad, nodding along to whoever was speaking to him. Saskia walked around the perimeter of the clearing, staring out at the crowd of stern, worried faces. There was Caird, already running over to greet Dubois. Owen was standing over a pile of rescued artillery.

And then she spotted him. Victor. He was leaning up against a banyan tree, dried MediGel streaked on his forehead. *Someone brought MediGel*, she thought, and then: *Victor's hurt.*

"Victor!" she cried, pushing forward into the crowd. She saw Evie and Dorian out of the corner of her eye, running to join her. "Victor, are you okay?"

He turned toward her, and his face broke out in the big, goofy grin she remembered from school. "You made it!" he said, lifting his hand up in greeting. The sleeve of his shirt was shredded, and his arm was marked with angry red welts, still visible even beneath the MediGel application.

"What happened to you?" she gasped, stopping a few paces away.

Victor shrugged. "Wanted to get in on the fighting."

"He held his own against a Drone," said a rangy, rough-voiced woman standing beside him. Kielawa, the other medic. A health pack was tucked under one arm. "Lucky I was here to patch him up."

"It barely grazed me," he said. "That Banshee was the real problem."

"No crap," said Dorian. "Considering all our supplies are burning right now."

"Not all of them," Kielawa said. "Command's gonna send a supply drop just as soon as they can get through the fighting outside atmo. That's why we met here."

"Then what?" Evie said. "We set up a new camp? There's hardly enough space."

Kielawa shrugged. "We scatter out into the woods. We should have been camped out like that from the beginning, but we needed easier access to run surveillance. Still, can't act like a proper military in a guerrilla war." She grinned. "Good job, by the way, blowing up that Scarab. All this—it means the Covies are *panicked*."

"Yeah," Dorian muttered. "I noticed."

Kielawa laughed and turned away, moving toward the steady trickle of soldiers pushing out through the woods.

"What the hell did you do?" Evie directed her question at Victor. "Did you seriously fight a Drone?"

Victor shrugged, the tatters of his shirtsleeve rippling against his arm. "I hit him square between the eyes. I think that counts."

"Looks like he hit you square on the arm," Dorian said.

Victor glared at him. "I'm fine." Still, he reached up, rather self-consciously Saskia thought, and brushed his fingers against the MediGel.

"So now what?" Victor said, dropping his hand. He swung his gaze around, studying the mass of soldiers like he was in command. "You think Command's really going to get a supply drop to us?"

Saskia frowned. Of course they would *try.* She had to believe that much.

"Let's hope so," Dorian muttered.

"Attention!" Commander Marechal shouted, his voice cutting through all the chatter, all the questions, all the faint panic circulating through the clearing. "Attention! We have to regroup! Join with your teams! Make a note of who's missing! Move!"

Saskia glanced over at the others. Her team. They'd found one another without even having to be asked.

She smiled a little, in spite of herself.

Meanwhile, the rest of the militia swirled around. Most of them had broken up into their teams as well, but the late arrivals stood on the outskirts, scanning the crowd. Saskia watched them as, one by one, they found their squads, the teams within them. One by one they ceased to be alone.

Squads. Teams. Family. She was starting to see what Owen meant, about how war swaps one for the other.

But interestingly, right now Owen was the only one of the entire militia who stood by himself, towering over them in his armor. This deep into the forest it looked burnished and dark. His expression was unreadable.

As the militia settled into their squadrons, Commander Marechal barked out, "Report!" And squad by squad, they reported those who had gone MIA: three from Blue, one from Red, one from Yellow, two from Green. When his gaze swept around to Saskia and the others, Saskia felt a faint guilt when she called out, "Local Team. All present and accounted for, sir."

Commander Marechal nodded, turned to the next.

In the end, thirteen soldiers were missing. Of those thirteen, only three were confirmed dead.

"Ten of us are still out there," Commander Marechal said, his voice muffled strangely by the thick leaves. "Our first mission is to recover them, get them fixed up. Because we are going to need all the help we can get."

The reverent silence erupted into sharp conversations.

Commander Marechal held up his hands. "I spoke with Command. The suborbital fighting is . . . intense. And it's only getting more intense—"

Everyone exploded with questions again. Saskia glanced over at Evie.

"Looks like we won't be getting those supplies," Evie muttered.

"Enough!" Commander Marechal shouted. "You all are soldiers. Act like it."

This was enough to snap the militia into a displeased quiet.

Commander Marechal took a deep breath. "Better," he said. "Command is not going to be able to get us the promised supply drop." He paused here, as if daring the militia to erupt into protest again. But there was only a stunned stupor that fell over the crowd, and Saskia felt a weight drop in the middle of her stomach.

"However, there was a supply drop made about three klicks from here yesterday afternoon that we hadn't yet been able to collect. This will be enough to last us until we complete the mission."

"The mission?" whispered Evie. "We already sabotaged the excavation!"

"I don't like the sound of this," Dorian murmured.

Saskia didn't either.

Commander Marechal looked over at Owen, standing a few meters away. "Spartan Owen will tell you more. He'll be leading the operation."

Owen shifted his weight from one foot to the other. Saskia might have thought he was nervous right now, that somehow he was revealing a flash of the person he might have been before ONI drilled fear out of him, but Owen didn't get nervous. She knew that much.

"If conditions are right, ONI will be sending a pickup in three days," he announced. "But before we can extract, we have to secure one thing."

"Oh no," breathed Saskia, and she could tell by the sudden electric restlessness in the air that the rest of the militia knew what was coming too.

"They want the artifact," Owen said. "That's our new objective."

Evie let out a long, low sigh. Dorian cursed. Even Victor looked a little queasy at the thought.

CHAPTER NINE

DORIAN

The plan to retrieve the artifact was simple. Go in shooting and grab it.

Okay, so there was more strategy involved. Owen had laid it all out in the clearing, the militia gathered in tight around him. They'd work in squads. Conduct a sneak attack. Hit them while their equipment was out. Punch a hole in their lines hard enough to gain access to the artifact and then hope for the best.

Oh, and leave the kids behind.

In a way it made sense; the rest of the squads had been near the site at one point or another, and they were working together to determine a best course of action. But regardless of the action chosen, it was going to be violent. And violence was what Owen and ONI were keeping Local Team away from.

Dorian was not as ready to go fight as Victor—and for good reason; he'd seen one too many times what the Covenant was capable of, and those marks on Victor's arm were just further confirmation. But at the same time, Dorian was sure there was an easier way to get at the artifact. All the reports said their explosion had driven it deeper underground, between the service tunnels.

There had to be a way to access it from underneath the Covenant. Using the service tunnels had worked when blowing up the drilling equipment; he was confident it could also work to their advantage in retrieving the artifact.

"Hey. Saskia said you wanted to see me?"

Dorian glanced up from the holographic map he'd been staring at for the last twenty minutes. He was ensconced in a makeshift lean-to, wedged beneath an oak tree. At least it wasn't raining.

"Hey, Evie," he said. "I did want to see you." He patted the mat of grass he was using as a cushion. Evie sighed and crawled in. She looked tired, dark circles blooming underneath her eyes. "You think you could get ahold of Salome?"

Evie blinked in surprise. "Salome? Why?" With her outdated, patchwork programming, Dorian wasn't totally surprised to find the militia hadn't been making use of her.

"I've been thinking," Dorian said, amplifying the map so that it flooded his lean-to with green light. "There might be a way to get to the artifact through the service tunnels."

Evie frowned. "You don't think Owen would have come up with that?"

Dorian sighed. "Owen is a soldier. He's working with a bunch of other soldiers. It's not like when it was just us and him and he had to keep us out of harm's way. So, yeah, he's approaching this like a soldier. But I just think there's got to be—maybe not an easier way, but a *sneakier* way."

Evie laughed, shook her head. "After everything, I'm honestly ready to just sit here, and let them take care of it. Then we can go back to the refugee colony, maybe use those full scholarships we were promised."

Dorian smiled at that, but he felt the emptiness in her statement. "And if they mess up the mission?" he said quietly. "If they don't get the artifact?"

"They'll get it," Evie said.

"Sure, probably, but it can't hurt to have a backup plan, right?"

Evie rolled her eyes. "Come on, Dorian. At the end of the day, we're civilians with some weird, specialized training in fighting and navigating terrain. This is their job, this is what they do. We might just be out of our depth on this one." She paused. "I mean, you're starting to sound like Victor."

He studied her, not sure how to put his doubts into words. It was clear to him ONI wanted that artifact—sure, the fighting out in space probably was bad enough they couldn't break through—but why send them on this suicide mission right after their camp had been destroyed? Evie read it as a quick errand on their way home, but Dorian saw it for what it was: an act of desperation.

He didn't think ONI *wanted* to leave them on Meridian if things went bad. But he could imagine it happening. They'd find a way through the fighting if the artifact was secured, because evacuating an asset of that value would become a priority. That, he was sure about.

So if he wanted a guaranteed ride off Meridian, he needed to find a way to secure the artifact. Owen and the rest of the militia probably were going to be successful. But after everything, he didn't want to put his future in someone else's hands. Not if he wanted to see Remy and Uncle Max again.

But looking at Evie, he just wasn't sure he could explain all that to her. She would dismiss him the minute he even hinted at the possibility that ONI might leave them stranded. So he just said, "What else have we got to do? It's just coming up with a backup plan."

Evie considered this.

"C'mon," he said. "No one's as bad-ass as you when it comes to hacking into that ancient Brume-sur-Mer system."

Evie grinned and her cheeks pinkened and she looked away, her hair falling into her eyes. Seeing her flustered from the praise was honestly pretty cute.

"So you'll help me?" he said.

"I'll try to get you in touch with Salome," Evie said. "Assuming she's even still functioning. And assuming we can find a computer."

"Remember, Dubois brought his data pad during the evac," Dorian said promptly. He'd already considered this and knew it would not be a wise idea for them to attempt to patch into her directly using the stations set up around town.

Evie laughed. "I see. And he'll let us use it?"

Dorian reached into his bag and extracted the data pad. It was an older model, beat up and scratched and ugly, but Dubois claimed it worked just fine. Dorian tossed it at Evie, and she caught it midair and turned it around in her hands.

"He just let you borrow it?" she said.

"I told him I was doing some prep work for the mission. Not exactly a lie, right?" Dorian grinned. "Besides, Dubois is cool. You know that. Anyway, get to it! Let's see what you can do."

Evie sighed. "I doubt we'll be able to connect to the town's comm system. Going to have to find another way." She switched on the data pad, and the light shimmered over her face.

"Owen was able to get in touch with ONI."

"Yeah, on a military channel," Evie said. "I'm sure ONI's got a signal beaming down here so they don't lose track of us. Or that artifact." She scowled a little. *At ONI*, Dorian thought, until he saw her tapping furiously at the screen. "Ugh, this is barely working! We'll never—oh, there it goes."

"Are you patched into ONI's channel?" Dorian asked.

Evie lifted her gaze at him. Then she broke into a peal of laughter. Dorian's cheeks burned.

"That's not something I could do," she said. "Not directly, anyway. I can tell just from a glance that it's way too secure. The good news, though, is that we don't need anything *from* the channel, we just need to *use* the channel, and that, I think I can do."

Her fingers danced across the screen. Dorian crawled around beside her so he could peer over her shoulder. The data pad's screen was filled with a cascade of code, Evie dancing through it so quickly he could hardly follow her movements. Her brow wrinkled in concentration. Dorian found himself holding his breath.

"I got it!" she cried. "I think."

"You think?" He looked closer. "The connection light is on."

"Yeah, but let me see if I can actually get in touch with Salome." She swiped across the screen, icons fluttering open beneath her touch. Code materialized in a separate window. Dorian sighed, leaned back against the trunk of the tree, and looked out at the makeshift camp that had sprouted up in the clearing. The supply box from ONI had contained a few tarps that they had stretched out into tents, with the thick tree canopy overhead providing cover from Banshee patrols. But mostly it had contained weapons.

No wonder Owen was leading a charge against the Covenant. Evie could barely get in touch with the Brume-sur-Mer infrastructure system. They were in a tiny town, and surely the UNSC was focusing on larger cities with a more immediate threat. With little food and water left, and limited resources to stage any kind of attack plan, the only thing they had going for them were numbers—and a Spartan.

What else was left but fighting it out for the artifact? Once the Brume-sur-Mer militia had the artifact in hand, they would immediately get bumped up on the list of ONI's priorities.

"Evelyn Rousseau!" chirped a familiar saccharine voice.

"You got her!" Dorian tore his gaze away from the camp. Sure enough, a two-inch hologram of Salome flickered in the air above the comm pad. She looked over at him and blinked her bright eyes. "Dorian Nguyen!" she said. "I did not expect to see you two." She frowned. "I did not expect to see anyone. The town has been invaded by the Covenant for some time now."

"We noticed," Dorian said. Then he grinned at Evie. "Thanks."

She smiled back. "Let's hope this plan of yours works."

"Plan?" Salome tilted her head, leaving a streak of light in her wake. Dorian wondered how long this comm pad was going to hold on. "I don't like it when the two of you have plans." She put her hands on her hips. "Also, you shouldn't be in this part of the forest. It's restricted according to a proclamation issued by the Meridian government on—"

"Salome," Dorian said. "We need your help with something. Do you still have a view of the town?"

Salome gave a little squeak of offense. "Of course!" she said. "I am the town's only artificial intelligence. What good would I be if I couldn't see it?"

"Hey," Dorian said. "I'm sorry. I just didn't know if the Covenant had cut you off."

Beside him, Evie covered her mouth to hide her laughter.

Salome sniffed in annoyance. "They don't even know I'm here," she said. "Don't think I don't see what they're doing. Digging holes all over the place."

"Yeah," Dorian said. "That's what we want to talk to you about." He grabbed the projector he'd been using to study the holo-map of the town. "There's one hole in particular that we're interested in. It's at Rue Coquillage and Rue Flot by the—"

"Oh, *that* one." Salome sighed and shook her head, her hair swishing like static. "Yes, that's officially been declared a danger zone. You should not be going there, Dorian Nguyen."

"I promise I won't," Dorian said solemnly. "I just want to see how it lines up with a map I have. Can you project your image for me?"

"As long as you won't go there! Only military personnel should enter the area."

Dorian looked up at Evie, who was still smiling. It was nice to see someone smile, after everything that had happened.

"You hear that, Evie?" he said. "Military personnel only."

"Noted," she said.

Salome didn't pick up on their sarcasm, though—someone had thoughtfully left that ability out of her programming. Her avatar vanished and a few seconds later was replaced by a grainy image of the Covenant's excavation site—or what was left of it. The shield was gone, and the massive Scarab platform lay in charred, melted heaps. A trio of jellyfish-like figures drifted around the wreckage, pulling out chunks of less charred, less melted machinery with their long, slender tentacles. They were obviously Covenant, but not like any of the species Dorian had fought before.

"What are they?" Evie breathed. "They look like they're . . . repairing it?"

Dorian felt a knot in his chest. "Well, then we better get in there quick, shouldn't we?" He activated his map, a simple green grid that shimmered over the image of the strange creatures. He rotated the map around, adjusting its position relative to the excavation site. Trying to find his way in.

"Salome," he said. "You have any views of the hole itself? Any way to show us what's underground?"

"It's *underground*, Dorian Nguyen," she chirped. "Why would you need to see it?"

Dorian rolled his eyes. "Look, if you can't do it—"

"I can show you the view from the service tunnels."

Evie glanced up at Dorian, an eyebrow raised. She was starting to understand.

"Perfect," Dorian said.

The image flickered and was replaced with a view of the service tunnels—or what was left of them after the sabotage mission. This particular stretch was in much worse shape than what Dorian and the others had trekked through as they fled from Covenant retaliation. The walls were blasted in, revealing striations of dark dirt and clay. The ceilings hung in tatters.

"There is no way we're getting down there," Evie muttered.

Dorian ignored her. "Salome, where's the hole in comparison to this tunnel?"

"Right here, Dorian Nguyen." A section of the image brightened, turning even grainier in the process. A piece of the Covenant Scarab had slammed through the tunnel, crashing through its reinforced walls. And something was in the dirt. Something shiny, something smooth. A faint curve of unblemished glass.

"Oh my god," Evie said.

"Salome," Dorian said, his chest tight. "What is that? That glass thing?"

A long pause. Dorian took a deep breath.

"I don't know," Salome said. "It appeared after the blast. It was originally encased in some black material, but the explosion stripped that away."

Dorian looked up at Evie. Her eyes were wide—with fear? Excitement? He couldn't tell.

"Told you there was an easier way," Dorian said.

"Absolutely not," said Owen.

"Are you serious?" Dorian shouted. "It's the same freaking move that we did to blow the excavation site up in the first place! There's no reason to march into battle and try to dig the stupid thing out!"

Owen enlarged the image and slid the focus on the tunnel itself, away from that strange curve of dark glass. "That tunnel is not passable," he said. "Look at it."

Dorian glared at him, refusing to look at what he knew Owen was showing him: collapsed walls, thick chunks of stone, destroyed structural beams.

"With respect, the Covenant isn't exactly passable either. It's not *safe* to—"

"I never claimed it was safe," Owen said. "But it plays to our strengths. The Covenant's presence here is already diminished, thanks to Blue and Green's valor during the sabotage. And it wasn't a large presence to begin with."

"How do you know that?" Evie asked, sitting quietly beside Dorian. He wanted to yell at her for staying so calm. How could she act like Owen was being reasonable?

"Same reconnaissance we've been working with since we arrived here," Owen said. "The plan was always to wear down the enemy until we could strike and sabotage their excavation efforts. Thanks to their attack on our camp, we have not been able to wear them down as much as I would have preferred, but the Meridian soldiers here are tough. They can handle themselves." He paused, ran one hand over his shorn hair. "If you want to help, you can work with Kielawa to prepare medical supplies for the evac."

Dorian threw up his hands. He couldn't believe this. Owen had been so cautious when they had worked with him before, always encouraging them to stay on the periphery, to not engage in any theatrics. He didn't seem like the type to just race into battle. For a second, Dorian wondered if this was the flip side of being the hand of ONI— having to accept marching orders when you didn't agree with them.

But then, Owen had been trying to protect Local Team all along, hadn't he? And he still was. No one expected *Dorian* to march against the Covenant. Or Evie, or Saskia, or even Victor. They were expected to stay behind and issue MediGel as people inevitably came straggling into camp bleeding and broken.

"The four of us would be going into the tunnel as backup," Evie said, and Dorian realized her calmness was a gift. She sounded so sure of herself. "The Covenant will be distracted by the fighting—just like when we blew up the Scarab, as Dorian pointed out. We can be in communication, and if it looks like you need us to try and extract the artifact from the tunnel, we can. Otherwise, you can continue as you originally planned."

Owen studied her for a long moment. Dorian held his breath.

"So how do you suggest handling the extraction of the artifact itself? This is an object of unknown origin. ONI requires certain protocols and special equipment when extracting an artifact of this nature. To avoid contamination. There's no way of knowing how it will affect you."

"If we learn the protocols and how to handle the equipment—"

Owen shook his head. "We have one pair of exo-gloves for extraction. One ionized lock-cube for field transport. These will be going with my team. Even if you were able to get to the artifact, there would be no way to safely extract it."

Dorian's stomach dropped. He hadn't even considered that—he'd been too busy worrying about the Covenant and the tunnels themselves.

Evie paused for a moment. Owen shifted his weight as if to stand up, as if to say that the conversation was over. But then Evie spoke.

"We're going as backup," she said. "We don't have to touch the object ourselves. If we get to it, we'll let you know, and you can send the extraction team to meet us."

Owen tilted his head. "I suppose that could work," he said.

"Thank you," Dorian said.

"But there's still the fact that the tunnel isn't stable."

Dorian let out a long frustrated sigh, pressed his hands into his forehead. But Evie remained as unflappable as always.

"That's true," she said. "But if we wanted a safe mission, we wouldn't have agreed to return here in the first place. We want to help save our home, our people, even if it means there's risk."

Dorian dropped his hands and stared at her. She sat with her hands folded in her lap, her spine straight, her expression clear. A brilliant move. She knew how to talk to adults.

Owen closed his eyes. "I suppose there is some value in your plan."

Dorian flashed Evie a grin.

"But you need to be one hundred percent aware that if that tunnel collapses, if you get trapped in any way, I'm not going to be able to save you. And if the Covenant is running patrols down there still . . . you'll be on your own."

"That holds true for the entire militia," Evie said. "Not just us. We're willing to put ourselves out there."

"I just need you to be fully aware of the situation before I agree to this plan."

Dorian looked at the image he was projecting over Owen's desk, the grid map, the overlay of the drill site. The shiny curve of alien glass jutting out of the dirt.

"And under no circumstances," Owen said, "do you attempt to extract that artifact on your own."

"Understood," he said.

CHAPTER TEN

VICTOR

They waited until the afternoon rains set in, smartly using the last vestiges of the rainy season to hide their passage through the woods. Victor led Local Team as they darted from tree to tree, moving quickly and silently. The wounds on his arm had almost healed, although they were going to leave some pretty cool scarring across his skin. Proof that he could handle himself in a fight.

The rest of the militia was out there somewhere, moving toward their own objectives. Part of Victor wished he could join them. He even knew the basic plan: They were going to form an invisible ring around the excavation site, drawing in tighter and tighter, picking the Covenant off one by one, until they were close enough to snatch the artifact up with the collapsible grav-pull drone ONI had included in the drop. It almost sounded like something from a holo-film, it was that cool. He knew he shouldn't think that way, but he just couldn't help himself.

Still, he had to hand it to Dorian. Without his little plan, they'd be back at the new campsite, just . . . sitting there.

Thunder rumbled through the clouds, bringing with it another surge of rain. Owen's voice crackled in his ear.

"Have you reached the entrance, Local Team?"

"Almost," Victor replied, looking at the map emblazoned across his HUD. The lens was blurred from the rain, but he could still make out the path. "ETA five minutes."

"Copy." Owen's line fell quiet. Victor glanced over his shoulder at Saskia, who was following up his lead. He could barely make out Evie and Dorian behind her.

And then he stepped out of the woods, onto the smooth flat surface of a road. Rue Pin.

Even with the rain he felt exposed. Naked. The road stretched in both directions, dark and empty and disappearing into the rain's thick haze. Across the way were the blocks of buildings. Warehouses and shipping containers. Whatever they once contained was abandoned now.

"All right, team," he said. "Stick to the underbrush. Let's go."

He stayed right on the edge of the forest, where they could afford a little cover and where they could keep an eye on the road. It remained empty, no sign of Covenant scouts. But Victor didn't let his guard down.

"Come in, Local Team." Owen again.

"Not there yet," Victor said.

"I want you underground before the op starts."

"I know." Victor shoved aside a tangle of vines, revealing the turn off to Rue Flot a few paces away. "I've got eyes on it."

"Good."

Victor gestured at the others to stop, still scanning the street. Rain pounded over the landscape, turning to mist when it hit the ground. Victor wiped at his shooting glasses, trying to clear away the steam and rivulets of water. In the haze, every building looked like a hulking Covenant ship, every shadow a creeping Covenant scout.

"What are you seeing?" Victor asked.

"Looks clear to me," Evie said.

"Same," said Dorian.

Saskia stepped forward, swinging her rifle around with her gaze. "Seems too quiet," she said.

"Maybe we just got lucky." Dorian hoisted up his gun. "I say we make a break for it."

Victor gave one last look around the street. "Agree," he said. Then, pressing the integrated comm on his helmet: "Spartan, we're going in."

"Happy hunting," Owen said grimly.

Victor nodded at the others. Then he sprinted out into the road, legs pumping. The rain pelted him. He could hear the others behind him: the pounding of their footsteps against the road, the puffs of their breaths. And the rain, of course, roaring all around them.

He swerved around the corner onto Rue Flot, and the entrance waited up ahead, a metal cylinder jutting out of the soaked ground. He ducked his head, pushed himself forward. The entrance was so close—

A shriek cut through the static noise of the rain. Behind him, one of the girls shouted and then opened fire. Victor whirled around, momentarily blinded by the rain.

A green bolt soared past him.

"A Grunt!" Saskia hollered, still firing.

"Spotted!" Dorian yelled.

Victor couldn't see anything in the rain. He fired in the direction of the plasma bolts, eager to cut off the Grunt before it could call for backup. The creature shrieked again and then materialized in the mist, loping toward them. It shot off another round from its plasma pistol. Missed.

It can't see either, Victor realized.

He lifted up his rifle, aiming for the methane mask all the Grunts wore. Water sluiced into his eyes. His fingers were slippery. He couldn't see *anything*.

And then he thought about the holo-films he used to make, how he'd shoot sloppy and the footage never came out. He had finally realized he had to calm down. He had to breathe.

And that was what he did. Took a deep breath. Wiped at his shooting glasses.

The Grunt swiveled its oversized head toward him, the mask like a target.

Victor squeezed the trigger.

The mask shattered; the alien flew backward. "Got him!" Victor said, and then he took off again, his heart pounding. The tunnel entrance seemed to pull away from him. He let out a shout of frustration and then he was slamming up against the entrance, yanking hard on the door. He dove into the stairwell, the *drip drip drip* of the rainwater echoing against the metal walls. Evie plunged in after him, then Dorian, and then finally Saskia, who pulled the door shut, immersing them in a sudden and impenetrable darkness.

Dorian cursed. "The explosion must have knocked out the emergency lights."

And they hadn't been able to bring a flashlight. Supplies were limited, and all three of the militia's flashlights had gone to the primary mission.

"I got it," Evie said. Then she went silent, and all Victor could hear was the dripping rainwater, the scrape of canvas. He felt unmoored, like he was buried in nothingness.

Then there was a paltry flare of light. The map projector. It cast everything in a thin blue glow. Victor could barely make out the faces of the others.

"This'll have to do," Dorian sighed.

"It'll be fine," Victor said, burying his fear. He tapped on his helmet. "Spartan, we're in."

The connection crackled. "Good. Proceed as planned. Keep me updated."

"Understood." Victor nodded at the others. "All right," he said. "Dorian, take it from here."

Evie handed Dorian the projector, and Dorian descended the stairs, sweeping the map from side to side. The light flickered over the walls, making every corner and angle of the stairwell seem to move.

"Could you hold that still, please?" Victor asked.

"How else am I going to see anything?" Dorian shot back. "It's going to be worse when we get closer to the explosion site." He paused. "Wish Salome would have mentioned the freaking lights were out. If I'd known, we could have insisted on one of those flashlights."

"Well, you kept telling her you weren't going down here," Evie said. "So that probably had something to do with it."

Saskia laughed, and Dorian made an irritated noise under his breath.

They walked single file through the dark, dripping tunnel, the flickering map light guiding their way. It threw strange shapes on the walls, illuminating the splotches of mold that crawled like some Covenant poison over the metal.

"How do you think the others are doing?" Evie said suddenly.

No one answered. Victor figured they just didn't want to think about it. Hell, he didn't really want to think about it, even though he did anyway: They'd just be falling into formation now, approaching the excavation site in teams of three or four, preparing to strike—

A clatter ripped through the tunnel, loud as an explosion.

"Sorry!" Dorian shouted. "That was me. Sorry." The light swung around. "I told you, I can barely see anything."

"What was it?" Saskia asked, peering over Victor's shoulder.

Victor couldn't see anything but the formless shadows of Dorian and Evie up ahead.

"Chunk of metal," Dorian said. Then he kicked it again, and the clatter rebounded off the walls.

"Stop," Evie said. "You want to call the Covenant down here?"

"I'm just trying to get it out of your way." Another scrape of metal against metal. "There. We must be getting close, though."

"You have the map up," Victor said. "You mean you don't know where we are?"

Victor could feel Dorian glaring at him.

"Yeah, I know where we are," he snapped. "What I don't know, exactly, is where the artifact is. *Exactly*," he added, before Victor could say anything.

"Fighting isn't going to help any of us," Saskia said. "And you know that the faster we secure this thing"—a pause, and Victor knew she was thinking *if we can secure this thing*—"the sooner we can get everyone else out of a firefight. So let's keep moving."

Her words left them sobered and quiet.

On they walked, this time without speaking, even when Dorian kicked debris out of the way. Victor resisted the urge to check in with Owen—he'd been given strict orders only to make contact if they had the artifact secured.

After a time, the air in the tunnel shifted, turning acrid and stale. Victor's boots squelched in thick patches of mud, and when he reached out to steady himself, his hand touched wet clay, not the smooth cold metal he was expecting. He jerked his arm back to his chest. "We're close, aren't we?"

"We're getting into the unstable area, yeah." Dorian's voice sounded far away. "There's a turn up ahead that's going to be the real trick. Then we should be there. At least we don't have all that dust like before."

Their pace slowed. More than once Victor scraped his head against the peeling strips of ceiling dangling overhead. The debris piles grew big enough to see even in the thin light of the map, and they rose up out of the mud and the grating like lopsided, crumbling mountains. Victor found himself thinking of Owen as they made their way through the destruction—Owen, having been defeated up above, lying dead at the base of the excavation site.

Could Spartans even die?

"Stop," Dorian said. "We're at the turnoff."

He had set the map projector on the ground in the entrance. There was no door, and the entrance itself was much too big anyway, a jagged, charred hole where the true entrance used to be. Victor slowed and peered in, his shoulder brushing against the edge, crumbling it into black ash.

In the quiet of their stillness, he could hear the distant thud of weapons firing.

"Let's hope we can do this fast," Evie said softly. "Give the other teams their best chance."

Victor nodded, but really he felt a vague guilt emanating from somewhere deep inside his chest. This was the second time he'd gone creeping underground while other soldiers were putting their lives on the line. Soldiers like his sisters. Soldiers like Dubois and Caird and even Valois.

Dorian knelt beside the map and turned it, light-shapes flashing over the destruction in the tunnel. Lining up the map to the actual tunnel.

"Here," Dorian said. "This is where the artifact should be. We're here." He pointed to a deceptively close place on the map.

"It's a straight shot," Saskia said.

"Yes, but according to the images Salome sent me, it's not a *clear* shot. You thought the debris was bad out here?" Dorian lifted the map, keeping it lined up, and stepped through the entrance. Immediately, Victor could see what he meant; rather than being swallowed up by the negative space, as it had for the duration of their walk, the light shone across a wall of blackened metal.

"We have to get through that," Dorian said.

Victor stared at the blockage. Thought about how the edges of the entrance had crumbled at his touch.

"Hold on," he said.

He picked up a chunk of metal from one of the debris piles; it had melted into something vaguely ball-shaped. Then he flung it into the blockage.

It tore through the debris with a cloud of ash and dirt. At first, nothing happened. Then there was a low, angry grinding. Dorian cursed and scrambled backward just as the debris pile collapsed, sending out an explosion of ash that clung to Victor's skin and coated the back of his throat.

"Nice job," Dorian choked out. "Now we're filthy."

"There's a path through, though." Evie grinned at Victor. "Nice job."

He shrugged. "Hey, you remember that scene from *Triple Retreat*? Just stealing the idea."

Evie laughed.

"Okay, that's great," Saskia said, edging closer to the entrance. "But is it safe for us to go in there?"

"Probably not," Dorian said. "But it's safer than being up there."

Victor glanced up at the ceiling. It was quiet enough again to hear the fighting overhead. Gunfire, the shuddery explosions of artillery. "We've got to do this fast," he said. He hoped they were able to do it at all.

"Agreed," Evie said, brushing past him. "Dorian, hold up the light. Let's see how much of a path Victor cleared."

Dorian did as she asked, lifting the map. Blue lines of light bounced over the wreckage inside the tunnel. Evie crept forward, twisting around the collapsed debris. Then she stopped.

"Closer," she said.

Dorian moved in after her, and after a moment's pause and a quick exchanged glance, so did Victor and Saskia.

Evie stood with her hands on her hips, gazing up at the debris. "I'm going to have to climb it," she announced.

"Be careful," Dorian said, edging closer with the light.

She pressed one foot against the debris. Shifted her weight. The pile held. She hoisted herself up, moving slowly, cautiously. It reminded Victor suddenly of the first time they had climbed a banyan tree together when they were children.

Her foot slipped, sending a twisted sheet of metal flying into the mud. "I'm fine!" she called out. Pulled herself up again. Victor found himself edging closer, his muscles tensed, ready to catch her if she fell.

But she didn't fall. A few second later, she vanished over the top of the debris.

"Light!" she shouted. "I can't see anything."

Dorian glanced at the others. "I'm not going over," he said. "Just up."

Victor nodded. Dorian crept cautiously up the side of the pile, holding the map in one hand. Victor held his breath, wondering if the debris could hold Dorian's weight.

"Can you see yet?" Dorian yelled, hoisting the map over his head.

"A little!" Evie's voice was plaintive, far away. "Can you get any more?"

Dorian's shoulder hitched, but he kept going, pushing himself up higher. Saskia made a worried noise. Blue light splayed across the top half of the tunnel, revealing the shredded ceiling, the bare spots of dirt and clay.

"I can see!" Evie said. "It's not bad, actually! And I think I see the—"

An immense clap of thunder rolled through the tunnel. The world jolted, clumps of mud raining down on Saskia and Victor. The debris pile scattered, all the metal glinting in the map light for one shuddering second before Dorian hollered and the light blinked out.

"Damn it!" Victor said. "That can't be good."

The sound of gunfire echoed overhead.

"Dorian!" Saskia called. "Evie! Can you hear us?"

The tunnel shuddered again. More rain of mud and, this time, the shredded remains of the ceiling, the sharp edges slicing open Victor's skin. He fumbled in the dark for Saskia. "We've got to get out of here," he said. "Those explosions, they're going to bring this whole place down—"

Suddenly, Owen's voice flared in his ear. "Local Team! Come in, Local Team!"

Victor activated the comm. "Owen?" he said, all his memorized protocol forgotten in the darkness. "What's going on?"

The ground shuddered again, throwing Victor sideways. He slammed up against something warm and yielding. Saskia screeched in surprise, then grabbed his arm. "Victor?"

"Have you found the object?" Owen said. Victor could hear the rattle of gunfire over the communicator.

"No." He gritted his teeth; Saskia was still gripping hard onto his arm, her nails digging into his skin. Where were Dorian and Evie? The light was still out. "We're almost the—"

"Things are not going well up here," Owen said. "We have no way of approaching the artifact. I can't—"

And then he cut out, and Victor heard the same gunfire, muffled now, spilling down from up above.

"What did he say?" Saskia's voice drifted out of the darkness.

"They can't get to the artifact." Victor swept his arm out, trying to feel for the debris pile. Something kept dusting across his head: dirt. "It sounds—" He couldn't bring himself to say it directly. "It sounds bad up there."

"Oh no," Saskia whispered.

"Dorian!" Victor yelled, his heart hammering in his throat. "Evie? Can you hear us? We need the light!"

More dirt showered down over them. Victor reached out in the dark for Saskia, wanting the comfort of knowing he wasn't alone. His hand graced against her arm, and she grabbed it, squeezing it tight.

"I hear you!" Evie shouted back. Victor let out a long sigh of relief. "I'm bringing the light over."

"Go," Saskia said in a shaky voice. "I'm fine. Get the light."

Victor moved toward the sound of Evie's voice. More dirt and mud and debris rained down on them.

"This tunnel is going to collapse," Saskia breathed. "We have to get out of here."

"As soon as we get the artifact," Victor responded into the darkness.

"The extraction team will never make it in time!"

A thin beam of blue light spilled over the top of the debris pile.

"Oh, thank god," Saskia said, dropping Victor's hand. She scurried over the pile, sending dirt and scrap metal sliding down. In the light, the dirt falling out of the ceiling looked like rain.

"Victor!" Evie called out as she helped Saskia over the mound. "Hurry! We've got to find a way out of here. Dorian says there's a closer exit at the end of this tunnel, but we have to hope it's not blocked."

"That's a relief." Victor heaved himself up onto the debris pile. It trembled beneath his weight. "But we've got to grab the artifact. The fighting's too bad up there. It's all on us."

Evie frowned, her face carved into strange shapes by the light. "The artifact? There's no way. Owen made it clear we weren't to touch it ourselves. And I know he would want us to put our safety first—"

Victor scrambled up beside her, panting a little. He looked down at the other side of the pile. What little of it he could see was clear. "We don't have a choice," he said. "We're going to have to risk it."

Evie stared at him with big shining eyes. Dirt crumbled around them.

"Are you serious?" she said.

He nodded.

Together, they scrambled off the top of the pile. Evie swept the map around until she found Dorian and Saskia.

"We have to get the artifact," Evie said to Dorian. "Without the extraction team." Victor braced himself for Dorian to protest, but Dorian just closed his eyes, took a deep breath.

"Owen's going to kill us," he said.

"We don't have a choice," Victor said. "We're the only ones who can do it."

"Do you even know where it is?" Saskia said. "Your map wasn't exactly . . . exact. I mean, I don't know if this tunnel is going to—"

Another explosion. Victor felt this one in the marrow of his bones.

"Yes!" Dorian shouted. "Look, we don't have time to stand around discussing it. I'm in!"

Evie tossed the map to him, and he bolted forward, lifting it high, shining it along the right-hand wall—what was left of it. Something deep inside the earth groaned, a sound like a giant waking.

For a paralyzing moment, there was nothing but darkness and blue light. And then something caught. A flash, like a fire flickering in the distance.

Dorian slid to a stop, swinging the light around. Another flash, brighter this time. It refracted the weak blue light of the map, throwing it in strange, iridescent shards around the tunnel. For the first time, Victor felt like he really saw where he was. He saw the destruction wrought by the explosions. Saw the deep gouges in the clay walls. Saw the constant, showering dirt.

"That's got to be it," Dorian said. "Victor, get over here and help me."

Dorian handed off the light to Evie, and she held it up. The refractions shimmered everywhere, dancing like butterflies. The artifact jutted out of the wall. It looked like a glass cylinder, maybe twenty-five centimeters in diameter.

All this trouble for a tube of glass.

"Let's hope this thing won't kill us," Dorian muttered.

The ground shuddered, sending with it a surge of dirt. Victor wiped it away from his eyes. "I'm willing to risk it."

"I guess I am too," Dorian said as the tunnel trembled again.

Victor stared at the artifact, his eyes stinging from the dirt. He took a deep breath, conjured up all his bravery.

Then ran over and grabbed hold of it.

He was prepared for it to burn his skin down to the bone. Instead, the artifact just felt cool and satiny to the touch. He pulled.

Nothing happened.

Dorian grabbed ahold of it too, then muttered, "We're in this together." Then: "Pull!"

They pulled.

"We can do this," Victor said. "Count of three."

Victor pulled with all his strength, his fingers pressing hard against the artifact's smooth shell. Beside him, Dorian groaned in exertion and then let out a string of profanity when the artifact remained in place. Victor released his grip and stumbled backward.

From deep inside the tunnel came a low, harsh creaking.

"Oh, that's not good," Evie said. "We've got to get out of here. If we can't even pull it out, we're never going to be able to carry—"

A sound like an explosion tore through the tunnel, and the ceiling shoved downward in an explosion of dust. Victor ducked, hitting the ground hard, his ears ringing. He lifted his gaze, panic squeezing his chest tight. Evie was right. They had to get out of here before the whole tunnel collapsed.

Dorian was the first one up, scooping out the dirt around the arti-fact with his hands. "Come on!" he said. "I bet it's just wedged in there."

"He's right," Victor said, getting shakily to his feet. He peered up at the ceiling, pressing dangerously low. "We don't have any other choice."

"Digging is going to take too long." Saskia brushed past him and walked over to Dorian. She put one hand on his arm, and he stopped and looked at her. In the aftermath of the explosion, everything was too quiet.

"What do you suggest, then?" he said bitterly.

Saskia pulled her rifle around on its strap. "If it's wedged in there," she said, "we need a lever to help pry it out."

"You're going to shoot it out?" Dorian said icily.

Saskia released the rifle's magazine, dumping her ammo to the ground.

"No," she said.

"You need a fulcrum," Evie said, suddenly understanding Saskia's plan. "Victor, help find a rock. Something to balance the gun on."

"It needs to be the same height as the artifact." Saskia was field-stripping her rifle, sliding the barrel away from the stock. Victor whipped his head around, following the path of the light from Evie's projection. She stopped it on a particular triangular-shaped rock a meter away from the artifact.

"How about that one?" she asked, just as Victor said, "That'll work."

They glanced at each other. Evie smiled at him, remembering all those hours spent combing over the rocks on the beach, making miniature mountains for his holo-films.

"Well, let's move it into place," Dorian said. The three of them circled around the rock and shoved. Unlike the artifact, it scraped easily across the debris.

The ceiling shrieked, sank a few centimeters lower.

"Hurry!" Evie called out to Saskia, who was balancing a loose piece of the tunnel's metal reinforcement on top of the rifle stock.

"I've got it." She darted over to the rock just as Dorian and Victor shoved it into place. Dirt fell down around them as the ceiling dropped even lower. Gunfire rang out on the surface.

Saskia jammed the piece of metal under the artifact, her face twisted in concentration. Sweat gleamed in blue drops on her forehead as Evie directed the light toward her work. Then Saskia picked up her rifle and wedged it under the metal, the two pieces balanced like a child's toy on top of the rock.

"Okay," she said, a little breathlessly. "Here goes nothing."

Another shower of dirt. Another creak of the ceiling.

She pushed down on the makeshift lever, and the artifact jumped in the wet dirt. Evie let out a whoop of celebration, but Saskia was still pressing down on the lever, wiggling it back and forth.

"Here, let me help," Dorian said, and he added his strength to

Saskia's. Once again the artifact jumped, this time sliding forward from its place in the wall. Clumps of mud showered down around it. Saskia pressed on the lever with her foot, and the artifact tilted downward.

"We've got it!" Dorian said.

"Victor, don't let it fall!" Saskia added, and Victor darted forward just as the artifact finally slid loose on the back of a mudslide. It landed easily in the crook of his arms, not heavy at all. He was also relieved that it didn't burn through his clothes or otherwise seem to immediately poison him.

"Good thinking." He glanced up at Saskia, but she was staring at the wall, her eyes wide.

"We've got to go now," she said.

And then Victor saw it. The crack where the artifact had been. And in the blue light, it was deepening.

"Straight ahead!" Dorian shouted. "If it's blocked, we're screwed, but we're not getting out otherwise. Evie!"

But she was already in front, running with the map hoisted over her head. Victor cradled the artifact against his chest as his feet pounded through the mud, his head tilted down to avoid the constant cascade of dirt.

"The shelter tunnels are better reinforced!" Dorian called out. "We get to them and we should be fine. But we've got to *run*!"

Everything was rumbling. Clumps of dirt exploded around Victor. One landed on his head, showering him in dust. He spit it out, kept running.

"I see it!" Evie screamed. "The exit!"

And then Victor saw it too. A door. This one hadn't been blasted away, although it hung open, revealing a sliver of light on the other side. The emergency lights were still up.

The earth groaned again, then roared. Dirt was piling up around them.

Evie flung the door open, flooding the collapsing tunnel with eerie white light.

Victor dove forward, the artifact pressed to his heart, eyes shut in a wish for safety.

CHAPTER ELEVEN

EVIE

The sound of the earth caving in was like the end of the world. Evie lay on the grating inside the shelter tunnel, listening to that sound echo around her. Mud and debris spilled in through the open door, piling up on her like a grave. But the shelter tunnel's infrastructure held.

Dorian cursed softly when the collapse ended, when they were drowning in silence again.

Evie pushed herself up to sitting and tried to wipe the dirt out of her eyes—but there was dirt on her hands, and it just made things worse. Her eyes stung and watered. Her mouth was full of mud. She spat a stream of it onto the grating.

"Spartan," Victor was saying into his communicator. "Spartan, come in." A pause. He clung to the artifact like a lifeboat. At first glance, it looked like a piece of polished glass. But as Evie stared at it, she saw a glow inside, pale and opalescent.

She shivered, trying not to consider what it might be doing to him.

"Owen!" Victor shouted. "We got it!" But he fell silent again, and his expression changed. Darkened.

Things had gone bad. The explosions. The gunfire.

The collapsing tunnel.

But at least Owen must still be alive, Evie told herself. At least all of them were.

"Understood," Victor said, then tapped the side of his helmet. He looked up at the others.

"What's the word, great leader?" Dorian said.

Victor, to his credit, ignored this. "We reconvene at the new campsite," he said. "Things . . . didn't go well up there."

"Can we get to a safe exit from here?" Saskia asked.

Dorian felt around on the ground, his head lolling. "Where the hell's the map?"

"I still have it," Evie said. The lines glowed softly in the emergency lights. Funny how brilliant they had been in the absolute darkness. She handed it to Dorian, who drew it out, the pattern of tunnels crisscrossing.

"Looks like we can get out at Rue Chêne," he said. "That's not bad."

Evie frowned down at the map. Rue Chêne. It was on the edge of the woods, so they'd be trekking quite a while to get to the campsite. She glanced over at Victor again. The artifact glowed faintly against his hands.

"Are you okay holding that?" she asked him.

"Yeah," he said. "It's cool to the touch. Want to feel it?" He held the tube out, and it threw off cataracts of rainbow lights.

"Be careful," Saskia said in a low voice. She looked up at the others. "I think we need to decide how we want to carry this thing. Victor, Dorian—you're the only two who have had contact with it so far."

Dorian gave her a dark look. "So what are you saying? We get the honors of being expendable?"

"What? No." Saskia glared at him. "I'm just saying, if the two of you hold it, that minimizes the exposure to the group."

"It hasn't done anything to me so far." Victor shrugged.

"It could eventually." Evie frowned, considering her words carefully. She hoped her suggestion wouldn't turn out to be a terrible one, but she also knew they had to get out of the tunnels fast. They couldn't stand around arguing about who deserved exposure. "That might be a reason for us to take turns carrying it. Even if it hasn't done anything now, long-term exposure could cause problems. Like radiation, you know."

The group fell silent. Evie looked over at Saskia, who was frowning, her brow furrowed.

"Maybe," she said.

"I'll take it for now," Evie said, swallowing a lump of fear. She held out her hands and accepted the strange glowing object from Victor. He was right; it was cool to the touch. Lighter than she expected too.

They set out, moving quickly through the shelter tunnels. Evie cradled the artifact against her chest and felt the rattle of something inside it. Not the light: That stayed put. But there was something else, something small and possibly broken, something that clinked against the glass with each of her steps.

She didn't want to think about what that something could be.

When they made it to the exit, Evie handed the artifact off to Dorian, since Saskia would be leading them through the woods. He looked down at it, frowning.

"A lot of effort for something so—" He stopped. "You ever been to the art museum in Port Moyne?"

Evie nodded, then laughed a little, despite everything. "Yeah. It's like those blown glass sculptures they have, isn't it?"

He tilted the artifact; the thing inside slid back and forth, moving invisibly through the light. "Let's hope it actually is some ancient alien crap, huh? If ONI wants it so bad, then it's got to help us out somehow, right? Use the Covenant's own obsessions against them."

Evie thought about the explosions, the incessant rattle of gunfire. Things going bad, all so they could get ahold of this tube of glass. "Let's hope so."

Saskia and Victor led them up the stairs; Evie followed behind Dorian. All of them had their rifles out.

Saskia kicked open the door. Evie ducked her head against the unexpected flood of sunlight.

"Ugh, I miss the rain," Dorian muttered. The artifact shimmered in his hands.

"That thing is a freaking beacon," Evie said.

"No kidding," Dorian said. He shifted around, grabbing for his bag; spangles of light flashed over the soft blowing grasses. "Good lord," he muttered.

"Let's keep moving," Victor said. "Dorian, try to hide that damn thing."

"Oh, I'm trying." Dorian crammed the artifact into his bag, but only about half of it fit. He sighed, wrapped his arm around the exposed half.

They made it to the woods without incident. There was a quietness out there that Evie didn't like, especially given that it was a late-season sunny patch. Normally insects and animals would be wailing from their invisible spots up in the trees, a sense of the world emerging from its rain-soaked cocoon.

But today: silence. Silence, and the occasional whiff of smoke.

Still, they made it through the woods without incident. No sign of the Covenant anywhere. But as they approached the campsite, Evie felt a queasiness in the pit of her stomach. It was quiet here too.

"You want to be the one to hand it over?" Dorian asked Victor, pulling the artifact out of his bag. "Since you did most of the hard work?"

Victor only shook his head, though, looking grim.

Dorian offered it to Saskia. She wrinkled her nose. He turned to Evie.

"Walk it in for us," he said. "We did good, and this plan would've never gotten off the ground without you."

He knew something was wrong too. She could hear it in the forced chipperness of his voice, the strained edges of his smile. And that was why she took the artifact from him, balancing it on her two palms, blinking down at the fragmented light. Even with the streaks of mud their fingers had left on the glass, it glowed like starlight.

They stepped into the camp, Victor leading the way. The queasiness in Evie's stomach turned sour. Her hands were shaking. She peered up at the tattered lean-tos, the precious few tents from the emergency drop.

At the *emptiness.*

And it *was* empty. Not entirely, but enough to be upsetting. The few people who were here were sitting in the mud, not speaking. Almost all of them were dotted with rough splotches of MediGel or biofoam, their expressions slack. Dubois was among them, and he lifted one hand in grim greeting.

"Oh my god," Saskia said.

"Owen told me it had gone bad—" But Victor didn't finish, just shook his head.

Evie curled her fingers around the artifact. Light bounced across the camp, and soldiers turned toward them, as if noticing them for the first time.

"Is that it?" Dubois called out. "Is that what we were fighting for?"

"Where's Owen?" Victor said, too loudly.

Evie found it hard to fill her lungs with breath. She cradled the artifact close to her chest, aware of everyone staring at it, their expressions wary and dark.

"Spartan!" shouted a man with MediGel drying over the left half of his face. It was Valois, the one who was always hassling Victor. "They did it. Probably poisoning themselves, the way she's holding that thing, but they did it."

Owen stepped out of the largest tent. His visor was up, and he looked exhausted—the first time Evie had ever seen him look that way. She'd seen him injured—horrifically so—but never so . . . defeated. He strode across the camp, his pace picking up.

"Set that down immediately," he barked.

Evie did as she was asked, sliding the artifact onto the ground. "We couldn't wait for the extraction team," she said. "The tunnels were going to collapse, and—"

"I understand," he said. "You disobeyed orders, but I can understand. Still, we have to minimize contact."

"We swapped who held it," Victor said. "Since it didn't seem like it was doing anything—"

"That was probably unwise, but there's nothing we can do about it now." Owen lifted the artifact up to his line of sight. It looked so small in his huge grip.

"It was sticking out of the side of the tunnel," Dorian said. "Thanks to Saskia, we were able to pry it out pretty easily, once we dealt with the debris."

Owen nodded. "Come with me," he said, whirling around, marching back toward his tent. Evie glanced at the others—did he mean all of them? Just Dorian?

"Let's go," Saskia whispered.

They cut across the camp. Evie could feel the stares of the surviving members of the militia sticking to them like spiderwebs. She couldn't look any of them in the eye.

Owen held the tent flap open for them as they ducked inside, one by one. Then he set the artifact on a big metal cube that she realized was the box the emergency drop must have come in. The five of them just stood around it, staring at it as it glowed steadily in the dim light.

"We lost seventy percent of the militia," Owen said.

A pang of sorrow shot through Evie's chest. Someone—maybe Victor—let out a sharp gasp. The others were silent.

"The Covenant were stronger than we suspected," Owen continued. "They had more support than our reports suggested. And the excavation site was too heavily reinforced for us to even attempt an extraction." Owen took a deep breath, his expression weary but focused. "We're lucky you came up with an alternate plan. Even if you had to disobey my order to carry it out."

Evie glanced at Dorian, who was looking down at his feet, his hair falling into his eyes, hiding his face.

"Why'd you do it in the first place?" Saskia said. "Go in fighting like that?" There was a quaver in her voice.

"Those were our orders based on the available intel," Owen said. "Sometimes intel is on point, and sometimes it's off—either way, we can't afford to make decisions based on anything else. There are millions of lives at stake. It's our job to keep Meridian from falling, and we have to do that based on more than a best guess."

Evie's pang of sorrow turned to a dull throb of unease. She understood the urgency, the importance, of their mission. And the last thing she wanted was for Meridian to fall to the Covenant. But something in Owen's tone still suggested that Command was looking to squeeze every last useful drop out of a militia that had—against all odds—outlived a one-way trip.

"Fortunately, in the end, we were successful." Owen sighed and turned his gaze on the artifact. "You proved yourselves capable soldiers."

Evie shifted her weight, crossed her arms over her body. Glanced over at Dorian. He looked up at the right moment and their eyes caught, and she wondered if he was thinking the same thing as she was: That, while the attack might not have been Owen's idea, it *had* been his to let them go into the tunnel after all, despite the danger.

"Do you know what the artifact is?" Victor said.

Owen shook his head. "I don't have a clue." He paused. "ONI has experts, of course, but it's looking like it might be difficult to make contact."

"Are you serious?" Dorian blurted out. "I thought this whole thing was their idea!"

"Yes," Owen said. "But as I just said, it's clear now that the Covenant forces here in Brume-sur-Mer, and likely on Meridian in general, are much stronger than we anticipated. Our fight here is one very small part in a very large theater of operations on this side of the moon. A lot of people need extraction right now, not just us. So we may be stuck here for the time being."

"What the hell?" shouted Dorian. "Getting this thing was supposed to be our ticket home!"

"Don't talk to him like that," Victor snapped.

The blood rushed through Evie's ears. She didn't want to think about this—the possibility that after all they had gone through they weren't even going to be able to get the artifact to ONI. She glided forward, knelt down in front of the metal tube. The artifact glowed steadily. Behind her, Dorian and Victor were bickering. She tuned them out, focused just on the artifact. Something had been inside of it. But it was impossible to actually see because of that bright light.

"Can I borrow the exo-gloves?" she asked.

"Leave it to the experts at ONI," Owen said.

Evie looked up at him. "They may not be able to look at it. I promise I won't do anything dangerous."

Owen frowned, but he handed her a bulky, gray pair of gloves. She put them on, the exo-material heavy and hot against her skin. Then she reached out and picked up the artifact. Tilted it to hear the *clink*. Tilted the other way. Another *clink*.

She thought of the gifts her father used to give her when she was a little girl. Clever puzzles she had to solve before she could access her real gift. It had been his way of encouraging her interest in problem-solving and computer science, but she'd always had a fondness for those physical puzzles.

And this artifact reminded her of one.

She tilted again, listened to the *clink*.

"What are you doing?" Saskia asked.

"Quiet," Evie said. "I'm thinking." She held the artifact between her two palms. No sign of movement inside. The surface was smooth. No seams. No cracks.

She tilted it. *Clink*.

She glanced up at Owen. "There's something inside. I'm trying to figure out how to get at it."

"I'm afraid this counts as doing something dangerous," Owen said.

"I have the gloves on." Evie gripped the artifact and twisted. Nothing happened. She moved her hands over the side of the cylinder, testing it.

The cylinder moved. The light inside flickered.

A shout came up from the others. Evie almost dropped the artifact in surprise.

"That's enough," Owen said. "Please put the artifact down. We don't have the protections in place that ONI has in their labs."

She looked up at him, her breath held tight in her chest. "Please," she said. "We can send whatever observations I make to ONI through the comms. They might be able to use it."

Owen frowned.

"I think it's a puzzle," she said. "Just a few more seconds."

Owen crouched down beside her. "Be *careful*."

She twisted again, in the same spot, but nothing happened. She hoped she was right, that this was a puzzle, and not a trap ... or that activating whatever was inside wouldn't do any harm.

She took a deep breath. So she couldn't see seams, but something in the artifact could move. She twisted again, back the other way. Another flicker.

The others were crowding in close; she could feel their breath on the back of her neck. She pushed the sensation away, however, focusing just on the puzzle.

She ran her hands up the length of the cylinder. Nothing.

She gave it a shake. Nothing.

She twisted again, in the same spot, and this time the light blinked out.

"Oh my god!" she shouted, dropping the artifact onto the table. It rolled sideways, clinking the entire time. Owen grabbed it before it rolled off the surface.

"We are obviously not getting the kind of data that would be useful for ONI," he said. "Even if there's nothing dangerous about the artifact itself, the Covenant could very well be attempting to track it right now. That's the last thing we need."

"Do they even know we have the artifact?" Saskia said.

Owen shot her a dark look. "If they don't know, they will soon enough."

"I was getting somewhere with it," Evie said.

Owen set the artifact down on the table. Even with the light out, Evie couldn't see the object inside. The glass was just dark, like the cylinder had filled with smoke.

"Let me try one more thing," she said. "Please. The Covenant could track the artifact to us regardless of what I do now. And maybe I can—deactivate it somehow."

Owen's frowned deepened. "I'm not sure that's how it works."

"It's worth a shot," she said. "If we have to hold on to it until we can deliver it to ONI."

A long pause. And then Owen nodded once. Immediately, Evie picked up the artifact and tried twisting again.

And this time, the top half of the cylinder twisted all the way around. The light blinked back on, even brighter than before: a shimmering, opalescent glare that stung at Evie's eyes. She twisted it to darkness. Twisted again, only halfway.

The light gathered into a point. Evie froze. The point of light brightened, streaming between her fingers. She glanced up at Owen.

"You've started some kind of reaction," he said urgently. "Stop it. Immediately."

Evie twisted, slowing her movements down. The light flickered, faster and faster the slower she twisted, until when she stopped it was flickering on its own, the light shimmering like static across her face. Panic rose up in her throat. "I can't get it to stop," she whispered.

"I don't think you need to," Victor said. "Evie, look."

She lifted her gaze off the cylinder and gasped. Geometric shapes floated in the air above them, dancing as if they were sparks of light caught on a sheet of metal. Circles and half circles floated into a triangle; dots spun around like stars.

"Keep going," Owen said. "I recognize this. It's a map."

"What?" Saskia said. "How do you know?"

"I've seen this Forerunner script, in this configuration, before. And it was a map then."

"Really?" Evie's heart pounded. "Can you read it?"

"No. But keep going. It should show us something soon."

Evie twisted, trying different patterns of movement. The cylinder spun more easily now, and the glyphs flickered and changed, orbiting one another like planets. Eventually they moved closer and closer, their edges bleeding together. Evie kept twisting. Slow, then fast, then slow again. The shapes merged into an enormous corona of light.

A *clink* rang out from inside the cylinder.

Immediately, the corona exploded into a million points of light that hung suspended, filling the tent. Evie jumped in surprise. But it wasn't an explosion at all.

"What the—" Dorian said.

"It *is* a map," Saskia breathed. "Of the galaxy,"

The dots of light drew together, forming a bright sphere that slowly carved into itself swirling gases of yellow and green. A planet. An extremely familiar planet.

"It's Hestia V!" shrieked Victor.

The phantom Meridian spun lazily around the gas giant, the features dimming into a smoky murk.

"What's happening?" Saskia said.

"Look," Evie said, because there was a single bright spot left on the Forerunners' concept of Meridian, a fiery beacon glowing in the northernmost part of Caernaruan, far on the top of the world.

Meridian stopped spinning. The light pulsed.

And then the image shifted, flattening out. Caernaruan spread out in front of them, the point of light still blinking, blinking, blinking.

Suddenly, a green holo-map snapped into existence. Evie turned around; it was Dorian, holding up his map projector.

"Let's find out where this stupid light is," he said, and zoomed out from Brume-sur-Mer's tunnel systems to the entire moon, then zipping over to Caernaruan. The green lines overlaid the image of Caernaruan, lining up perfectly. Dorian zoomed in on that blinking light. It shimmered over a net of lines on the map. A city.

"Annecy," Dorian said, reading the map's label. "It's pointing to Annecy."

And then, abruptly, the glowing image of Caernaruan vanished in a flash of white light, leaving only Dorian's map. The artifact itself went dark and lifeless. Evie stared at it for a long moment, then set it down carefully on the table.

"Now what?" Dorian asked, breaking the silence.

Owen looked up at them. "I'm contacting ONI," he said. "You were right. They're going to want to know about this."

There wasn't much to do at that point but go back out to the camp and find a place to wait for Commander Marechal's orders. It was raining again, a faint drizzle that only hinted at the storms that swept through the area during the height of the rainy season. *Still, it's just enough rain to be miserable*, Evie thought as she burrowed beneath a pile of wide palm trees someone had brought in for shelter. The drizzle turned the dirt from the cave-in into a sticky, dark mud, and Evie wiped at it disconsolately, succeeding not in cleaning it off but just in smearing it worse. She wanted to complain, but if she looked up, she saw soldiers resting out their injuries and their grief, and she felt sheepish in her discomfort.

"I can't believe Command sent them out there like that," Dorian said softly beside her. He sat with his arms thrown over his knees, his expression dark. "I thought it was weird that the commander and Owen were being so adamant about the attack."

"They're soldiers," Victor said. "They knew what they signed up for."

Dorian rolled his eyes. "Look around you, man. Every single squad lost someone." He paused. "Except for us."

"Just because we didn't fight," Evie said.

Victor looked down at the dirt. "Weren't allowed to fight," he muttered.

"And thank god for that," Dorian said. "You think we would be here now if we'd gone into that battle? We'd be dead, or injured, and we wouldn't have secured that thing." He jerked his head back toward Owen's tent, where they'd left the artifact.

Victor scowled and opened his mouth to protest. But Saskia interrupted him.

"Dorian's right," she said. "And now their deaths weren't totally in vain."

They went quiet at that and sat without speaking as the rain picked up. Finally, the mud on Evie's skin started to streak away.

About an hour later, Owen came charging out of his tent. "Evie," he said. "Commander Marechal and I need to speak with you."

Evie straightened up, her heart pounding. She exchanged quick glances with the others, wondering if it was obvious how nervous she was.

Owen tilted his head toward the Command tent.

"Good luck," Dorian whispered.

She shot him an angry look—was he *trying* to make her more nervous?—and then jogged over to Owen. Together they walked into the tent. Commander Marechal was sitting at the desk, a holo projection lighting up the murky interior. Evie put her hand to her forehead in a salute, and Commander Marechal nodded. "At ease."

She dropped her hand, but her shoulders were still tense with anxiety. The air in the tent was muggy and thick from the rain. She could barely breathe.

"Thank you for joining us," said a female voice. The holo flickered, and Captain Dellatorre materialized in the air above the desk. Evie felt a jolt of fear, a jolt of excitement.

"Yes," Commander Marechal said. "Thank you. Please, have a seat."

Evie glanced at Owen, but his face was impassive. She slid into the rickety chair set up beside the projection of Captain Dellatorre.

"Spartan-B096 has informed me of the success of your mission."

Evie said nothing, just squeezed her hands together in her lap. She would hardly call the loss of 70 percent of the militia a success.

"He also informed me that you managed to activate the artifact." Captain Dellatorre pressed her lips into a wan smile. "That should have been done under the controlled conditions of a laboratory."

A silence hung over the dark, humid tent. Evie realized she was expected to respond.

"I understand that," she said softly. "But with the delay in getting the artifact to ONI, I thought—"

Captain Dellatorre waved one hand, the light of the holo trailing after her movement. "You disobeyed a direct order. Or rather, convinced Spartan-B096 to disobey a direct order."

Evie forced herself not to look over at Owen.

"You were deeply lucky the artifact wasn't a weapon—or something worse. There is a reason we have protocol for handling these objects."

Evie took a deep breath. Out of the corner of her eye, she could see Commander Marechal watching her, and she felt vaguely dizzy.

"I understand," she whispered, her cheeks hot.

"Do not do it again."

Evie sat as still as possible, her fingers prickling from being clenched so tight. "I won't."

"Good." Captain Dellatorre lifted her chin imperiously. The light from the holo was burning Evie's eyes. "Now. To the matter at hand. Rousseau, I invited you to this briefing because you did crack open the map inside the artifact. You showed an aptitude for interacting with Forerunner technology. And that may prove useful."

Evie's anxiety shifted. What did that mean?

Captain Dellatorre gazed out through the holo-projection. "I'm saddened to report that conditions above your position have worsened."

Captain Marechal frowned. "In what way?"

"The fighting has grown even more intense. The Covenant is managing to penetrate Meridian's orbital lines and funnel more and more forces groundside—just as you experienced today."

Beside her, Owen shifted his weight.

"And unfortunately, extraction off Meridian is impossible at the moment. For everyone." She paused, tilted her head toward Evie. "Including our youngest team members."

At first, Evie didn't quite grasp what Captain Dellatorre was saying.

No extraction. No way off Meridian.

"Are you certain?" Commander Marechal asked. "My group's been through a lot as it is, and we still have the Covenant bearing down on us. That artifact itself could be a damn beacon."

"I understand," Captain Dellatorre said. "Which is why ONI has decided to send you to Annecy. You are stranded on the moon, but transport north should be manageable."

The tent seemed to collapse in like a black hole. The entire reason Dorian had even come up with the backup plan was to get them off Meridian faster. And now they were going to be heading deeper into the fighting? She blinked rapidly, trying to hold back tears. Commander Marechal was leaning forward, speaking with Captain Dellatorre about the details of the plan, but their voices seemed to meld together into gibberish. She looked up at Owen. His gaze flicked toward her, just for a second, and she saw the sympathy in his eyes.

"Rousseau," Captain Dellatorre said, jerking Evie out of her fog of panic.

"Yes, ma'am." Evie straightened up.

"My scientists are curious to know more about the artifact. Could you please go over how you were able to activate it? In detail, please."

Evie's thoughts were a confused jumble of fear and confusion. She opened her mouth, unsure where to start. Everyone was staring at her.

"It was a puzzle," she began, her voice shaky. "And I did my best to solve it."

Thirty minutes later, Commander Marechal had called the remaining members of the militia together, ready to relay Captain Dellatorre's orders. Evie found the rest of Local Team, still shaky from the meeting in the Command tent.

"Is everything okay?" Saskia asked. "What's going on? What's this meeting about?"

Evie shook her head. "It's not good."

"What do you mean?" Dorian said.

"I've got new orders," Commander Marechal said, clomping into the center of the encampment. "We're leaving Brume-sur-Mer."

"Oh, wow, seriously?" Victor laughed. "Why were you keeping that from us, Evie?"

Dorian, though, only frowned. "He said leaving Brume-sur-Mer. Not leaving Meridian."

Victor's laughter vanished. "What the hell does that mean?"

Saskia shushed him, led the group up to where the rest of the survivors had peeled themselves away from their resting places and into a ring around Commander Marechal and Owen. Evie's throat was dry.

"We've made contact with ONI," Commander Marechal said. "And I have some bad news."

Dorian twisted around and looked at Evie. She just shook her head, hopeless.

"They can't get us off Meridian. Not right now, at least."

Angry voices rose up from the militia, an intense rumble of discontent. "So what are you going to have us do?" someone shouted. "Just sit around here until the Covenant come and pick us off one by one?"

There was a surge of angry agreement. The commander looked unfazed.

"The artifact we recovered contained a map," he said, and then launched into a brief description of what Evie had accomplished earlier. "And because we are presently stranded here on Meridian," Owen said, "ONI has decided to send us to Annecy. We'll be moving out immediately, so as to avoid Covenant retaliation—they're already scouring the area around the original camp, so we have to act fast."

Saskia gave a sharp inward gasp, and Evie instinctively reached over and grabbed her friend's hand. She felt that fear herself.

"Did they tell you that in there?" Saskia whispered.

Evie nodded grimly.

"What the hell's in Annecy?" yelled Dubois.

Commander Marechal sighed. "We don't know. It will be our job to find out."

"I'm not asking about what that map is directing us to," he snapped back. "I'm asking what the hell's in Annecy. Is it Covenant-occupied? Abandoned? What?"

"Soldier, you're being impertinent," Commander Marechal snapped. "The city was evacuated yesterday. As such, we don't have a full picture of what—"

Groans erupted from the group. The commander held up his hand, yelled, "Enough! I'll remind you that we were sent to Meridian to secure whatever the Covenant was after. But the object in Brume-sur-Mer isn't what they were after, at least not ultimately. Ergo, our mission has not been completed."

Owen stepped forward. "Sir, if I may . . ." When Commander Marechal nodded, he turned toward Dubois and the rest of the survivors. "Extraction isn't possible right now with the Covenant orbital presence. You all know we cannot stay in Brume-sur-Mer. Our options here are limited."

Dorian stepped forward. "I've got a question."

"No one can be extracted," Owen said. "Not even Local Team. But all of you are capable of handling yourselves."

"That's not what my question is about," Dorian said coldly. "I wanted to know how we're getting to Annecy if the Covenant are after us here and orbital transport's blocked. It's on the other side of the moon."

A couple of militia members agreed, and Owen smiled slightly, just for a flicker of a second.

"We are aware of that, Nguyen." Commander Marechal activated a glowing map of the forests surrounding Brume-sur-Mer. Vast areas of it were marked bloody with red light; Evie realized that was Brume-sur-Mer itself and the original camp. Covenant-controlled territory. "If you will stand down, as is expected of you, I will explain the situation."

Dorian stepped back, his cheeks flushed red.

Commander Marechal looked out at the crowd. "I understand that you are upset," he said. "I understand what we have been through. But we have orders, and we have protocols, and we aren't going to dissolve into chaos because you are unhappy. Now"—he gestured at the map—"we will hike north through the woods, following this trail here." A blue line lit up on the map. "It's not a true trail, but we've determined it will get us through the woods in optimal time. This will take us to Desmarais, where we will load up on an in-atmo cargo freighter. The pilot is part of the Meridian Air Force and will get us to Annecy in a couple of hours."

The commander switched off the map. "She will drop us in Annecy, and we will proceed from there. Command will attempt to maintain contact with us to ensure immediate extraction of anyone who requires it once we break atmo." He looked coldly at Dorian. "Including Local Team.

"Our options are limited here, as Spartan Owen stated. All of us have suffered due to the charge on the Covenant excavation site, but this war has called for desperate measures since the beginning."

Evie noticed Saskia looked over at Owen when the commander said this, although she could not read her expression.

"*Suffered?*" sputtered Kielawa. "More than half of us are *dead*."

Commander Marechal's face hardened. "What did I just say about protocol, Kielawa? All of us will be dead if we don't rendezvous with the pilot in Desmarais. The Covenant will stop at nothing to retrieve the artifact currently in our possession, and you damn well know it. We have to stay one step ahead of them."

For a moment, the woods were silent. Then the militia erupted into angry yelling.

"Is Command serious?"

"A freighter? Really?"

"They're sending us into another death trap!"

"And they're just abandoning these kids? Are they kidding?"

Commander Marechal responded by giving a loud shout of anger.

"This is our best chance for survival," he said. "Fifteen minutes. Pack up what you can carry and move out." He slung the rifle around to his back. "And by the way, those *kids* are the only reason we're getting to leave Brume-sur-Mer at all. If it weren't for them, we would be preparing to march on the Covenant again. Now move!"

There was a pause, a held breath. Then the militia scattered throughout the camp, gathering up weapons and rations, leaving the tents. Commander Marechal turned to Local Team.

"Thanks for vouching for us," Evie said quietly.

"I only said it because it's true," Commander Marechal said. "Now, you heard what I said. Pack up and carry out. I'll be transporting the artifact."

And then he stomped away, stooping down to pick up his comm pad. Evie glanced at Saskia, who looked pale and worried.

"I've always wanted to see Annecy," Evie said with a strained smile, but Saskia only stared at her.

CHAPTER TWELVE

SASKIA

Saskia had gotten very familiar with the forest around her parents' house in the time before the invasion. She had been able to navigate through the tangled copses of trees, the heavy underbrush. After the invasion, when she and the others had found themselves stranded outside the town shelter, she had led them through the woods with a confidence she didn't always feel but could always, at least, fake. Sometimes they had to clear a path, but there was always the start of one, a thin area where people had walked before.

On their way to Desmarais, there were no such trails.

They were nineteen troops in total, a number that seemed so small when she had finally counted it but which seemed enormous now that they were wading through waist-high ferns, hacking away at vines as thick around as a man's forearm. The old-growth trees towered over them, their trunks covered with parasitic plants that created a second canopy that caught what little rain made its way through the treetops. The militia walked single file, Owen at the front, Local Team behind him, and then what remained of the four squads, with Commander Marechal bringing up the rear. Saskia walked right behind Owen, untangling the felled branches he sliced away with a Covenant energy sword he had somehow acquired during the earlier battle. The branches fell Saskia's way with blackened edges, smoke sizzling on the damp air.

"How much longer?" Dorian mumbled behind her.

"I have no idea," she said, flinging a wad of vines into the undergrowth. "I don't even know how long we've been walking."

He didn't try to talk to her further, thank god. She was too exhausted to navigate such a deeply wooded area and speak with someone at the same time. Her leg muscles burned, and her feet sent shooting pains up her splints every time she pressed them into the ground. Her vision blurred; her mouth was dry. She wanted to curl up in a bed—a real bed, not a cot, not a pile of rain-soaked palm leaves—and sleep.

But she couldn't. So she walked.

She had no sense of how long they had been walking. When Owen halted and threw up a fist to indicate that the others do the same, she thought they had arrived. Except they were still deep in the woods. There were no signs of civilization, just the greenery crushing in around them and the constant shriek of insects.

"Something's coming," Owen muttered.

Saskia's chest seized up.

"You four, get close," he said, holding out one hand, as if he could sweep Saskia and the others into the safety of his armor. "Victor, give the signal."

Victor nodded, then stuck two fingers into his mouth and let out a loud, piercing whistle. Saskia huddled close to Owen with the others, her rifle out. She peered through the scope and saw only green. A rustle as the rest of the militia formed two tight concentric circles, weaving as best they could through the dense growth.

Saskia held her breath, one eye squeezed shut, the other watering as she stared through the scope.

"Careful, careful," Owen said softly. "They're close."

"How can you tell?" Saskia whispered.

Owen didn't take his eyes off the woods. "I hear them. I hear—"

And then Saskia heard it too, a deeper pitch to the rustling. Leaves scraping against armor. The guttural whisper of an alien tongue.

"Get down," Owen hissed, and opened fire.

The plasma fire was returned immediately, purple streaks that scorched the underbrush. Saskia hit the ground, her elbows sinking into the mud. The militia fired out in their ring, the gun blasts erupting like fireworks in the forest.

With a piercing, unison cry, the Covenant charged.

Saskia fired furiously at them between the spaces of the militia's legs, the recoil from her gun shuddering up her arm. These were not Grunts coming after them, but the imposing, leathery-skinned reptilian creatures the UNSC called Elites. When Saskia had first learned about them in school, they were called Sangheili.

And she had fought one before.

And survived, she thought, sliding another magazine into her rifle. From her vantage point, she counted ten figures total: Four of them were definitely Elites, but the rest look liked massive bears walking on their hind legs, firing heavy iron weapons toward the militia. *The others are Jiralhanae. Brutes*, she thought, remembering the holos from school and from her training at Tuomi Base.

Ten to nineteen. And she had the nineteen on her side. It was a strange feeling, to be the one doing the outnumbering for once. Though she knew from her parents that the odds still weren't in their favor in this fight.

Owen had broken away from the crowd and charged straight into the remaining pair of Brutes, who swung their large weapons up and out, attempting to slice him open with the jagged, serrated edges affixed to their stocks. He caught their blows with his energy sword, drawing forth great sprays of sparks. The militia moved in tighter, giving him cover fire as the Elites directed their attention toward him.

And, like that, Saskia understood what Owen was doing. He was making himself into a distraction.

"He's giving us an opening to run," Saskia said, her voice trembling.

"No way." Victor gritted his teeth, his gun firing off at a tremendous, earth-shattering speed. "I'm not running."

"He's trying to protect us," she said, feeling hopeless. "He knows we can't take them with these weapons, and we can't just stay here to die." She swung her head around, looking for Dorian. But Dorian crouched beside Evie and Farhi, the muzzles of their rifles blazing with white light. At least the Brutes had been beaten back. And it didn't seem like a single member of the militia was missing.

Yet.

Saskia grabbed her rifle and leapt to her feet, finger squeezing tight against the trigger. She joined in with the rest of the militia, firing into the knot of Elites swarming toward Owen. Two of them peeled off and strode toward the militia. They both wore armor that flared with energy shielding as it deflected the bullets, sending them careening dangerously out into the forest. And one of them had the same kind of energy sword that Owen wielded.

"We won't be able to defeat them!" Saskia hollered. "They're too powerful!"

The one with the energy sword roared something in the clicking Sangheili tongue and raced toward her. She had a sudden flashback to the day when she had led all the Brume-sur-Mer survivors to the for-est, only to be confronted by an Elite. She had only survived that fight with luck, really. She doubted she could manage a trick like that again.

The Elite swung its energy sword at her as the other fired into the rest of the militia, who returned a wall of bullets that sent the Elite slamming back into a net of vines. The Elite with the energy sword twisted around and barked something in its language, which the sec-ond Elite returned. It was strange, but it sounded like the same combative tone Saskia used to use when her parents asked her to stay in her room during weapons demonstrations. The same tone that fre-quently meant she was planning on ignoring them completely.

Commander Marechal shoved his way through the crowd, urging the soldiers forward.

"Run!" the commander barked, blocking their view of Owen, who was engaging the crowd of Elites. "Get to the rendezvous point!"

"We're not leaving him behind!" shouted Saskia.

"Go!" Owen roared.

Saskia fired once more into the melee of Spartan soldier and Covenant Elites. Then she did exactly as Owen asked. Her bare feet pounded against the ground, and as she passed Evie and Dorian firing into the Elites, she grabbed hold of Evie's arm and pulled her forward with her.

"What are you doing?" Evie squawked.

"Getting us out of here, like Owen ordered!"

"We can't leave him!"

Owen picked up the limp body of one of the Elites and hurled it into the crowd that had massed around him.

"He can take care of himself," Saskia said. "Let's *go*." She pulled harder on Evie's arm, and this time Evie relented.

"Dorian!" Evie called. "Victor!"

"They're over there," said Mousseau. "Good luck getting them separated."

And that was when Saskia saw. The two of them were in the middle of the brawl with the Elites, throwing their guns sideways at Elite heads, getting dragged down to the forest floor by powerful, muscle-corded arms. Owen sprang into action with a spray of bullets, and Victor and Dorian scrambled to their feet. Victor had a bloody streak across his forehead. Mousseau grabbed him and pulled him forward, dragging them away from the fight.

"Let's go," Caird said. "I'm getting us out of here."

"We can help!" Victor said, shrugging out of his grasp.

"None of us can help," Caird hissed, pushing them forward. "Blue squadron will be right behind you." She shoved Victor toward Saskia, and she caught him. The blood pulsed out of a wound across his temple. Did they have MediGel? She couldn't think about that, not until they got to the rendezvous, not until they were safely in the air.

She grabbed Victor and yanked him forward. Dorian had already caught up with Evie, and the two of them weaved through the woods, ducking away from blasts of wayward plasma fire. The Elites were too focused on Owen to notice them or the other militia members who had managed to peel themselves away from the fighting. And so they took advantage of the break and ran, pushing themselves as far as they could through the thick, murky tangle of the forest. Saskia could hear the plasma fire behind them, ringing out through the woods. Was it getting closer? She could only hope it wasn't.

"How much farther?" Evie gasped.

Saskia shook her head. Glanced over at Dorian, who was running with a grim, fatalistic determination.

"No idea," he said, not looking at her.

"It's just a couple of kilometers," said Commander Marechal, approaching behind her as he led the militia toward Desmarais. "We were close before. Now we've just go to—"

A dark mass plunged down from the trees, growling and carrying a fat, heavy-looking weapon equipped with a curved, vicious blade. The last Brute. In one lunging movement, the blade arced through the air and sliced across Commander Marechal's midsection. He crumpled, disappearing into the tall grasses.

Dorian screamed, stumbling to a stop and then ducking to avoid the trajectory of the Brute's weapon, still red with blood. The creature lunged forward, growling in its unfamiliar language, bringing its weapon to bear, moving to make Dorian its next victim. Saskia stumbled backward, unloading her rifle directly into the exposed base of the alien's neck. The others nearby joined her attack, pumping rounds into the massive beast. It felt like they fired forever, and with every jerk of her rifle, Saskia thought of Commander Marechal falling beneath the Brute's heavy blade.

And then, finally, the Brute collapsed like a falling tree.

"Run!" she screamed, jumping around its body. "Let's go!"

She held her rifle tight as the militia streamed past her. The *pat pat pat* from Owen's rifle continued to ring out in the forest. At least they hadn't lost him too.

As soon as the last militia member had passed, Saskia followed behind them, sweeping around her gun, looking for more deadly surprises to drop out of the woods. The trees seemed to press tight together, as if they were hemming her in. She whirled around and stumbled her way up to the rest of the militia. The sound of Owen's gunshots grew fainter. The forest closed tight around them. The air was so thick with humidity it felt unbreathable, and Saskia's lungs ached as she surged forward. She wondered if Owen was still fighting the Elites. She couldn't hear his gun at all now, but they were so insulated by leaves and vines, the quiet meant nothing.

And then the forest ended.

It was as if an enormous knife had come down and carved out a blank space among the trees. Houses dotted the grass, little metal cubes of the type used by early settlers. Most of them had been sealed shut.

"Is this it?" Saskia jogged over to Dorian. "Desmarais?"

"It's the outskirts," he said. "That pilot should be here somewhere."

As if in response, the door to one of the houses slid open with a creak and out stepped a woman in old military fatigues, a rifle strapped to her back. She squinted at the militia with an appraising look.

"Where's Commander Marechal?" she said. "And the Spartan?"

Farhi stepped forward. *The de facto leader*, Saskia thought, now that Owen was still fighting and the commander was dead. She still couldn't quite grasp the reality of what she'd seen. How suddenly he'd gone down. How lucky the rest of them had been to escape.

"We got attacked by a lance of Elites on the hike here," Farhi said. "Spartan Owen stayed behind to fight them off. As for the commander—" She took a deep breath. "A Brute got him. Surprise attack."

The woman pressed her hand to her heart, a small gesture of grief. Then she swept away a piece of hair that had fallen out of her braid. "We've got a small window for takeoff. The Covies run a regular perimeter sweep, and we'll be pushing you out in the five minutes while they're looking the other way."

Saskia slunk closer to the edge of the woods, her head cocked. She thought she'd heard something beyond the trilling of insects. Some kind of . . . snap. Not a rifle shot, at least. But the sound of something breaking—

And then someone shouted, "Get down!" just as a massive figure erupted out of the woods in a spray of tree leaves and broken branches. Owen.

In one liquid movement, Owen twisted in midair, shooting a wall of bullets into the dark shadows lurking behind the boundary.

"Guess we won't be waiting after all," the pilot hollered before swinging her rifle around and firing off into the woods. The rest of the militia followed, just as a trio of Elites burst out shooting at Owen. Saskia squeezed the trigger on her rifle, although it seemed the bullets just dissolved into the woods without touching anything.

"Get them to the freighter!" Owen bellowed, firing over his shoulder. "I'll be there!"

"You heard the man!" said Farhi. She yanked out her pistol and fired several shots toward the Elites. "Lead the way!"

The pilot responded by letting loose a cloud of gunfire. "This way!" she screamed. "Got it set up behind the houses!"

A stream of people stampeded toward the untouched neighborhood. Saskia got swept up in the group as they surged forward, and she struggled to get her footing on the damp, slick grass. Plasma fire streaked overhead, leaving trails of smoke in the air. Behind her, the Elites shrieked in their native tongue.

A bolt whizzed past her head and struck Mousseau square in the back, sending him tumbling forward. Saskia screamed and stumbled down beside him. Blood oozed out of a charred hole in his shirt. In his skin.

"Get up," growled a familiar voice. A huge hand grabbed the back of her shirt and jerked her to her feet. She went limp, imagining the Elite's sharp claws shredding deeper into her flesh. "We have to clear out of here *now*. That means leaving him."

Behind her, Owen nodded grimly, fired off a couple of shots. The

Elites were still coming. And there were more than three of them now too. Saskia counted at least six scrambling over the grass as she jumped to her feet. Owen gave her a shove forward and then resumed firing. Through the haze of plasma smoke and fleeing bodies, she spotted a flash of metal. The freighter. People were already cramming aboard. She pumped her legs and arms even faster, her lungs screaming.

"Right behind you!" Owen shouted.

The freighter's engine ignited. Farhi hung out of the hatchway, arm outstretched toward Saskia, her eyes on a point behind her. On the Elites, she was sure.

"Jump!" she yelled, eyes flicking back to her for just a second.

She jumped, caught her hand, slammed her feet against the hatch stairs. Farhi pulled her into the freighter, and she pressed up against the cool metal wall and closed her eyes. Gunfire outside. The freighter lifted, the pilot's voice crackling over the speaker—Saskia couldn't make out what she was saying.

Owen. Were they leaving Owen behind?

But then there was a clank, and the freighter tilted, canting to the side. Saskia grabbed hold of the wall to keep from tumbling sideways.

"Clear," Owen said.

"Let's get the hell out of here," the pilot said, and this time Saskia understood every word.

CHAPTER THIRTEEN

DORIAN

They flew through low atmosphere, the freighter slicing through the clear air just below the clouds. Dorian stared out the little portal window at the vast expanse of blue sky. From up here, Brume-sur-Mer was a speck of dust in the distance, and there was no sign of the Covenant. No sign at all that Meridian was at war.

Victor, Evie, and Saskia had all made it aboard the freighter safely, and he was grateful for that. They were sitting together toward the back, sprawled out on the floor in the cargo area because all the seats were taken up by those with injuries. More injuries. Dorian had even watched Caird drag Dubois up the hatchway earlier, his arm black and bleeding from a plasma bolt. The sight of Dubois's usual jovial expression twisted up in pain had jolted him in a way he didn't expect.

But Dubois wasn't the only one who'd been shot, and Dorian heard from Kielawa that they were running low on biofoam. Over the constant whine of the freighter's engine were the occasional bursts of pained groans, and Dorian wished more than anything that he could block them out.

They were in the air for a long time. Had to be, with the way they were flying so low. No one really talked, and Dorian couldn't blame them. He knew he and the rest of Local Team had gotten off easy. No injuries other than cuts and bruises, no deaths. Not because they were so great either. Just because they were lucky. Because Owen kept making sure they stayed out of harm's way.

He knew they shouldn't be here. ONI's whole justification for sending them to Brume-sur-Mer was that they *knew* Brume-sur-Mer and their job there had made sense. But Annecy? What good were they going to be there? Yeah, it was nice of Owen to tell Command that Local Team could take care of themselves. But in the end, they had been promised one thing and delivered another.

They were just supposed to go to Brume-sur-Mer. Now they were stranded, and ONI didn't seem to give a damn.

A few hours into the flight, Evie came and sat down next to Dorian. She cradled a sleek black case to her chest.

"So he got it here safe and sound." Dorian sighed.

"He sure did." Evie set the case gently beside her. The artifact was in there, secured behind two locks. Owen had asked her to manage it once they were on the freighter, since she was the only one out of the militia who had some familiarity with the thing.

"What do you think we're going to find there?" Evie said, her face faintly lit by the glow from the locks. Dorian reached over and dropped the flap back over the opening.

"Who knows," he said.

"Owen told me that ONI thinks the actual artifact may be split into parts. If the Covenant figure out where we are, they're going to come after us. So they can get this, the first part"—she nodded at the box—"and then whatever's in Annecy."

"Great." Dorian leaned back against the wall so he could feel the comforting rumble of the freighter's engine.

"I hope whatever it is," Evie said, "it's easy to get. I mean, they said the city was evacuated. Lucky them."

"Seriously. Imagine getting out of there with time to spare." Dorian laughed, even though it felt bitter in the back of his throat.

The freighter flew on. The sunlight coming in through the windows dimmed and then darkened completely, leaving them with only a few watery emergency lights. Evie fell asleep with her arms wrapped around that stupid artifact. Saskia was snoring softly across the way, along with basically everyone else on the freighter. But Dorian couldn't sleep. His thoughts kept churning wildly through his head.

And then he felt the shift in altitude as the freighter began dropping toward the surface. He stood up, picked his way around the sleeping soldiers to a window. He figured even with the evacuation, Annecy's AI—if it still remained active and intact—would keep the basic grid up. It was always something, to see a city lit up from above. Granted, the biggest city he'd ever seen was Port Moyne, when Mr. Garzon was first teaching him to fly. He figured Annecy would look like a galaxy in comparison.

But nothing appeared in the window. There was only the endless sweep of black, the ghost of Dorian's reflection in the glass. He frowned. Picked his way over to the other side of the freighter. Nothing.

"What are you doing?" Owen asked. His voice was quiet, but Dorian jumped when he heard it anyway.

"Wanted to see Annecy from above." Dorian looked over at Owen, his armor making him a shadow monster in the dim lighting. "Didn't Commander Marechal say ONI had told him it had been evacuated a day ago? The grid should still be up, right? For stragglers."

"Is that what he said?" Owen asked.

"I thought so." Dorian frowned. Owen always got cagey when they talked about ONI, but this wasn't getting at anything classified. The commander had told all of them this not even twenty-four hours ago.

God, it felt like a lifetime ago.

"Perhaps there was already an attack," Owen said carefully.

Dorian's chest seized up. "What the hell? You mean you're flying us straight into a war zone? After what *just happened*?" He glared. "Aren't you in communication with ONI anyway? Why didn't they tell us to turn around?"

Owen held up one hand. "I have been, and I haven't heard anything. It was simply a guess. It's just as likely the infrastructure has been shut down."

People were stirring, groaning, pushing themselves up. Dorian glanced around at the militia, at the dried biofoam patchworking their faces, at their tattered, blood-and-mud-streaked clothes. Everyone looked like they'd aged years since the attack on the excavation site.

"You wouldn't take them straight into battle," Dorian said, turning back to Owen. "Who cares what ONI says?"

"ONI is focused on keeping humanity from going extinct," Owen said brusquely. "So that's why I listen to them."

Dorian's face went hot.

"Something you need to learn," Owen said, "is that self-preservation stops being so important when the preservation of your entire species is on the line. This isn't just about you or me or the soldiers on this freighter. It's about every human being in the galaxy. It's about understanding that as a soldier, you might just have to sacrifice yourself for peace."

Dorian looked down at his hands, his thoughts fluttering between angry, probably ill-conceived retorts and memories of Remy and Uncle Max. They were supposed to be safe now. But Owen's words made Dorian realize that they weren't. Not as long as the Covenant were gunning for humanity.

And then he thought about his parents, two people he hadn't thought about in months. He didn't even know if they were alive—he hadn't received a transmission from them since before the attack. He'd always felt like they'd abandoned him when they joined up with the UNSC. For the first time, it occurred to him that maybe they'd done it for his protection, even as they left him behind.

A sacrifice.

The whine in the engines shifted as the freighter switched over to hover.

"We're touching down already?" Dorian broke away from the Spartan—and his own complicated thoughts—to press his hand against the window. It was completely dark outside save for a few red flares sputtering against the shadows. In their dim light, he thought he saw the hulking boxes of buildings off in the distance. But he couldn't be sure.

The pilot's voice boomed through the freighter. "Welcome to Annecy," she said, and there was a brittleness to her voice that Dorian did not like. Had she been there before? "I hope you've got your coats because it's cold out there."

The militia groaned at that. "Figures ONI would send us to the top of the world and not even get us jackets," grumbled Kielawa. "Guess we'll have to scavenge for them."

"Hopefully there's something left to scavenge from," muttered Valois.

Dorian felt a twist of paranoia. "Why wouldn't there be?" he asked. "It was just evacuated a day ago."

Valois chuckled. "You really believe that?"

And like that, the twist of paranoia became a deadweight in the bottom of Dorian's stomach. "Why wouldn't I?" he asked, trying to keep his voice steady.

Caird shrugged. Something in her seemed to have dimmed with Dubois's injury. "We had this saying in my family. Got it from my great-grandmother, who fought with the Insurrection. You never take ONI at their word."

The hatch hissed open, and frigid air blasted through the freighter, much to the mumbled protests of the militia—except for the remaining members of Green Squad, who slapped each other on the back and made a big show of expressing their love for that bone-chilling Caernaruan breeze.

Dorian shuffled over to where Evie and Saskia stood with Victor, all three of them taking stock of their meager belongings. "Something's up," Dorian said.

"What are you talking about?" Victor popped up the lid on the box of ammunition in his bag, then immediately frowned at its contents. "I hope there's a supply drop somewhere."

But, Dorian realized, putting his thoughts into words felt a little too paranoid. "It's just weird, all the lights being out. Don't you think? Brume-sur-Mer wasn't like that even after the invasion."

"Yeah," Evie said. "Salome kept things running. Those infrastructure AIs usually do, don't they?"

"Weapons ready!" Owen shouted. "We don't know what we're going to find out there."

Victor sighed and tossed the ammunition back into his bag. "Lot of good they'll do us."

"We'll find more ammunition," Saskia said. "It's a city."

Dorian racked back the slide on his rifle and tried to shake his uneasy feeling as they marched off the freighter and into the frigid dark. Wind swept across the open landing pad, slicing at Dorian's bare arm. He gritted his teeth together, trying to keep from shivering.

Fortunately, Owen activated a light on his suit, a beacon to lead the team across the open. *Risky*, Dorian thought, but they didn't have much of a choice, did they? They were lucky they had weapons.

They moved quickly, feet skittering across the smooth concrete surface. Stars swirled brightly overhead, their patterns distorted by blurs of red and pink light. The battles raging above Meridian. Dorian had never been in a place dark enough to see them before. The thought made him shiver almost as much as the cold.

"Approaching a structure," Owen said, voice staticky from the wind. Dorian's eyes had adjusted enough to the darkness that he was able to better make out the building up ahead. It didn't quite look right, though.

Beside him, Evie gasped.

"It's been destroyed," she whispered, and instantly the dark lumps in the distance sharpened into focus. Half the building was rubble, the metal twisted into monstrous shapes that rose up off the landing pad like claws. Owen's light swept over the damage, creating sharp shadows that made Dorian's skin crawl.

Someone let out a low whistle.

"Heading left," Owen said, guiding them toward the part of the structure that was still standing—mostly. The top half was jagged and torn, and it took Dorian a moment to realize that the roof had been ripped off.

"What happened here?" Saskia said. "What weapons could . . ." Her voice trailed away. "It can't be safe for us to be here."

"Oh, calm down," said Valois. "Annecy was one of the first cities hit. Six months ago. Too little too late evacuating the place yesterday." He gave a cruel, rumbling laugh.

"Six months?" Dorian shouted.

Several people shushed him, and Owen's light swept over the teams, landing on Dorian like a spotlight. "We need to be quiet," he said. "You know that."

"Six months?" Dorian whispered to Valois. "That can't be right."

Valois smirked. "Trust me, kid. I was here." He leaned in close. "Guess you don't know everything, do you?"

"Stop screwing around with me," Dorian snapped.

Valois's expression hardened. "I'm not screwing around with you. This whole area was the first one hit, although there are rumors that the fighting in atmo has been going on for even longer. UNSC and the Meridian Special Forces were deployed to put a stop to it. Survivors were shipped off to refugee planets. And the government did everything they could to tamp down on the news. They weren't totally successful, but a bunch of backwater high school kids wouldn't have been paying attention, right?"

Owen sent a couple of Red Squad members ahead into the chewed-up structure as reconnaissance. The others all huddled close, backs together for warmth, but Dorian slipped away from the group and headed toward the collapsed building. His head buzzed. *Trust me, kid. I was here.* Six months ago? Valois was a jerk, but he'd never been a liar. How could Meridian have been under attack for six months without anyone in Brume-sur-Mer hearing about it? Unless Valois was right, and the news had been heavily guarded somehow. Brume-sur-Mer was on the other side of the world. But beyond even that, Owen had *told* them that the fighting had only been going on for a week, up outside the atmosphere. Nothing grounded.

What the *hell*?

"Dorian!" Evie hissed from behind him. "What are you doing? We can't split up."

Dorian stared at the piles of twisted, melted metal.

"He lied to us," Dorian said.

"What are you talking about?" Evie sidled up next to him and activated a little palm light that cast a small sphere of blue illumination over their feet.

"Owen," Dorian said. "When he told us that Brume-sur-Mer was one of the first hit. He lied to us."

"Why, because this place is bombed out? It's been three months."

"No." Dorian's mouth was dry, his voice scratchy. "Because Valois told me he was here when it happened. *Six* months ago."

The wind picked up, whistling mournfully as it blew through the rubble.

"Valois told you that?" Evie shook her head. "He's messing with you. We would have heard about it."

"Not if they kept it quiet."

"They?" Evie laughed. "You sound like the insurrectionists in our history book."

Dorian rolled his eyes. The wind buffeted against him, sending goose bumps running up his legs. "If they were trying to avoid a panic," he said. "If they thought they could keep it contained. I could see it. We were on the other side of the moon, so they wouldn't have even had to be that successful for us to not notice. But Owen should have told us. He shouldn't have claimed Meridian had just been fighting for a week." Dorian squeezed his fingers around the butt of his rifle. "He shouldn't have lied to us." He gave a bitter laugh, looked over at Evie in the darkness. He could barely make her out in the starlight. In the battle light.

"Makes you wonder who else is lying to us," he said.

"Don't," Evie said.

"Nguyen! Rousseau!" Farhi shouted. "Get your asses back here. We're taking shelter." She strode across the open space, shining a light in their faces. "Don't run off like that. This isn't that beach town you grew up in. You don't know this place."

"Don't know a lot of things," Dorian muttered, but he followed Farhi anyway.

Dorian woke with the sun. Easy to do when there wasn't a roof to block it out. The light came spilling in, pinkish and not any warmer than the night had been. At least they'd managed to find some emergency blankets, the fabric lined with liquid heaters. This place had been some kind of travel center, a hub for freighters and automatic cars. The supplies had all been pretty much ransacked, but Valois knew his way around, found the blankets tucked away in a cabinet on the rickety second floor.

Of course Valois knew his way around. He'd been here before.

Dorian wrapped the blanket around his shoulders and blinked up at the sky blossoming with streaks of pink and silver. He kept waiting for a Covenant ship to mar the view, but nothing flew overhead. There weren't even any birds.

He sighed, dropped his head back down. Yellow Squad was on patrol, and he spotted Caird leaned up against a big picture window, the glass miraculously still in place. Everyone else was still sleeping, piled up next to one another for warmth. Dorian stood, stretched. Dragged the blanket with him as he walked over to the windows.

He knew what he was going to see there in the soft dawn light, but the shock still raced through him like lightning. The travel hub was situated on a hill overlooking Annecy. These things usually were, Dorian's mom had told him once. One of those useless facts she'd shared with him before she joined up with the UNSC.

But Annecy just—wasn't there.

Dorian could see where the city had once been. Roads crossed over the softly rolling hills, intersecting the blackened frames of former buildings. Wreckage lay in monstrous heaps, more of that twisted metal and molten stone. The image unrolled all the way out to the horizon.

"Sure is a sight," said Caird.

Dorian jumped, then pulled the blanket more firmly around his shoulders, straightening his spine. "What was the point of evacuating a day ago?" he said, the question dry on his tongue because it wasn't the question he really wanted to ask—*why hadn't Owen told them the truth?* "Were people really still living here?"

"Yeah, they were," Granger said. "People don't like giving up their home if they can help it. And the outskirts of the city aren't as bad as . . ." She gestured at the view. "But with us here, we risk the Covenant coming back, and it was safer to give the orders. We'll see how many people listened."

Dorian stared out at the remains of the city. From this distance, they looked like ash.

"Did the city really fall six months ago?" he asked.

Caird hesitated. "Yeah."

Dorian closed his eyes against the sting of the truth.

"Look, I'm sorry. The information was classified. I only know it because my CO back then was from Calais, about a hundred kilometers away. Said Annecy got blasted from out of the sky. He'd been home on leave when it happened, so my whole team got looped in on the information control." Caird laughed, shook her head. "Imagine that. Home on leave and you see the opening shots of a months-long battle."

"Yeah," Dorian muttered. "Imagine that."

Caird sighed. "I know it's a shock. But they had the Covenant quarantined in this area and they wanted to avoid panic." She reached over and put a hand on Dorian's shoulder, and it sat there, a dead-weight. When he didn't respond, she dropped it and then ambled away, starting the final patrol of her shift. Dorian pressed his hands against the cold glass.

Six months. *Six months.* The thought burned in his head until he couldn't stand it anymore. He spun around, went over to the place where Saskia and Evie and Victor were sleeping. *Six months.* What had he been doing six months ago? Working with Uncle Max, writing songs, skipping the last class of the day so he could go down to the beach for a few more hours before the rainy season set in. All the while this city on the other side of the world was burning.

He knelt down and shook the others awake, jostling them and hissing, "Get up! Get up!" Evie was the first to respond, her eyes fluttering open. She peered at Dorian like she didn't quite recognize him. "What's wrong?" she said.

"Get up," Dorian said. "I need to show you something." He shook Victor and Saskia at the same time, more roughly than he ought to. Saskia moaned and swatted at him. Victor's eyes flew open.

"What the hell, man?"

"He says he needs to show us something," Evie answered, pushing herself up to sitting. "Wow, it's cold in here."

"Keep the blanket," Dorian said. He gave Saskia one last shove, and she rolled over, groaning.

"What do you want?" she said.

"Get up," Dorian told her. "We've got to talk to Owen."

"I thought you wanted to show us something," Victor said.

"Yeah, well, that too."

Now that all three were awake, they roused themselves quickly, their training kicking in. Dorian stood a few paces away, arms crossed over his chest to keep out the cold air. When they were ready, he led them over to the windows.

"Oh my god," whispered Saskia, the first one to respond at all.

"We knew it was destroyed," Victor said, wrapping himself more tightly in the blanket. "You woke us up to show us this?"

"No," said Evie, her face ashy and pale. "No, it's because it happened six months ago. Is that what you're getting at?" She turned to Dorian. "The city's been like this for six months."

Dorian nodded once.

"What are you talking about?" Victor snapped. "The invasion started three months ago."

"No, it didn't," Dorian said.

Saskia tore her gaze away from the ruins of Annecy and blinked at him, her eyes shining. "What are you saying?"

"Owen lied to us when he said Brume-sur-Mer was one of the first hit. When he said the fighting had only been going on for a week. He *lied*."

Victor and Saskia stared at him. Evie kept gazing out the window, her fingers pressed lightly on the glass.

"Why would he do that?" Saskia asked.

"That's why I woke you up," Dorian snapped. "I think we need to go ask him."

"Are you sure this happened six months ago?" Evie whispered.

Dorian glared at her, annoyance flaring up in his chest. "Yes!" he said. "And I didn't just hear it from Valois. Caird confirmed it, and we can trust her. Owen *lied* to us, and it makes me want to know who else has been lying to us."

"Dorian," Evie said softly.

"Don't act like you haven't thought it too," Dorian said.

Victor sighed. "You're acting paranoid. There's no reason to think—"

"Six months!" Dorian shouted, gesturing out the window. "Our world has been under attack for six months, and we didn't know anything about it. I'm not going to sit here and pretend like we weren't being lied to."

Silence. The space around them felt suddenly enormous, and Dorian felt very small. The lightening sky overhead exposed him, exposed all of them. And all he wanted in that moment was to be on a ship heading back to his uncle.

"I'm going to find Owen," Dorian said. "You can come with me or not. But I'm going to get some answers."

He whirled around, skirting the remainder of the militia, all of them sleeping beneath the softly glowing blankets. They could sleep anywhere, he thought. He hadn't seen Owen all morning, and he hoped he was still in the building. Not that Dorian wouldn't set out across the ruins to confront him.

He heard the patter of footsteps behind him, and when he glanced over his shoulder, he was surprised to find Evie and Saskia, their expressions determined. Even more surprising was Victor, strolling behind them with his hands in his pockets, his head dipped down.

"You're gonna get your asses kicked," Victor said sheepishly. "Couldn't let that happen."

Dorian rolled his eyes.

"He's not going to get his ass kicked." Saskia sighed. "But I do hope we can get some answers."

CHAPTER FOURTEEN

EVIE

They found Owen holed up in a narrow little room in the center of the building, the walls crumbling and half-melted around him. He was talking with somebody, Evie could tell, but it was through the comm in his helmet rather than the comm pad he'd been using before.

"Must be classified," Dorian said, seething.

Owen hit the side of his helmet and the visor slid away. "You should be sleeping," he said. "Getting your energy up." He paused, taking them in. "All four of you. You're my only intact team."

Evie felt a pang in her chest.

"Yeah, because ONI won't let us do anything," Victor said. Saskia nudged him hard in the ribs.

"We need to talk to you," Dorian said. "It can't wait."

Owen's eyes betrayed nothing. Evie wanted to put a hand on Dorian's shoulder, to try and calm him down. It wasn't exactly helping their case that he was acting like he didn't understand the chain of command. Like they were just a bunch of scared, confused kids stranded in the middle of an alien invasion.

But before she could move, Dorian stepped forward, into the room. Owen sighed.

"Fine," he said. "I was finished with the briefing anyway."

"Briefing?" Victor said. "About what? What are we going to be doing?"

"Let's hear what you want to talk about first." Owen stepped forward, guiding Dorian back out into the hallway. "More structurally sound out here."

"So why were you in there?" Dorian asked.

"Better security." Owen's mouth twitched a little. "Relatively speaking."

They stood in a semicircle out in the hall, cold wind howling around the corners. Evie shivered; she wished she'd brought the blanket with her. Who cared how it would look.

"It's about Annecy," Dorian said. "We know you lied to us."

Owen didn't react.

"Valois and Caird told Dorian that Annecy fell six months ago," Evie said softly. "But when we found you in Brume-sur-Mer, you said the Covenant had only been attacking Meridian for a week or so."

"Of course, we hadn't heard anything ourselves," Victor said. "Nothing in the newsfeeds."

Dorian glared at him. "I explained that."

"He's right," Owen said, after a pause. "It wouldn't have been in the newsfeeds,"

Saskia took a deep breath, looking as if she'd just been punched in the stomach. "So it's true," she said. "You lied to us."

"I was following orders," Owen said. "Information about the land attacks on Meridian was to be kept in quarantine. UNSC did not want panic. Civilians were kept out of the loop unless they were in an affected area."

"What are you saying?" Evie's voice felt dry. "Are there parts of Meridian that don't know we're under attack at all? *Still?*"

Owen fixed her with a clear gaze. "It's certainly possible."

"There's a chance the colony could be glassed!" cried Saskia. "You of all people—"

"Understand what happens when people panic," Owen said. Evie glanced at Saskia, wondering what else she had learned about Owen's origins. She had shared what little she knew while they were at training. He'd been a war orphan. "We can't even evac military personnel from certain parts of Meridian right now. Do you think we can afford to divert military resources toward transporting civilians off-world? Any weakness in our armor against the Covenant would lead to a bloodbath. You want me to treat you like adults? Like soldiers under my command?" He looked hard at Victor. "You want to *fight*? *That's* the reality. That's the calculus of war. And it's what's kept humanity alive so far."

Evie took a step back as Owen brushed past them toward the rest of the militia.

"People have a right to know," Dorian said, his voice low and angry. "If we had known that the Covenant were targeting Meridian locations, you think I would have gone out on a boat with—" He stopped, took a deep breath. "People—my friends—are dead because we were unprepared. Because we *didn't know.* And you just—just kept lying to us. Because UNSC told you to."

"And to protect you," Owen said, turning. "If I had thought it was prudent to share the history of the attacks with you, I would have. But it was irrelevant to our survival in Brume-sur-Mer. It is, quite frankly, irrelevant to our mission here." Something in his expression darkened, flickered, returned to normal. "ONI has a potential location for the second artifact, based on the images of the first artifact's map that I sent them. And I told you, you're my only intact team. Given that fact and your previous experience, I think you're going to be our best option for making contact. But you have to understand that I can't tell you everything I know. I will *never* be able to tell you everything I know."

Dorian's face twisted with anger, but Evie stepped forward, her hand on his arm. "We aren't actually in the military," she said. "Things might be different now, but before . . . we were just kids. And we were scared. And you did lie to us."

Owen stared at them, his eyes hard and glittering. "All four of you know how fraught an evacuation can be. Now imagine an entire world trying to leave the surface of Meridian—and flying straight into Covenant forces."

Evie stepped back, her cheeks burning. She hadn't even considered that possibility, despite living through it herself.

"I've watched the Covenant use evac vehicles for target practice," he said flatly. "When I lied to you back at Brume-sur-Mer, it was to focus your attention on the matter at hand, not on hypotheticals that could get people killed. Meridian has not fallen yet, which is why we are here—to prevent that from happening. The people on this world have a chance to survive if we do our jobs right."

Evie felt numb. She understood better why ONI had sequestered information about the earlier attacks, even if the lie still stung.

But Dorian, she could tell, was even more furious. "You still lied to us."

"Sometimes," Owen said, "a lie is the only difference between people living or dying."

Dorian spat. He jerked his arm away from Evie and stalked down the hallway, his footsteps echoing off the crumbling walls. Evie watched him go, her chest twisting. Part of her wanted to go after him.

She was hungry, and cold, and still covered with mud and dirt from retrieving the first artifact. She had no idea when she would be clean again. When she would be safe.

"We shouldn't be here," she said softly.

Victor made a scoffing noise. But Owen said, "You're right. You shouldn't. But you are now. And you have to decide what you're going to do about it."

Dorian had stopped at the end of the hall, near a gouge in the wall. The wind pushed his clothes and his hair back. Evie wondered what he was looking at. If the wreckage that was Annecy looked any different from this angle.

"We need to know what the Covenant are trying to find," Owen said. "We need to evaluate how much of a threat it is. If you want to save the people of Meridian, that's how you do it. You have to under-stand that the magnitude of this war is far, far bigger than the four of you and the people you love. It always has been. You're not just scared kids anymore, and I think you know it."

Evie looked away from Dorian, at Saskia, who said nothing but gave a gentle nod, a minuscule *I'm in.*

"Yeah," Victor said. "Of course we do. Dorian's just—"

"Scared," Evie said, maybe too defensively. "Just like all of us."

Victor looked away.

"That's good, to be scared," Owen said. "That's what's going to keep you safe when we go out into Annecy."

Evie wanted to protest. Wanted to refuse. She wanted to arm herself with knowledge, ask Owen all the questions that were populat-ing the fringes of her brain. *How many lives had been lost? How far had the invasion spread? When would ONI—when would Owen—lie to them again? Did they really have a shot at saving Meridian?*

But she knew it would be pointless to do or ask any of those things. Not here. Not now. Not with the Covenant closing in on whatever artifact lay out there in the ruins.

In the end, only three of them went out into the city with Owen. Dorian stayed behind, his fury radiating around him. He said he would help Green Squad scavenge the area, looking for supplies, and Evie knew he would. More than anything, Dorian cared about the well-being of the people around him—that was why he was so furious about the lie in the first place. She knew he thought that knowing about the invasion would have prevented the death of his friends. She saw the anger in his expression, the distrust. The *hurt*. She felt that hurt herself every time she looked at Owen. She understood why he'd done it—after all her experiences, the UNSC's decision did make some sense to her, which was why she wasn't about to give up her responsibility. But was flat-out lying the best solution? Surely the UNSC could have found a way to share information about the invasion in a way that would allow people to prepare, rather than just going about their lives to be blindsided.

One good thing was that Saskia had managed to find a beat-up old reconnaissance vehicle in a hidden militia depot, bulky and armored with a turret fixed to the back. Saskia smiled when she came driving in with it, seeing Owen, Evie, and Victor standing out in the cold, dust from the demolished buildings blowing up in miniature tornadoes.

"A Warthog," she said. "I used to ride around in one of these with my parents. And even better, there's a huge stockpile of ammo in the back."

"We're extremely lucky you found that," Owen called out as she pulled to a stop in front of them. "Makes it a hell of a lot easier to get to the coordinates." He kept acting like the conversation earlier that morning had never happened. Evie rankled against it, this military way of pushing aside the things they didn't want to think about. But she didn't say anything either. After all, her mom had done the same thing.

"I've got to say, I don't think I'll miss fighting my way through the woods," Victor said as they crawled into the Warthog.

"It'd be nice if we had some jackets, though." Saskia smiled at Owen. "Mind if I man the turret?"

Owen sighed. "That's a pretty dangerous position to be in."

"Well, that's not a no." She crawled into the back of the vehicle, bracing herself against the mounted machine gun there.

"If you're going to do it," Owen said, "hang on and don't fire until I tell you to. That turret has serious recoil, so be prepared for it."

Evie wondered how Saskia could so easily act like nothing was wrong. Victor too. Didn't it *bother* them? The broken buildings of the city loomed over Evie like tombstones, and she wondered how many people had died here during the invasion. It was one of the first hit, Dorian had said, which implied it wasn't the very first. Could the UNSC have saved lives, at least here, in these early days, by alerting the people of Annecy?

Focus on the mission, she told herself, and despite her lingering hurt, she reminded herself what Owen had told them, that what they were doing now was how they would save Meridian. A way to ensure the lives lost in Annecy—and within their own militia—wouldn't have been in vain.

Owen turned over the engine, and the Warthog rumbled down the side of the hill, heading into town. Evie leaned forward against the back of the front seats, her arms wrapped around herself to keep out the cold. She actually thought she preferred the forest to this. At least they had been dressed appropriately.

"So where are we going?" Victor said.

Or is that classified? Evie thought.

"Eastern side of the city." Owen tapped a comm control on the Warthog's dash, and a map of the city flowered into existence. A pale green dot blinked in the upper left-hand corner. "We'll see how accurate that is, though."

"Would ONI give us the wrong coordinates?" Evie shouted over the wind.

"Only if they made a mistake."

"I meant on purpose." Evie felt vaguely dizzy.

Victor shot her a dark look. "Stop trying to be Dorian," he muttered.

"Why do you think they would do that?" Owen asked.

"They're clearly okay with lying when it suits them." The words were out of her mouth before she could stop them. "Even when it means excessive casualties. Maybe they decided we'd serve them best as a distraction while the militia—"

"Evie, stop." Saskia leaned down, one hand gripping the turret, her mouth close to Evie's ear. How she'd managed to hear the exchange over the wind and the rattle of debris beneath the Warthog's tires, Evie had no idea. "Let's focus on the mission."

"You're right," Evie said, and she knew Saskia was. But Evie didn't like operating in this world of secrets and classified information. It wasn't just about the UNSC keeping the invasion a secret from civilians either. ONI had led Owen and the militia straight into a death trap with limited intelligence. How could she blindly trust them after that? If it hadn't been for Dorian's backup plan, they'd probably all be dead, and the Covenant would have the artifact, which, for all ONI knew, was a world-destroying super-weapon.

For the first time in a while, Evie was glad to be getting out of this life soon. She was going to be a computer scientist, where all the answers were laid out in front of you if you knew how to look for them.

She leaned back in the seat, teeth chattering a little. The husk of the city flashed by. Buildings jutted like stalagmites out of the charred ground. Unrecognizable lumps of debris marred by a single untouched sign for a breakfast restaurant, the letters flat without the energy to make them glow. Evie thought of the destruction the Covenant had wrought on the main street back in Brume-sur-Mer. It was nothing compared to the wreckage of Annecy.

And she'd had no idea it had even happened.

Owen turned the Warthog down a narrow alley. The vehicle barely fit between the two towering brick walls, the only remains of whatever buildings they'd once belonged to. He killed the engine.

"Is this it?" Victor said doubtfully.

"No," Owen said. "But we're continuing on foot. Easier to stay hidden."

Evie's frustration and anger was replaced then by the old squeeze of fear. She wrapped her fingers around her rifle. "You think the Covenant's here already?"

"I think it's not safe to assume anything." Owen paused. "Regardless of what ONI might say."

He jumped out of the Warthog, and Evie just sat stunned.

"See?" Saskia dropped down beside her. "He understands."

"Does it matter if we can't trust him or ONI? He lied to you too," Evie said.

"Yeah, but I understand why he did it." Saskia put her hand on Evie's shoulder. "We've got to trust him if we're going to get out of this alive. We can be as angry as we need to be later, but for now we've got to trust—"

Gunfire exploded on the other side of the building. Saskia and Evie both slouched down in the seat, instincts kicking in. Footsteps against the cement. A pant of breath.

It was Victor.

"Grunt," he said. "Owen got him. Are you two coming or not?"

"Let's go," Saskia said, and she climbed out of the Warthog. Evie took a deep breath and followed.

Victor led them around to the other side of the wall, in the blackened pit where some part of a city had once been. Now there was just Owen clutching his rifle, the body of a Grunt splayed out in front of him.

"I knew it," he said. "We've got to be careful. The fact that there's a Covenant presence this far out from the coordinates—" He glanced over at Evie and Saskia and Victor. "Remember your training. This is just like Brume-sur-Mer. Stick to the shadows. Stay hidden."

He turned and gestured for them to follow, skittering up close to the wall. They lined up behind him single file, the way they always did in the forest. It felt strange to fall into position without Dorian, though, and Evie wondered if it would ever be the same between them again. He'd been angry enough that she could imagine him trying to find a way off-world, though she doubted he'd get far if Meridian really was in as bad of shape as ONI made it seem.

She tried to shove the thought aside, the way of a soldier. Because she *was* a soldier now, creeping through a war zone. There would be time to process all this later. If they managed to get out alive.

They picked their way through the ruins, running across the open spaces to duck behind piles of debris. The cold wind blew up clouds of white dust that made Evie's eyes sting. At least the movement kept her relatively warm.

Owen held up a fist, stopping them in their tracks. Then he gestured them closer.

They crouched down behind a slab of gray stone. Owen reached into the hard case fixed onto the armor of his thigh and pulled out the artifact. The light inside pulsed like a star.

"What's it doing?" Evie blurted, before slapping her hand over her mouth. She'd never seen it pulse like that before.

"The coordinates are dead ahead," Owen said in a low voice. "I wanted to see how this would react."

The light brightened, faded, brightened, faded.

"It seems like there's a connection," Saskia whispered.

Owen nodded, then lifted his head over the top of the stone. The wind was whining through the demolished buildings, keening low and haunting. It was all Evie could hear.

"Not seeing any hostiles," he said, slipping the artifact back into the case. Evie wanted to reach over it and pull it out again—she was fascinated by that pulsing light, fascinated by the secrets the artifact could hold.

But Owen was already moving forward, jogging over the piles of shredded garbage that rose up in the wind, swirling like ghosts.

"Let's go," he said.

Evie took a deep breath, stood, followed. Owen was a blur on the debris fields up ahead. She hated being out in the open like this, but there was no place to duck behind and hide. Whatever had happened here had left an empty space in the middle of the city, insulated by strips of white foam and sparkling swirls of broken glass.

"What is this stuff?" Saskia whispered, kicking a wad of foam.

"Not sure," Victor muttered. "It kind of looks like insulation, but the smell is more . . . sterile?"

Owen stopped, lifted one hand. *Over here.* Evie broke into a run, her heart hammering. Owen crouched down on the ground, pulled out the artifact. Immediately, a glare of light flashed out over the open space, bright enough that Evie stumbled, momentarily blinded. Panic crept up her spine. How far had that light traveled?

More importantly: Had the Covenant seen it?

She blinked the dots out of her vision and took off again. "Why'd you do that?" she demanded as she stumbled up next to Owen.

Saskia came up behind her. "What *happened*?"

"The artifact is reacting strangely," he said, his voice frustratingly calm.

Evie scanned the area around Owen. More of that strange white debris. It drifted up into piles beside them, swirling and then settling, dusting across the hulking shoulders of his armor. As Evie approached, she saw a soft purple-pink light reflected in his visor. Her chest seized up.

"They beat us to it," she said, suddenly aware of the energy shield blocking their path.

"Maybe," Owen said. "Maybe not." He pointed at the ground, and Evie moved closer and saw that there was an enormous hole carved into the broken, blackened cement. A Covenant energy shield arced over the hole, sealing it tight.

"Why 'maybe not'?" Saskia asked. "They've clearly been drilling here."

"If they'd already taken the artifact, there wouldn't be a shield over it," Owen said. "There's no excavation equipment here anymore either. No Locust, no Scarab. But they are protecting something down there."

"Which means they beat us to it," Evie said softly. "But it's probably still there."

Owen looked up at her, his face hidden by his visor. "Exactly."

"Also explains why there are only scattered patrols in the city; if they can't extract it—"

"It means they've been focusing their efforts somewhere else," Saskia finished.

Brume-sur-Mer, Evie thought. But now that they'd extracted the artifact, how long would it be before the Covenant set their sights on Annecy?

Owen stood, switched on the light embedded into his helmet, shone it down on the shield. Evie expected it to just reflect back, but instead they were able to get a better glimpse of what lay beyond the shield, in that huge hole. Stairs. Smooth gleaming walls. An opening of some sort—no, she realized. A doorway.

"It's a building," she gasped.

Owen nodded, the light bouncing over the shield, revealing more flashes of the structure: strange carved glyphs, smooth gray walls made of stone.

Evie became aware then of a strange humming sound, something vaguely mechanical. She grabbed her rifle and whipped her head around, surveying the open space and finding only that white debris. "Do you hear that?" she whispered.

"Yes," Victor said, gripping his own gun. "What is that?"

The humming intensified, filling up the air around them. And then Owen cursed.

Evie jumped; she'd never heard that from him. He whipped off the case containing the artifact and immediately the humming stopped, although the case was still vibrating, the material rattling against the palm of his glove.

"I didn't even feel it," Owen said, sounding slightly dazed.

The vibrating seemed to be getting more intense. Evie reached out for the case, but Owen clutched it more tightly and shook his head. "It's not safe."

"Nothing about this is safe," she snapped, and when she pulled on the case, he let it go. The vibration rumbled up through her fingers, into her arm. She tried her best to ignore it and slid the case open.

There was no flash of light like before, but the light inside the cylinder was shimmering violently, bouncing strangely against the glass walls. Evie took a step closer to the excavation site. Held the case up toward it.

The case jerked out of her hand, went flying sideways. Evie stumbled with the force of its movement and hit the ground hard, close enough to the energy shield that she smelled the sizzle of its power.

"Got it," Owen said. She peered up, and he was holding the case in one enormous fist. It lifted itself up, trying to pull away from him, but he was able to hold tight. "It wants to get to that structure."

"What if we let it go?" Victor said. "That was some intense force. I wonder if it could break through the shield—"

Reddish plasma bolts suddenly streaked past them, raining down over the shield and the rest of the dig site like comets. Owen leapt away from the shield and began firing; the artifact slumped back to normal. Evie scrambled to her feet and fired off a round of bullets, aiming at the tall, shaggy figures barreling toward them. Jiralhanae, howling and firing as they approached.

"Run!" Owen roared, and they did, Evie and Saskia taking the lead, Victor laying down cover fire. They had to get to shelter. The plasma bolts lit up the shadows around the ruins.

"There!" Victor called out, pointing at the ragged remains of a steel wall. Evie pumped her arms faster. She could hear Owen shouting behind them. Shouting orders? She couldn't hear over the adrenaline, and so she ran, her lungs burning, until she could duck behind the wall.

"Figured it wouldn't be unprotected for long," Saskia murmured as she reloaded her gun. "Not after Owen took out that Grunt nearby."

"And now they know we're here," Evie gasped. "Always the

perennial problem with us." She stood up, peered around the wall, firing wildly. Owen was racing toward them, Brutes following. She counted three of them.

"Run!" Owen roared. "We've got to lose them in the city. Now!"

Evie twisted back around the wall. "Did you hear that?"

Saskia and Victor nodded wildly.

"Well," Evie said. "Let's go."

And so they ran.

CHAPTER FIFTEEN

VICTOR

Victor slouched down in a pile of ash and dirt, the softest place in the entire city. He took a deep breath, but the cold air just stabbed at his lungs. He never thought he'd say this, but he missed Brume-sur-Mer and its sweltering humidity.

"Do we know where we are?" Saskia asked, sitting a few paces away on a chunk of broken stone. She squinted up at the sky. "Better yet, does Owen know where we are?"

Does it matter? Victor thought, although he stopped himself from saying it out loud. He wasn't Dorian, for god's sake. He was still trying to toe ONI's military line, but he didn't like not knowing about the true start date of the invasion any more than the others. He understood that there were things Owen couldn't tell them—hell, there were things his own *sisters* couldn't tell him. He never expected Owen to sit them down and spill all of the UNSC's secrets. What bothered Victor was the idea that Owen had kept information from them that the other members of the militia already knew. If they could fight alongside people like Caird or even Valois, they could know that Meridian had been under attack for the last six months instead of the last three. At this point, Victor knew that their work on Meridian merited more respect than that, and Owen knew they could take care of themselves.

"I think the most important question," Evie said, "is whether or not the Covenant know where we are."

That elicited a murmur of agreement from Victor and Saskia both. Victor pressed himself back into the dirt and stared up at the brilliant blue sky. They'd been running for at least half an hour, weaving around half-demolished buildings, ducking behind felled trees and piles of broken bricks and glass and stone, trying to confuse the Brutes' scent tracking. They'd lost them pretty quickly but had kept running to be sure they were in the clear, weaving around on top of their own steps. Now, Victor knew, they were lost, and without any real equipment to help them survive or get them back to camp.

He hated to admit it, but this wouldn't have happened in Brume-sur-Mer.

"So now what?" he said.

Evie and Saskia looked at him. "We're going to have to find our way back," Saskia said. "If we can get up high, I bet we can see where the transport center is. It's on a hill."

Victor grinned at her. "Good point."

She smiled back. It still made him feel all fluttery in his chest.

"I wish we had the artifact," Evie said, gazing off into the distance. "It was so *weird*, wasn't it, the way it pulled at the excavation site like that? Like it wanted to be there."

Victor nodded. "Yeah, I thought the same thing." He looked over at Saskia. "What about you? Do you know of any technology that can do that?"

Saskia laughed a little. "Does it matter? We're dealing with Forerunner tech with that thing. It's not something we're ever going to understand."

Victor's cheeks warmed. "I know that," he said. "I just thought—"

"I think the artifact is more than a map," Evie said. "I mean, I don't know what, not without getting to the dig site. But if it was just supposed to get us here, I don't know why it would be freaking out like that."

"Maybe it wanted to make sure we definitely went inside," Victor said.

"Right," said Evie. "So what's inside?"

They went quiet. The wind stirred the dust around, and it glinted in the bright sun. Victor still couldn't get over how much *light* there was here, despite the constant chill. It was like the sun couldn't do anything to warm the air.

"We ought to try to find some warmer clothes," he muttered.

"I don't think we're going to be finding anything here." Saskia gestured at their surroundings. "I mean, *look*."

She was right; they might as well have been resting in some ancient alley, worn down by time. Buildings lay in heaps of rubble, twisted metal frames clawed jaggedly toward the sky. Nothing even looked remotely like a city, let alone a store.

"Well, I hope Dorian found something, then," Victor snapped. "Might as well do some good if he's not going to help out."

"If there were something there," Evie said. "I'm sure Dorian would find it." But Victor knew her well enough to hear the shiver of doubt in her voice. And why not? Dorian had been *livid* about Owen lying to them. For good reason, Victor had to admit, even if he didn't like the way Dorian expressed it. He had lost the most out of all of them during the invasion.

"Oh," Evie said after a moment. "Oh my god, I just had a thought."

"About clothes?" Victor said.

"No." Evie stood up and paced around the debris, her fingers tapping along her thighs. Victor recognized this particular maneuver; it was what she did when she was on the verge of a breakthrough. "Look, it's clear the Covenant found the Forerunner building—the structure, whatever it is—before us. The space has been cleared out; it's protected behind an energy shield."

"They were guarding it," Saskia added.

"Well, sort of." Evie stopped pacing and looked up at her. "The Jiralhanae must have been patrolling, but they weren't nearby. That light flash would have drawn them instantly, and it took them a while to get there. So there's a presence, but they're only watching the perimeter. That means the Covenant aren't too worried about someone swooping in there and taking off with something."

Victor nodded, the pieces starting to fall into place for him too. It was just like when they were designing robotics for class last year. "So we're not looking at an *artifact* here, not like the one from Brume-sur-Mer."

"Right," Evie said. "Saskia, is this making sense?"

"It is," she said. "But what do you think is down there? Some kind of building?"

"Yes," Evie said. "But there's got to be more to it than that, right? It can't just be *a building*—I mean, why would the Covenant be protecting it, then? It must have some other purpose, something they can't get to work—"

"And you're thinking the Brume-sur-Mer artifact is the key," Victor said.

Evie shrugged. "That thing wanted to be in the structure, that's for sure. I mean, it flew out of my hands."

"Yeah, and it went straight for the shield too," Saskia said. "Owen caught it before it hit, but—"

"It wanted in the building," Evie said. "There's got to be a connection between the two things. I just—we have to figure out what."

"We'll need to get past that shield," Victor said. "Take it in there."

"Yes," Saskia said. "That doesn't sound dangerous at all."

Victor blushed. "We just escaped a pack of Brutes. I think we can go into a building." But then he sighed. "It is a weird alien building, though, so you may have a point."

"*May* have a point?" teased Saskia.

Victor's blush deepened. He wondered if she was flirting. Probably not.

"Once we get back to camp, we can take a look at the artifact," Evie said. "Victor, you can help me—you didn't look at it much before, and you were always the hardware guy."

Victor smiled. "I guess you could say that."

"Then it's settled." Evie paused, looking up at their surroundings. "Now we just have to figure out how to get back."

An hour later, at the point when the wreckage had all started to look the same and even Victor was about to give up hope of ever getting back to the camp, voices echoed through the buildings. Human voices.

A very familiar human voice, in fact: Dorian's. He was out scavenging for Green Squad, and he came around the corner of a fallen building with his gun hoisted and a supply pack strapped to his back.

"So you didn't die," Dorian said, lowering his weapon. "We weren't sure."

"What's that supposed to mean?" Victor asked.

Dorian laughed bitterly. "Owen came back here an hour ago. Said he lost you. I figured he was just lying again, and ONI had fed you to the Covenant as part of their grand master scheme where everyone dies painful, horrific deaths but they win the war."

"Seriously?" muttered Saskia. "You need to let this go." She didn't say it loud enough for Dorian to hear her, though.

As it turned out, they had been closer to the camp than they realized. Dorian led them through a narrow gap in a nearby wall, and the landing pad gleamed dead ahead, the transport station glittering in the sunlight.

From there, they made it back to camp in fifteen minutes, straggling one by one into the main atrium. The place had been transformed in their absence; a heating unit hummed steadily in the corner, warming the room to a halfway decent temperature. Jackets were laid out on the floor, ripped and dirty but still *warm*—Victor grabbed one and threw it around his shoulders as soon as he spotted them. The camp itself was empty, though.

"I heard you found something." Dorian stretched out on top of one of the blankets. "Some kind of structure? A building?"

"Yeah," Evie said. "Underground. Where is Owen? We need to talk to him."

Dorian scoffed. "A lot of good that does."

"Dorian," Saskia said. "He didn't lie to hurt us. We're going to need your help."

Dorian jerked up to sitting, his hair falling into his eyes. He looked exhausted. They probably all did.

"Those lies cost my friends their lives," Dorian snapped. "They cost how many lives in this city? In case you haven't looked around, it doesn't look like the UNSC really knows what it's doing on Meridian. Or if they do, they're doing a terrible job of it. If they'd been open to my plan in Brume-sur-Mer, sixty lives could have been saved. And I made that plan not even knowing *half* of what's going on in this world. And yet you all are willing to keep parroting this lie that it's okay because the adults know better? They don't. And, Evie, I know you know it too."

Evie crossed her arms, glancing up at Victor.

Saskia sighed. "It's not about the adults knowing better," she said. "It's about looking at the bigger picture. It's about understanding that even more people could have died if they'd tried to evacuate into the middle of a Covenant blockade—"

Dorian rolled onto his back, twisting away from them.

"Fine," she muttered. Then, louder: "So where is Owen? We do need to talk to him, like Evie said."

Dorian gestured loosely. "Out back with the others. They're running drills."

"And you're not training with them?" Victor frowned.

"Clearly not."

"Come on," Evie said. "Let's go. Let him have some space."

"He shouldn't be talking like that," Victor said once they were in the corridor and out of earshot. "I mean, yeah, Owen shouldn't have lied, but what does Dorian propose we do? Without the UNSC we'd all be—"

"I can see where he's coming from," Evie said, which didn't surprise Victor at all. These days she was always taking Dorian's side. "I mean, his friends died, Victor. None of us went through anything like that. And he was right. If we had known about the attack, we could have been better prepared."

"But that wasn't Owen's fault," Saskia said. "It was the government keeping the attack from us for our own good. By the time Owen came along, Dorian's friends had already—" Her voice faltered. "He's being unfair."

"Yeah, you're right," Evie said. "But the point is that Owen *is* the government. He has to keep their secrets and carry out their orders. If

Dorian disagrees with the UNSC, with ONI, he also disagrees with Owen. And I don't blame him. Seeing Annecy in this state ... I have questions too."

Victor listened to their conversation, trying to work out his own feelings. He knew in the military you couldn't know everything. Security issues. But three months ago, they'd been in an active war zone, with a slim chance of surviving—what if something in their rescue and escape plan hinged on them knowing something that ONI didn't want them to know?

Honestly, thinking about it just made him exhausted. Victor—and it seemed like Saskia agreed with him—wanted to bypass processing this entire situation and skip straight to the only logical conclusion: They would have helped the UNSC anyway, because the UNSC represented humanity's best chance of survival. It was like Owen had said. Their lives weren't the only ones in the galaxy. There were millions of others to factor in too.

They stepped through the jagged gap in the wall, out onto the landing pad. The militia was divided up into their squads, all of them sparse and painful to look at. Owen barked orders, offered tips of improvement.

The case, with the artifact, was still clamped to his thigh.

"We should be out here running drills with them," Victor said. "Going over Owen's plan."

"We *should* be looking at that artifact," Evie responded. "If we can take it back to that structure, we might be able to study it, get some answers."

Saskia nodded. "But Owen will never agree to that—it could compromise the whole mission if we get caught by the Covenant."

"Well, that's why we're not going to get caught." Immediately, she cut through the landing pad toward Owen. Saskia and Victor hung back while she and Owen spoke, Evie gesturing wildly, pointing at the artifact, then at the city, then at the sky. Owen kept shaking his head, but Evie stayed on him, her gestures growing more and more emphatic. Typical Evie—not even a Spartan could stand in her way when there was a problem to be solved.

"What do you think ONI's gonna want us to do?" Saskia asked.

"Huh?" Victor went still. "ONI?"

"With the last artifact, they wanted us to literally take it. But we can't take a building. There's got to be something more to all this."

Across the landing pad, Owen handed Evie the case. Then he barked out Farhi's name.

"Huh," Victor said. "Looks like we're about to do some investigating."

Evie jogged up to them, breathless. "Okay," she said. "It took some convincing, and Farhi's going to come along in case we run into the Covenant—"

"So a babysitter," Victor said.

Evie shot him an annoyed look. "We're lucky he's letting us go at all—this is a huge risk we're taking. Farhi stepped in and mentioned we could scout out if the Covenant presence has been beefed up at the site since our last run-in with them. That and telling him we'd be in and out as quickly and quietly as possible was the only way he'd let us go. He did like our theory, though. He's already working with the rest of the team to figure out how to get access to the structure. Saskia, you want to help us, or do you want to run through the plan with the militia?"

Victor resisted the urge to offer to let her take his place; he'd prefer to be here, helping Owen come up with a strategy. But Victor had always been good with hardware. Probably better for him to take a look at the artifact.

Saskia tilted her head, looked out at the landing pad. "I think I'll stay here," she said. "It's important one of us knows the whole plan of attack, and I doubt Dorian's going to show up any time soon. Plus it's probably best you go in with a smaller group to avoid being seen. I'll be more help to you this way." She nodded at them. "Good luck."

Victor zoomed in on the dig site on his helmet. The energy shield was a white mass in the center of his field of vision.

"I'm not seeing anything," he said. "Looks clear."

Farhi's voice crackled in his ear. "Looks clear from where I am," she said. She was perched up on the second floor of a nearby building with a sniper rifle, keeping an eye out for Covenant scouts. "You two be careful."

"Acknowledged."

"Okay." Evie rustled beside him, behind the last source of cover for the next forty meters. "You ready?"

Victor pulled out his rifle, cocked it into place. "Go for it."

Evie took a deep breath and slid open the case. A pale glow flooded between them, a sphere of light about a meter wide. She eased out the cylinder. The light flickered but didn't flash like it had earlier that day, which was what Victor had been bracing himself for. He breathed a long sigh of relief.

"Yeah," said Evie. "Let's just hope this light isn't enough to draw them."

"Is it vibrating?" Victor asked.

"A little." Evie held it up between them. The light was diffused, but that flicker made Victor feel like he was back in Mrs. Alvarez's chemistry class. That damn light had never been fixed. Never would, now.

Evie grabbed the cylinder and twisted, the way she had when she discovered the map. The pieces slid together, and the light blinked out.

"Oh." Evie frowned. "So it's not going to show us the map again."

"Well, we're here," Victor said. "I mean, that kind of proves your theory, right? That it's not just a map. It served that purpose, so now it's got something else to do."

Evie nodded. Through the haze of night vision, Victor could see the movement of the artifact in her hands, a faint blur where its edges should be. He wished they'd had their full complement of equipment, instead of whatever people had been able to carry with them as they raced through the forest. A nanoscanner, or even just a computer—either could have given him some insight. Hell, if they'd had time to take the artifact to the Brume-sur-Mer high school, he bet he could have hooked it up to the JDI machine and gotten a read on its electromagnetic waves. *Something.*

"I think we should go closer," Evie said. "I'm leaving it in this state, though. I'm curious to see what happens."

"I'll lead the way," Victor said, tapping his helmet.

They picked their way across the field of trash and destruction. Even with Farhi keeping watch, Victor was aware of how exposed they were, how disadvantaged. He had to admit he found the idea of a babysitter less irritating now that they were out in the open.

Evie yelped, her voice echoing out into the darkness. Victor cringed, tightened the grip on his gun.

"Everything okay?" Farhi said, her voice staticky.

"It's moving," she hissed, more quietly. "Oh god, it's pulling me toward the—"

She shoved past him, her arms jutted out in front of her, the artifact pressed between her palms. The light pulsed. He couldn't look at it directly.

"Evie!" He followed after her, grasping out with one hand—but she was running too fast. Or being *dragged*, really. Somehow she managed to stay on her feet, but her legs kept splaying out from underneath her, and she twisted around and looked at him with a stricken expression. "I'm trying!" he cried.

"It's pulling me!"

"What the hell's going on?" Farhi said.

"It's the artifact," Victor panted, running after Evie. "Not the Covenant."

They were almost to the energy shield. Evie smothered a scream. The artifact jerked in her hands, and then, to Victor's horror, she went flying straight to the energy shield.

"Drop it!" he shouted.

Instantly, she hit the ground. The artifact streaked forward, slammed into the energy shield in a blast of heat and light. Victor flew backward, his ears ringing. He was too stunned to move, his gaze fixed on the brilliant night sky.

"Okay, that's enough," Farhi said over the comm. "I have no idea what just happened but that light is going to call the Covenant. We have to get out of here. Now."

"Agreed." Victor sat up, fumbled around in the debris for his gun. Evie shifted up ahead, dragging herself to her feet. She rubbed her forehead. Then she let out a cry and scrambled toward the shield.

"What is she doing?" Farhi said.

"I'll get her!" Victor responded. He clambered to his feet and fol-lowed after her, heart pounding, afraid she was going to fling herself against the shield, but she slowed and knelt down at its edge.

Victor stumbled to a stop beside her.

"Look," she breathed.

At first, he thought she was talking about the artifact, which had bounced off the shield and lay undamaged on the ground, its light pulsing violently. But then she pointed toward the shield, and Victor followed the line of her finger to see a dark spot clouding out along the shield. It consumed the dome for one terrifying moment, and then went dark.

"We've got to get in there," Evie said.

Victor couldn't disagree.

CHAPTER SIXTEEN

DORIAN

N o way in hell," Dorian said.

They were outside in the cold because Saskia had insisted on talking to him privately. He figured it would be about that damn suicide mission to get into the Forerunner structure, but he had gone along anyway because Saskia had gotten this pleading look in her eyes and because Dorian honestly didn't have anything better to do. He and Yellow Squad had swept the entire transport station twice already. If they were going to scavenge, it would mean going out into the city. And Dorian wasn't ready to do that again.

He wasn't ready to do anything that would be a risk. Not for Owen. Not for ONI. He was tired of risking his life for people who didn't give a damn about him.

Saskia, at least, did care. He knew that much. Same with Victor and Evie, but they were holed up with Owen and the team leaders, planning their approach for gaining access to the building. Better than storming the place, at least, although Dorian wouldn't be surprised if that was what they wound up doing.

"Why not?" Saskia said a second time. Dorian was trying to ignore her. But she put her hand on his shoulder. "Well?"

"You know why." Dorian swept her hand aside. "We aren't supposed to *be* here. There's no reason for us to risk our lives on a mission that was never intended for us."

Saskia tilted her head, frowning, the wind blowing her lank hair into her eyes. Dorian's own hair was limp and greasy as well. What he wouldn't give for a bar of dry cleanser, much less a steam shower.

"What we did on Brume-sur-Mer," Saskia said. "That wasn't a mission intended for us."

"Oh, come on!" Dorian whirled away from her, his face hot with anger. "We were saving our families."

Silence save for the constant howl of the wind.

"Your families," Saskia said softly.

Dorian closed his eyes. "This is not the same. You had people you cared about in that town. This is just . . . errand running for ONI."

He heard her footsteps on the broken concrete as she walked around in front of him. "Our home is more than a town," she said. "This place"—she swept her hands out wide—"it's part of Meridian. If we can find out what's in that structure, and how it relates to the cylinder, we can keep the Covenant from getting to it. We can keep them from glassing our home." She shook her head, eyes damp. "Don't you want this to be our home again?"

Dorian stared at her, anger surging inside him. "This isn't going to be our home again," he snapped. "Every single survivor is settled in at the refugee colony. Why the hell would they come back here?" And he gestured out at Annecy too, at the rubble and debris, the shattered buildings, the hollow, echoing emptiness. "And besides, if we remove the artifact, the Covenant will have no reason to *not* glass this place. They've already won."

"Why are you being like this?" Saskia asked. "Is it just because of Owen?"

And there it was, the truth, hard and stinging like the wind. Her question hung in the air between them, ringing in his ears.

"You can't keep holding that against him," Saskia said. "I know you're angry. I was angry too. But he had good reasons—"

Dorian rolled his eyes. "They always have *reasons*." He paused, looked out over the rubble. "I don't know why you trust him. Why any of us did. We should have listened to those damn stories our grandparents told us about the Insurrection. Owen was created to do whatever the hell the UNSC says."

"He wasn't created," Saskia said. "He was a kid once. A war orphan."

Dorian didn't look at her. The information left him faintly stunned. "How do you know that?"

"He told me." Saskia walked over to Dorian's side, put her hand on his arm. He didn't shrug her away; her palm was warm, a comfort in the biting wind. "He didn't tell me much, but he told me that. He told me ONI trained him. Did things to him."

Dorian laughed, although it tasted sour on his tongue. "So you're telling me I should trust the UNSC because they snatched up an orphan, broke him down, and created a war machine from the parts?" He found himself thinking of Remy, ten years old. Orphaned, broken down, re-created. He shivered. Not, this time, from the cold.

"Look, I'm not defending what the UNSC did," Saskia said. "But they made him what he is. They made him a hero. Think of how many lives he's saved—how many people didn't become orphans because he was there to fight for them." She took a breath, her cheeks flushed. "Think about what would have happened to the people of Brume-sur-Mer if he had never shown up! We wouldn't even be here to have this conversation because no one would have made it off Meridian alive. Including Remy and your uncle."

Dorian was silent.

"Owen told me that, when it happened, when they—trained him, they gave him a new family. And I think something like that has happened with us." Saskia smiled, although she looked exhausted. "We can't do this without you."

Dorian sighed, pushed a hand through his greasy hair. This was such a Saskia thing, her obsession with family. All because her parents abandoned her.

But the thing was, he understood it. His parents had abandoned him too. All for the UNSC, all for their stupid senseless protocols that said it was okay to lie to a bunch of scared, grieving teenagers. Sure, Dorian had Uncle Max and Remy, but there was still a space in his heart that his parents had gouged out when they boarded that UNSC recruit ship.

Owen had made him think, stupidly, that maybe they'd done it to protect him. But Owen had also lied.

"I'm not asking you to do this for Owen," Saskia said. "I'm asking you to do this for Evie and Victor. They're going down there regardless of whether you come with us or stay here. But we've been through so much together. You really think we should split up now?"

"When they're about to do something incredibly stupid?" Dorian glanced at her.

She smiled like she thought he was joking.

"I mean," he said, "they're about to head down into some alien structure without any kind of protection. It's pretty stupid."

Saskia shrugged. "I guess. That's why they need us there to help them. Maybe that's the trick. Maybe we can do all the stupid stuff we want as long as it's the four of us. We've survived this long as a team."

Dorian stared at her. With her unwashed hair, the dark circles under her eyes, the filthy scavenged clothes, she looked so different than she had back before the invasion. He'd never even really talked to her before the attack. Now she was treating him like he was family.

Because he was family. They all were. As much as he hated to admit it, maybe Owen was right about this one thing. They'd survived something together, and that forged bonds that nothing else could. They were his family, and he wasn't about to be like his parents and abandon them.

"Fine," he said. "Let's go be stupid together."

The entire militia—what remained of it, anyway—set out at sunset, bundled up in jackets and armed with every weapon and piece of equipment they'd managed to put together. It wasn't much. The three remaining Blue Squad members manned the Warthog, the only piece of good luck on this entire trip as far as Dorian was concerned. Although even that made a peculiar sputtering noise anytime they drove over some particularly sizable debris, so Dorian spent the whole march waiting for it to cut out.

At first, things were quiet, just Meridian's ragtag militia and the emptiness of the city. But then something big and loud whined through the sky, leaving bright trails in its wake. Energy arced between two parallel cylinders. Everyone hit the ground, guns ready. Fortunately, the ship didn't loop back around to them, just kept barreling toward wherever it was going.

"That's not good," Evie said softly.

"It never is."

"No, I mean, they didn't have ships before." She frowned. "The site wasn't being watched from above. There were only ground patrols."

"Agreed." Owen, eavesdropping with that supersonic hearing of his. "But we knew this was likely to be the case, after we first encountered them at the site and then you"—he cleared his throat—"breached the shield."

"I didn't mean to," she said.

"We need to proceed with caution," Owen said, pushing forward through the group. They set out again, moving through narrow side streets, keeping their eyes on the sky and the shadows. A pair of Banshees swooped overhead, moving in the opposite direction from the dropship. Whatever they were doing, it wasn't surveillance. They would have seen the group heading into the city.

Dorian took a deep breath, resisted the urge to turn around.

Eventually, they came to a stop in a particularly demolished area situated on the top of a hill. The metal frame of a ruined building jutted out of the ground, its walls replaced by shredded white material that clumped together, plastering the frame like a faded old skin. Zabinski parked the Warthog behind the wall and began distributing equipment.

"We've got a clear view of the Forerunner structure site from here," Evie said. "And that building gives us a little cover."

Dorian felt a surge of curiosity despite himself. By that point, the sun had set completely behind the distant hills, but the night wasn't nearly as dark as it was down at the transport center. He drifted closer, creeping to the wall's edge. No one tried to stop him—not that he would have listened anyway. He peered around the corner.

"Holy sh—" he sputtered, slamming back around to cover. That caught some attention: Both Owen and Farhi jerked their heads up at him.

"What are you doing?" Farhi said.

"What did you see?" asked Owen, and even Dorian had to admit that was the better question.

"Nothing good," he said.

He peeked around the edge of the wall again, his heart

hammering. Even without the HUD of his old helmet, he could clearly make out the scene below.

The bombed-out space between the hills was *crawling* with Covenant soldiers.

There were ground troops marching in formation, heading off into the city. A pair of Locusts, like the one used in their excavation three months ago back on Brume-sur-Mer, crawled over the ground. A Banshee floated in the air, casting bright lights down over the entire scene. Fully armed Elites stood in a ring at the center of the space. A strange berobed figure sat near them, hovering in what appeared to be some sort of chair. It looked vaguely human compared to the rest of the Covenant species. But then it turned its head, and Dorian saw that its neck was longer, more serpentine. He gasped and jerked back behind the wall. In all his time fighting since the invasion, he'd never seen one of the San'Shyuum—the Prophets, as they were called. They didn't fight. Just led the Covenant in their endless holy war.

"Looks like our activities here have drawn more attention," Owen said to Evie, who stepped away from the wall, her face pale.

"We expected this," Farhi said.

"Not to this degree." Owen gestured and the militia gathered around him. The wall rose up against the night, their only cover. Dorian kept staring at it, waiting for it to topple.

"We giving up on this?" Valois said.

Owen shook his head. "We can't. We've just got to learn from our past mistakes."

Dorian smothered a laugh. "Too bad we don't know the tunnel system around here."

"The shield's down," Victor said. The activation light on his helmet was blinking. Must have zoomed in on the view. "It's a straight shot into the hole if we can make it."

"They've got a Prophet down there, for god's sake," said Valois. "With about a million bodyguards. I'm not the only one who sees that, right?"

"I say we stick with the original plan," said Farhi. "Snipe at them from the surrounding hills, like we talked about, while the kids sneak in. The shield being down actually makes it easier."

A low rumble of suggestions started up from the group. Dorian glanced over at Evie and Victor. The two scouts. He thought about what Saskia had told him, about them being a family. Whatever crazy idea Dorian came up with, he wasn't about to let them go down there alone. All of them, or none of them.

Somehow, seeing all those Covenant troops down below had just cemented that fact for him. Weird how that worked out.

Owen stepped up. "If we do go forward with it, I'm going down there with them. Farhi, you'll lead the strike here."

Farhi nodded, gave a quick salute.

"I'm going down there too," Dorian announced suddenly. "The four of us, we work as a team, and Evie and Victor are going to need more reinforcements. You know a few gunshots from up here isn't going to pull away that entire setup down there."

Owen looked over at him. "Fine."

"I'm going too," Saskia said, stepping up beside Dorian. She glanced at him. "Like he said. We're a team."

"All right, then." Farhi clapped her hands together. "It's been decided. Blue, Red, Green, Yellow: You know what to do. Local Team." She looked at them. Somehow Dorian, Saskia, Evie, and Victor had managed to clump up together. "Happy hunting."

CHAPTER SEVENTEEN

EVIE

vie took deep, measured breaths, as if she were about to sit down for a final exam. She knew that every time she had undertaken some mission since the invasion, she had put herself at risk. Surveilling Brume-sur-Mer, accessing Salome's interface, blowing up the drill site—all of these things had been dangerous.

But never before had she run right into the middle of a Covenant-occupied zone.

This is so stupid, she told herself.

But she knew she was going to do it anyway.

They were waiting at the base of the hill, in a pile of dusty debris. Owen crouched between Evie and Victor, with Dorian in front and Saskia to the rear. Evie felt safe here, in her little nest of rubble. She knew she was about to throw all of that safety away.

"Position?" Owen murmured softly into his comm. Evie couldn't hear the answer, but it made Owen say, "Good. Yellow Squad: position?"

Evie listened to this litany as she breathed, trying to imagine herself successfully racing across the open field and diving into the structure. They got one shot to do this. One shot to prove her and Victor's theories.

"Ready," Owen said, still speaking into his comm.

Evie's chest constricted. Light from the Covenant encampment spilled through the transparent hunks of melted detritus currently keeping her hidden.

"Like we talked about," he murmured. "Green Squad, get ready—"

Evie twisted her fingers in the fabric of her jacket, wanting something that could ground her.

"Initiate," Owen said, and immediately there was the *rat tat tat* of UNSC military rifles. The air flooded with surprised shouts of anger in at least three different Covenant dialects. Evie resisted the urge to stick her head out from the garbage pile to see what was happening in the war zone. Instead she listened: to the whine of a Banshee engine, no doubt circling overhead for the shooter; to the pulse of plasma weapons and the rattle of human rifles.

"Blue Squad," Owen said. "Initiate."

Evie pressed one hand to Dorian's back. He twisted around, debris shifting around him.

"You ready?" she whispered.

"I'm doing this for you," he whispered, and something tightened in her chest.

"Green Squad," Owen said.

Dorian nodded at her, then glanced at Owen, who gave him the go-ahead. He slipped out of the debris pile. Evie still couldn't believe that he'd volunteered to scout out the situation.

"Initiate," Owen said.

The sounds of war rattled around them. Gunfire, plasma cannons, the eerie sound of Banshees: All of it sent goose bumps crawling over Evie's skin. She glanced over at Victor; he was staring straight ahead, his expression fierce and determined.

The debris rattled; Dorian stuck his head through.

"About half the Elites are still there," he said. "The Prophet guy is gone, though, along with his bodyguards."

"Makes sense," Owen said. "They'd protect him at any cost."

"It looks like they've sent the ground troops to suss out our people." Dorian leaned back on his heels. "So it's better, but not great."

"It's what we've got," Owen said. "Lead the way."

Dorian nodded, but he was looking at Evie. She gave him a smile she hoped was brave.

He slipped out through the debris, and the rest of them followed, sliding into the smoke and noise of the open air. A maze of fallen chunks of buildings separated them from the excavation site, illuminated by the blasts of plasma fire.

Dorian gestured, leading them forward. The smoke and dust choked at Evie's lungs, and she squeezed the grip of her rifle so hard her fingers ached. Seven meters to get to the dig site. Without being seen.

Dorian stopped at the edge of the zone, before all the debris got flattened out. He and Owen traded places. Despite the cold air, Dorian's face was gleaming with sweat.

"It's wild out there," he said.

Evie still couldn't see, but the constant rattle of the gunfire exchange seemed to bleed together into one massive noise, a vibration echoing through the hills.

Owen looked back at them, his visor reflecting the light of the battle.

"I'm going to lay down cover fire," he said. "There's a clear space between us and the structure—the Elites have fanned out to deal with our snipers." He paused. "Evie, you ready for the artifact?"

She took a deep breath. The artifact. The key component of their plan. She only hoped she could count on it to do what it had done before.

"I'm ready." She swung her rifle back around on its strap.

Owen handed the artifact to her. It wasn't vibrating yet, but the light inside danced wildly, almost to the rhythm of the gunfire.

"Focus on the goal," Owen said. "And look out for each other."

And before they could respond, he was on his feet, striding into the battle, firing his rifle.

There was a pause, a half second of hesitation. Then Evie darted forward, cradling the artifact to her chest. She didn't look back to see if the others followed; she only did as Owen told her, and kept her focus on the goal. It was easy, since she was running toward a hole in the ground, the only spot of darkness in the entire vista laid out in front of her. Plasma fire shot around her, lighting up the sky. The artifact began rattling against her chest. Owen was right; the Elites weren't ringed as tightly around the structure, but they were still there, firing their powerful stationary turrets up into the hills.

And then one of them was turning, its mandibled face twisting toward her, followed by the muzzle of its weapon. Panic coursed through her; she couldn't drop the artifact, and so she couldn't get to her gun. Why had she run forward without checking if the others were with her? What if she was out here alone, racing toward this monstrous soldier, its weapon about to fire—

And then Saskia dove in front of her, firing off her rifle. The Elite stumbled backward, Saskia's bullets lighting up the shielding on its armor. "Keep going!" Saskia screamed. "I've got this!"

Evie forced her gaze away from the Elite and pressed on. The vibrations from the artifact ran up her arms, making her shoulders ache. A little closer—

A shout in an alien tongue; the Elites were circling back. At least three of them, moving toward the entrance of the structure.

The artifact yanked Evie's arms forward.

"Now!" she screamed, praying the others would hear her.

And they did. She felt a hand on her ankle, an arm around her waist, another on her arm.

The Elites lifted their guns in unison.

And Evie's feet lifted off the ground.

She didn't move as fast as she had the night before, not with all the extra weight of her friends. But her theory about the artifact was correct; it wanted to be at the structure. And she felt it *calibrate* in her hands, some shift in the vibrations, and then, in a blink, she and the others barreled straight through the formation of Elites, plunging down into the dark of the dig site. Dirt billowed up around them. Someone was screaming.

The entrance to the structure rose up in front of them, a carved stone leviathan of sloping angles and straight arches. Evie squeezed her eyes shut as they flew across the threshold—hadn't there been an energy shield over the door?—and then she dropped the artifact and landed hard on a cold stone floor, her breath knocked out of her body, a warm weight resting on top of her.

She blinked, groaned. Her arm muscles burned.

She heard a slap of flesh against stone and a string of curses.

"I can't believe that worked," Dorian said, breathless. He was sprawled out next to Evie on the ground. "You okay?"

"I've been better." She moved to push herself up, but her arms trembled beneath the weight of her body. Hands gripped her hips: Saskia, pulling her up to standing.

"Thanks," Evie said, rubbing her arms. She blinked, trying to take in her surroundings. The structure was dark. The only light came from the artifact, which lay about a meter away, its light pulsing softly.

"Were we followed?" Dorian said. "Those Elites were right behind—"

"No," Owen's voice boomed and echoed in the small space. "And it looks like they won't be joining us. Certain Forerunner technology only responds to humans . . . looks like this structure follows those same rules. The energy shield over the door opened to admit us, and then closed behind us."

Evie turned around, still trying to rub the soreness out of her arms. She wanted to ask Owen more about the Forerunner technology he'd met in the field, but they had a job to do. And he probably couldn't tell her much anyway.

Owen ducked through the threshold and then straightened; as small as the space seemed, the ceiling was vaulted up high. Evie tilted her head back, but she could only see darkness.

"Even so," Owen continued, "we're going to want to do this as fast as possible. Let's not push our luck here."

Evie took a deep breath. They needed to start with the artifact. She gestured for Victor to join her, and then she picked up the artifact.

"It's not vibrating anymore," Evie said. She gripped it tight and then twisted.

Immediately, the stone walls of the room lit up, light seeping into the carved glyphs that spiraled out across the stone. It ran in rivulets, streaming toward a sculpture that was set into a sconce in the wall, its strange curves overlapping one another in disconcerting ways. Light flowed up the sculpture, pooling around a gap in the sculpture's design. A hole.

"Wow," breathed Saskia, her head tilted back, her face lit by the light. "Have you seen anything so beautiful?"

"I'm not liking the look of this," Owen said, taking a heavy foot-step toward the illuminated sculpture. "We need to act quickly and determine what this is. Protocol says we need to find a way to ensure whatever technology exists inside this place doesn't fall into Covenant possession. Just because they can't enter right now doesn't mean they won't be able to soon, and then eventually find a way to leverage this technology. So that needs to be our focus."

But Evie barely heard him. The artifact was warm in her hands, the pulse of light pressing against her palm, as steady and comforting as a heartbeat. She drifted toward the sculpture. Lifted up the artifact. It felt like she was supposed to insert the artifact, but it wasn't the right shape.

"What do you think?" Victor asked. "You think the artifact is some kind of activation device? That alone might keep the Covenant from accessing anything in here."

"The light is the same color." She tilted the artifact. The light didn't move the way it did outside the structure, but rather pulsed steadily in its center. She frowned. She had to play with it to get it to access the map; maybe this was the same situation? She twisted the artifact again, and this time it elongated in her hand, the glass moving almost like liquid as it transformed into an octagonal shape. Some kind of nanotech, maybe? It didn't look anything like human nanotech, that was for sure.

"Holy crap," Victor said.

"Are you two okay?" Owen asked.

"We're fine." Evie lifted the artifact—not a cylinder anymore, she thought, but a key, oddly shaped but perfectly designed to slot into the sculpture. She glanced over at Victor. He nodded.

"Only one way to find out what this place is," he murmured.

She took a deep breath, slid the key into place.

For a half second, nothing happened. But then Evie felt a weight pressing on her, as if the air had grown heavier. She reached out to steady herself against the wall, but her hand dipped into it, the stone a cold, sticky gel that clung to her skin. She screamed but did not hear it, only saw it—a metallic shimmer on the air that spiraled out of her mouth and exploded against the ceiling. She yanked out her hand, whipped around, panic squeezing her throat shut. Victor was no longer beside her—where the hell had he gone? There was Saskia, but she looked strange, elongated, her skin shimmery. And Dorian, his torso pressed into the wall, sinking straight into the stone. Evie screamed his name, and this time she tasted it, like blood at the back of her throat.

She lunged toward him, one hand reaching out—but she was on the ceiling now, hanging upside down like a bat. There was Victor, flattened out in the corner, black liquid streaming out of his open mouth.

And then Evie was splayed out on the floor, vomiting up stomach bile and the meager rations she had eaten a few hours earlier. Her head throbbed with a stabbing, intense pain. She retched, struggled to sit up. A wave of dizziness swept over her.

"We've got to get out of here now."

Evie lifted her head to find Owen towering over her, the artifact in one hand. His stiff posture revealed his concern.

"You're not sick," she whispered. Was she the only one? No, she could hear Victor gagging beside her. He was curled up, his face ashy and beaded with sweat.

"That thing did something to you," Owen said. "Can you stand?"

Evie shook her head, but she tried to push herself up anyway. Her arms trembled, and she lifted her head in a swoon. The doorway felt like it was across the world. Saskia was pressed against the wall, rubbing her head. Dorian was hunched over, vomiting into a corner.

And then Evie was flying. No—she was being carried. Owen carted her out of the structure, into the trench of dirt and mud outside. The hole. Gunfire popped overhead. The Covenant and the militia were still exchanging fire. Owen deposited her in a little carved-out section of dirt, keeping her out of sight. "Don't move from here," he said.

She slumped back, the dirt cool and soft. Her nausea was subsiding, but there was still a sharp, shooting pain lancing through her temple. She closed her eyes. Tried to ignore the rattle of gunfire on the surface.

Quickly, Owen brought out the others. They were all slumped and pale, hair damp with sweat, eyes fever bright.

"How are we—" It was difficult to talk. She tried to form words, but it felt like her mouth was full of cotton, and she couldn't tell if she was moving her tongue the right way. "How are we going to get out—"

"We're waiting," Owen said, crouching down in the dirt. He deactivated his visor. Unlike everyone else, he looked fine. No sign of sickness. "As soon as it's clear, as soon as you feel better, we'll make a run for it."

The gunfire exchange raged on overhead. Owen picked up his rifle, moved toward the entrance of the dig.

Evie just sank deeper into the dirt.

Three hours later, they were back at the camp, after a harrowing sprint through the last vestiges of the gunfight. Evie sat on top of her blanket with Saskia, drinking a tin of stale water. She felt significantly better than she had before, although her headache was still hanging on, a faint pain behind her right eye. Saskia seemed tired, but the color had come back into her cheeks, at least.

"That was—not what I expected to happen," Victor said, settling down beside them.

"What did you expect?" Saskia asked.

"I don't know." Victor stared down at his water. "Not that."

Farhi stomped over to them. "Spartan Owen needs to talk to you." She studied them, her expression unreadable. The tables had turned, Evie thought: Because they were sniping from afar, none of the rest of the militia had faced any injuries. It was just them. Sickened by a few moments spent in an alien room.

"Now," Farhi added, before crossing her arms, waiting for them to move. Evie stood up, legs shaking a little—she was still feeling weak from the sickness, as much as she didn't want to admit it—and headed toward the office in the center of the building. That was always where Owen was when he wanted to talk to someone.

Dorian, shockingly, was already there when the others arrived, slumped at the table looking annoyed. Owen had set up the comm pad, the holo projector turned on, shining a beam of light into the air. Evie crept into the room, slid into the seat next to Dorian. He glanced at her, gave her a weak smile.

"Feeling better?" he asked.

She nodded. "You?"

"Nah."

Owen cleared his throat. "Thank you all," he said. "ONI has asked us to debrief with them."

Evie felt a shudder of trepidation—ONI? Of course it made sense, but she didn't want to think about what ONI would ask them to do, given how far the artifact from Brume-sur-Mer had taken them.

The holo shimmered with encryption static, and then a sharp, familiar face materialized. Captain Dellatorre. She smiled brightly at the group, and Evie's trepidation grew stronger.

"Spartan-B096 has filled me in on some of what happened," she said. "But as he was unaffected by the event, my science team and I would very much like to hear your experiences." Three additional holos flickered on. "Allow me to introduce doctors Salo, Chapman, and Faraday."

Each of the scientists nodded at the mention of their name. Dr. Salo, a broad-shouldered woman with a pile of thick, dark hair, smiled stiffly. "We're very interested in knowing what happened."

No one spoke. The captain's hologram crossed her arms and stood very patiently, eyes flicking as if she were looking around the room.

"Someone's gonna have to speak up," Owen said. "I've told them everything I know. All I could see was what you four looked liked from the outside. And that's not terribly useful for us to figure out what happened in there." He shifted his weight. "It's imperative that ONI fully understand what just happened. To make sure you four are safe, and to assess the possibility of the Covenant turning that structure—whatever it is—into a super-weapon."

"What did we look like from the outside?" Saskia asked.

Owen's expression hardened. "It's hard to describe. Each of you looked . . . different. But all of you looked like you were being tortured."

Evie sucked in a breath. It had felt like torture, hadn't it? But then, she had barely understood what was happening to her. What was happening to the room—

"I'll go first," she said, leaning forward in her chair. Captain Dellatorre looked at her expectantly. "Once we inserted the artifact into the structure it felt like—like I was hallucinating."

The others made murmuring noises of agreement, and Dr. Faraday raised an eyebrow. "Hallucinating? Did you see anything? Figures? Shapes? What?"

"No, no," Evie said. "Well, sort of. I saw . . . sounds. Tasted them too. I saw Dorian melting into the wall. I saw—" The images flickered through her thoughts. "The wall melted into something else. Everything was merging together."

"Yeah," Saskia said. "I saw that too. It was almost trying to pull me in with it. Terrifying and painful."

Evie looked at Saskia. "You saw the same thing?"

"Yeah," Victor interrupted. "I saw Dorian embedded into the wall. And I was walking on the ceiling. You were too, Evie, and you looked all—distorted. Like a damaged holo-recording."

"Jesus," Dorian muttered. "We all saw the same thing."

Blood rushed in Evie's ears. "A shared hallucination?"

"Perhaps." The voice of one of the scientists cut through the confusion—Evie didn't see which one. "Spartan-B096, it seems their experiences line up with your reports as well."

The other scientists murmured in agreement.

"What?" Evie almost jumped away from the table. "You saw all this too? But—you were unaffected!"

"It didn't make me sick," Owen said. "But I saw the . . . distortions, I would call them. Not just saw them. Experienced them. I had to . . . swim through the air to get to the activation device."

"The sculpture you described," Dr. Chapman said. "Correct?"

"Yes."

"And what was the room like after Spartan-B096 removed the key from the activation device? What did do you notice?" asked Dr. Salo.

Evie shook her head. She didn't remember anything about the room afterward. She'd been too sick. She only remembered the area outside, the soft dirt. It had seemed normal.

"It was changed," Dorian said.

"What?" Evie looked over at him. "What do you mean?"

"I mean, it was changed." He shook his head. "I thought I was still hallucinating since I felt like such garbage, but... there was a big indentation in the wall, where Saskia had been."

Across the table, Saskia's face went ashy.

"The ceiling was lower. It looked different—the way the floor looked. And the room just—"

"It felt different," Saskia whispered. "I thought that. Like the air molecules had changed. You know how the air gets before a thunderstorm?"

Evie could hardly breathe. What had they done? She should never have inserted that artifact into the sculpture.

"It was only the room, though," Evie said, breathless. "Outside was fine—"

"I observed that as well," Owen said. "None of those changes seemed to happen outside the structure."

"It's a containment unit," Saskia whispered.

Everyone turned to look at her. She lifted her gaze, her eyes wide. "Don't you think? Like what my parents would use, when they were testing weapons—" She froze.

"Weapons?" said Captain Dellatorre in a flat voice. "You think this is a weapon?"

"I don't—I don't know. I just—doesn't it seem like that, to you?"

"Perhaps," the captain said.

"I don't know." Evie tapped her fingers against the table. Her mind whirred. "Especially since what we experienced was *real*. Isn't that the kind of effect that can happen if there's a slipspace drive failure?" Her heart was pounding. She wished she had paid more attention in her physics classes, but she'd always been more interested in running code to fix problems than unraveling the theoretical fabric of reality. However, she had read something once about failures with slipspace drives that sounded similar to what she had experienced in the structure. Slipspace was a compressed dimension of reality that was used by starships for faster-than-light travel, but it wasn't as precise or as safe as humanity would have preferred. Was their experience connected to slipspace—a kind of breakdown of the physical world at a molecular level?

"You think we went into slipspace?" Dorian asked.

"No," Saskia said. "We couldn't have. It would have been much more dangerous. Right?" She looked at the scientists for confirmation.

"Absolutely," said Dr. Chapman. "And your experiences don't quite line up with the experiences of entering slipspace directly."

"That's what I thought. But I do think—" She looked up and met Evie's eye. "I think the device is interacting with slipspace somehow. And that changed our reality."

"How is that even possible?" Victor said.

"It's alien tech," Evie responded. "I think Saskia might be right. I think we—"

Made a huge mistake. She kept her mouth shut.

Saskia leaned forward, her face twisted in concentration. "We talked about this in Mrs. Veitola's class. I remember. There's a process that molecules can go through, where they *change*—it's tied into slipspace somehow. Dammit!" She shook her head. "I spent hours cramming for that test."

"I remember that," Victor said. "It's a chemical process. It's supposed to be slow, though. It takes millennia."

"You're talking about Kulpinski's theorem," interrupted Dr. Chapman, his voice brimming with excitement. "That may not be totally relevant here, but the notion of changing molecules—" He turned away from the meeting, asked, "You're getting all this down, right?" to someone out of view.

"This has been a fascinating physics lesson," Captain Dellatorre said. "But I think we need to get away from the theoretical for the sake of time. What would be the purpose of such a device? One that could change molecules?"

"We would need more information before we could even begin to guess at something like that," Dr. Salo said. "Perhaps the Forerunners used it for travel, or—"

"Or as a weapon?" Captain Dellatorre raised an eyebrow. The whole room went quiet. "Frankly, we aren't concerned with what the Forerunners used the tech for. The Covenant want this thing. Clearly, they were unable to make it work without the Brume-sur-Mer artifact, and likely can't even access it, which gives us the upper hand. But we have to ask ourselves what the Covenant would want with such technology." She paused. Static ran through her holo. "We have to assume they'd be using it as a weapon."

A weight dropped in Evie's stomach. The blood rushed through her ears. A weapon. Of course. They'd been able to turn something about it on and off inside that structure. A power like that was unimaginable.

And in the hands of the Covenant?

"If they found a way to harness whatever happened in that room..." Victor said slowly, "they wouldn't have to glass Meridian. They could do something so much worse. Tear it apart, or—"

"Not just Meridian," Dorian said. "Any world in the galaxy. They could do whatever the hell they wanted to the entire human race." He laughed bitterly. "No more war, right? Just shift molecules around until we never even existed."

Captain Dellatorre gazed out at them from her holo. "This is worse than we feared."

"So extract us!" Evie shouted, forgetting all protocol. "And the artifact. They can't activate it unless they have the artifact."

"For now," Owen said. "There's no reason to think they aren't working on some other means of activation."

"Then what are we supposed to do?" Evie cried.

"It's a bit premature to assume that this structure could be used as a weapon in its current state," Dr. Faraday said. "Most recovered Forerunner technology had strictly utilitarian use, and this technology more than likely restricted the structure itself for some enigmatically practical purpose. The real risk is that the Covenant would find a way to leverage the technology and weaponize it, as the captain mentioned. There's only one way to know if they can."

"We need to be able to study the structure," the captain said, her voice unwavering and calm in the surge of panic filling up the room. "Owen, do you think it would be possible for us to secure the activation device in the structure itself?"

"And a piece of the structure's wall," added Dr. Chapman. "If it is a containment room."

Owen frowned. "The activation device, possibly—it appeared to be separate from the building itself, and should be removable. As for the walls—" He shook his head apologetically at the scientists. "I can't promise that."

"Please try," Dr. Chapman said, and the other two nodded in agreement.

"Very well," said Captain Dellatorre. "Get us the activation device, the artifact from Brume-sur-Mer, and attempt to retrieve a piece of the structure's wall. We are working on a plan of extraction—hopefully we should have an entry point within three days. That doesn't give you much time."

"Then it's true," Dorian said suddenly. "Meridian … it can't be saved."

He didn't sound angry or upset, only resigned. The truth of what this meant for humanity was etched on his face. "It's over once we take the Covenant's super-weapon away. But if we don't take it—"

Captain Dellatorre ignored the breach of protocol. "Spartan-B096, please notify us when preparations are complete. Dismissed." The holo-light disappeared, casting them in half darkness.

Owen turned to the group. "You all have had to grow up fast these last three months, I know. I'm sorry that had to happen and I'm sorry for the people you've lost." He zeroed in on Dorian, who glanced away. "But I told you, this war extends beyond the fate of one people, one world. This is about preventing our own extinction. The Covenant will stop at nothing to wipe out every colony until there's nothing left of our species. If they find a way to use the technology in that structure, the last twenty-five years of fighting will be for nothing." He paused, looking over the group. "We cannot let this power fall into the hands of the Covenant."

CHAPTER EIGHTEEN

SASKIA

We have to do that again?" asked Caird.

Owen shifted uncomfortably, his armor swallowing the flicker of firelight. The heater they'd been using had finally died, and one of the soldiers from Caernaruan built an actual fire with debris from the inside of the transport center building. Smoke rose up in a thin white line through the starry gap in the ceiling, bleeding out into the cold night air.

"Yes," he said.

Groans went up from the militia, grumbled complaints and strings of creative profanity. Only Local Team stayed quiet. Saskia didn't know about the others, but she couldn't get the debriefing with Daniella out of her head. The activation key for a potential super-weapon had been buried beneath Brume-sur-Mer for millennia. Entire lives had played out on top of it, no one ever the wiser.

She was grateful that her parents hadn't known.

"The kids almost died last time," said Kielawa. "They came back here looking like they were infected with a damn plague virus. Now you want to saw off a piece of that building and put it on a ship with us?"

"The sickness wasn't spread through infection," Evie said.

"Yeah?" Kielawa shot back. "You sure about that? You been tested?"

Evie scowled and wrapped her arms around her chest.

Saskia patted her gently on the shoulder. "It's fine," she whispered. "Nobody thinks we're infected with anything. I mean, they're sitting with us."

"She's kind of right," Evie said.

Saskia frowned. Another thought she didn't want to have.

"It's not just the artifact that's the problem," Caird said. "The Covenant had that place on lockdown last time. And they had a Prophet there, so they gotta be serious about getting that thing. Whatever we go back to, it'll be worse than last time. And they'll be ready for us."

"Understood, but those artifact samples could be the key to ensuring humanity's survival," Owen said grimly. "The best thing we can do here is come up with a plan that will keep us as safe as possible when we extract them. Farhi, what's the status on supplies?"

Farhi strode up beside the fire, sighing. She pushed her greasy, dark hair away from her face. "Not great," she said. "Weapons are all in working order, but we're running low on ammunition, which means another shootout like a few days ago probably isn't going to work."

This elicited more groans. "At least we know that works," someone muttered.

"Food rations are running low, which is why it's a good thing ONI's extracting us. We've still got the Warthog, some miscellaneous supplies we've scavenged. Nothing great. We're working with leftovers here."

Owen sighed. "I see."

"There's no way ONI can send a care package?" someone asked.

Owen shook his head. "They can't get through. All the focus is on getting ready for extraction."

"Nothing will be left to extract if we're dead," Kielawa murmured, turning away.

At that, the grumbling started up again. Saskia leaned her head against Evie's shoulder. She was suddenly very tired.

"I feel like they don't understand what's at stake," Evie muttered.

"They didn't see it," Saskia said. "And it's not something that's *that* easy to explain either."

"They want to get home, though," Dorian said. "That's enough of a motivation for most people."

Farhi clapped her hands together. "Enough!" she shouted. "We've got to work together on this." She sighed. "You know what we're up against. We've got to be clever. Owen? What's the plan?"

Owen nodded. "First things first: I will be leading the excavation, along with Local Team. They've actually been in the structure, so we'll let them continue that mission. We were lucky last time, when we made it past those Elites stationed around the site. We weren't carrying equipment either. We need to dispatch with any guards as quickly as possible."

A murmur of assent went up from the crowd. Saskia thought about the terror of racing across that vast empty space, hooking onto Evie's leg so they could be pulled into the structure. It had all happened so fast she had barely been aware of the battle going on around her.

"Our best bet is to utilize the Warthog," Dubois called out. "Drive straight into the area, firing from the turret. We've still got plenty of ammunition for *that*, at least."

Farhi pointed at him. "Good call."

"We've got that civilian fuel cart too," Dorian said. "Remember, we saw it sitting out on the landing pad? It'll get us an explosion."

Dubois laughed a little. "Is it always explosions with you?" he asked.

"What the hell's that supposed to mean?"

"That's actually a good idea," Owen said. "Set a fire. Control it so our excavation team can make it through." He paused. "This is a transport center. There must be fire suppressant around here somewhere."

"Yeah, there is," Farhi said. "Caird grabbed it before she made this thing." She kicked at the fire crackling at his feet. "Pretty good stash, if I remember correctly, right, Caird?"

"Great stash," she said.

"Good." Owen pointed at her. "You're going to be in charge of building this fire. It's going to be a barrier between us and the Covenant. Make a team to help you."

Caird saluted.

"The rest of you will help corral the Covenant forces where we need them, and watch out for aerial attacks."

All of this was sounding more and more familiar to Saskia. In fact, it sounded an awful lot like a pitch she'd heard her parents give a pair of suspicious-looking clients. Those clients had been interested in subterfuge too, under limited resources. And what was it her parents had told them?

"Smoke!" she cried out, remembering. "The smoke can help mask us."

"She's right," Caird said. "If we can get a smoking agent in that fuel, it'll make it harder for the Covenant air to know what's happening on the ground—their Banshees won't be able to see what's happening on the ground. It does mean we'll have to be careful, though. Don't want any of us passing out."

"Of course not." Owen surveyed the militia, what little remained of it. "The next question is the matter of actually securing the artifacts. This is Forerunner technology, which introduces some ... complications. The most significant of which is that it's designed to last for millennia."

Several people groaned in frustration. "*Now* you tell us ..." someone muttered behind Saskia.

Owen held up one hand. "That's not to say this is impossible. One thing that's working to our benefit is that the structure let us in, but not the Covenant. Why that's the case isn't clear, but it does mean that we'll have time on our side."

"Acknowledged, but we still won't necessarily be able to carve out a chunk of the wall," Farhi said.

"True," Owen said. "Which brings me to my second point. Given the age of this structure and how advanced the race is that made it, it's likely that most natural phenomena will not damage a Forerunner installation like this one. And that means there's a real possibility that we won't be able to burn it, freeze it, or even blow it up. However, it *is* likely that some parts of the structure are designed to be extractable. At the very least, we might be able to cut some parts loose if they are embedded in natural material, which isn't uncommon given what we've seen. So we need to get creative. We need to find our strongest tools. Pull from our own supplies, see what we can scavenge. I've still got the Covenant energy sword, and there must be some devices used by this transport center that could help." He folded his arms. "Any thoughts?"

For a moment, everyone was quiet. Then Kielawa called out, "I have my medical kit with me. There's a bone saw in it, with a precision laser blade. Can't promise anything, but—"

"No, that's good. What else?"

"We found a tension steel cutter in the garage out back," Caird said. "It's got a gravitic binder for tearing through starship hulls. Must have belonged to the station's rescue crew."

"That will work well if the Forerunner structure cooperates," Owen nodded. "We're lucky we found this place. It might just be the advantage we need to get this job done."

Slowly, the militia began shouting out suggestions—the various knives and tools they'd managed to bring with them or devices they'd found throughout the transport center and in the town below. Saskia felt a surge of pride that they were coming up with a plan of action so quickly. They would have to actually implement the plan, of course, which was a different task altogether. But still. It was going more smoothly than she had thought.

She just hoped the rest of the mission would as well.

Saskia jerked awake, her heart thudding. *We're under attack*, she thought. *They've found us.*

"Rise and shine, sweetheart." Valois leaned over her, grinning wildly. "Call just came down from ONI. They've got an extraction path cleared."

"What?" Saskia sat up, but Valois was already moving down the line, shaking people awake one by one. She looked over at Evie, who was rubbing the sleep out of her eyes. "I thought it was going to be in three days?"

"Guess not," said Victor. "Looks like we're finally getting back to the base."

"But we've barely figured out what we're going to do," Saskia said. "We haven't had time to scout or prep properly—"

"Probably not a lot we can do to prepare now anyway, right?" Evie asked. "We know what it looks like down there. We know there's a

Covenant presence. We know what we're grabbing." She gave a small, shaky smile, and Saskia knew she was terrified too.

They actually had a plan—a really good one, even, and one that the Covenant wouldn't be expecting it. But what worried Saskia was the possibility of what the Covenant might have done to prepare since their last run-in. For all the militia knew, there could be a whole Covenant fleet around the structure now, and it wouldn't matter what kind of plan they had come up with.

"Pack up!" shouted Farhi as she strolled through the transport center. "Take what you need! Leave what you don't! We'll be heading straight to the extraction point as soon as the mission is complete. We've got a window, and once it closes, it may not open again. Ever."

Saskia stood up and shook out the last of her sleepiness. She grabbed her rifle and the remaining ammunition. She was going to have to make it last this morning.

They met up outside, in the usual place. A thin line of pale pink dawn light appeared on the horizon, making the lines of everything seem soft and indistinct. They were already dividing themselves up into their teams: the firebugs next to the fuel cart; the corallers over by the Warthog; and the excavators. Local Team. In addition to the assortment of knives, ropes, and field materials the soldiers had scrounged up from their own supplies, there was a bundle of civilian tools that had been scavenged from the transport center: an insta-crete jack, a construction-grade laser, and the tension steel cutter Caird mentioned. They also managed to find a transport cart for the sculpture, which was good, since they didn't know how heavy it would actually be. Who knew if any of these things would be useful in the end? But it was all they had on hand, and Saskia told herself it would be enough.

Owen and Farhi emerged from the building. Owen jumped on the Warthog, turned to face the pockets of the militia that formed each team. A pale streak of sunlight shone out over the militia, highlighting their faces.

"We're doing this a little earlier than we planned," he said. "But we've got a solid plan. We're familiar with the area. And as soon as we're done, we'll be collected by ONI." He tapped his helmet. "I've been in contact. Window's clear and they are still on their way. Most of the fighting has pushed off from over Annecy. For now. We still need to act fast, though, now that we have the Covenant's attention. Let's get in, get the samples, get out."

This was greeted with a kind of contemplative quiet, a silence that matched the dim dawn light. Owen nodded at Farhi.

"Firebugs, corallers, you know what to do," Owen said. "Excavators, get in the Warthog. We're going straight there."

The firebugs piled up on the fuel cart, started up the engine, and rumbled toward the city. Saskia crawled into the Warthog, pressed in with both Local Team as well as the corallers, which consisted of the three most vicious fighters in the militia. They sat up on the back of the Warthog, hanging on to the turret as it bounced through the city. Saskia watched the buildings materialize in the dim light and replayed the plan in her mind—the million and one things that could go wrong. The biggest was that they had to use the Brume-sur-Mer artifact—the very thing that they couldn't let fall into Covenant hands—to access the site and get whatever ONI needed. Plus, while Owen had some experience with Forerunner structures, none of that experience was with *this* structure. No one, not even he, knew how it might respond now that they had activated it. The sculpture might not even be extractable, and even if it was unactivated, what if removing it triggered something just as bad? What if the structure was programmed to self-destruct upon removal of the sculpture, or upon being damaged—which was exactly what would happen if they removed a chunk of the wall? Even thinking about any of those possibilities sent a phantom pain winding through Saskia's skull. Still, there were more mundane dangers. About a million of them, it seemed.

The Warthog slowed to a stop about half a kilometer from the dig site. "Excavators," Farhi said. "Here's where we leave you."

Saskia glanced at Evie, who was sitting beside her, hoping for a bit of reassurance. But Evie looked as terrified as Saskia felt.

"It's going to be okay," Saskia whispered, wishing she were telling the truth. "We've got this."

"I hope so," Evie whispered back.

They climbed out of the Warthog: Evie, Saskia, Dorian, Victor, and then finally Owen, who saluted with two fingers, signaling to Farhi that it was time for her to drive off, around to the western side of the site. To Local Team, Owen gestured to the left, and they moved forward through the strips of that white foam substance that was everywhere in this part of the ruins. Saskia swatted it away from her face, cursing every time it blocked her vision. She could hear the Covenant up ahead: the whine of vehicle engines, the chatter of their language.

"Sounds like a party up there," Dorian muttered. Victor hushed him. But he was right. And Saskia could tell that Owen knew it too.

They stopped, right on the edge of the clearing. Owen motioned for them to fan out along the perimeter. Saskia squeezed Evie's hand, gave her a little wave of support, and then took up her position. She squatted down behind a particularly large piece of steel rubble, took a deep breath, and looked out at the dig site.

It was worse than it had been the day before. Elites were everywhere, barking orders at Grunts and Brutes, who were already moving out into the hills. The two Banshees from the day before were sitting on the ground, flanking the hole, which, thank *god*, still did not have a shield across its surface, but only because there was now some kind of structure built up over it instead. Not the Scarab that had been at the Brume-sur-Mer site, but some other kind of device designed in the Covenant's strange, organic style. Large leglike pillars rose around the hole's perimeter, jutting upward into a canopy-like chassis, which held a rounded pod that sent pulses of light down into the hole where the structure lay. A scanner, perhaps, trying to unlock the structure's secrets.

Saskia wished she could talk to the others, but they had no comms and now they were too spread out. She didn't dare move, not when there was no way to synchronize all of the militia's actions. And so instead she considered what now appeared to be a major alteration to their plan: this machine, whatever it was, crouching above the hole. This was why they needed those extra days. They knew the situation at the site wouldn't be identical. They needed to scout, to gather information. Then act.

Not that there was anything she could do about it now. So she took a deep breath and waited.

It didn't take long. A shout rose up from the other side of the clearing, zips of plasma fire.

Followed by the deep, thunderous roar of an explosion—the fuel cart.

The fireball billowed up, illuminating everything in angry red light. The Elites guarding the structure began screaming wildly at one another, while a pair of floating, tentacled creatures drifting near the scanning device swirled together, moving for cover. Saskia could hear the corallers in the distance, pinning down the Covenant, buying her time. But where were the others with the fire suppressant?

The fire spread across the clearing quickly. The white debris ignited easily, the scraps bursting into flames before the fire had even touched them. "Oh, that's not good," she muttered, fear sliding up her spine. That debris was all over the place. She was sitting on top of it. There was no way the firebugs were going to be able to control the fire—

Saskia scrambled to her feet and ran along the perimeter of the clearing. The thick smoke billowed over her, choking her, making her eyes water. She crouched down, trying to avoid it.

"Saskia!"

She turned; she could barely see Victor through the smoke. He was a silhouette, gliding toward her. Saskia coughed, pressing herself against a nearby stone.

"What are you doing?" Victor put his hand on her elbow, peered down into her face. "Are you okay? Why did you leave your position?"

"Did you see that fire?" she hissed, pulling him down to the ground, out of the path of the smoke. "It's moving too fast."

Even with her watery vision, she could see in Victor's expression that he had noticed it too. "Caird is capable," he said. "She'll handle it."

"Of course she's *capable*," Saskia said. "But she wouldn't have expected the fire to move this fast. There's no way she's able to clear the path for us—"

Gunfire exploded nearby. Saskia and Victor both hit the ground—which was covered in that white flammable material. Saskia shrieked, pushed it away, clawing for the dirt underneath.

"Owen!" shouted Blanc, one of the firebugs. "We've got a major problem!"

Saskia looked over at Victor, her hands still full of the white debris. "I told you."

"Owen! Local Team! Do you copy?" Blanc's voice bounced around through the smoke. Saskia spun around in place, kicking up debris and dirt.

"Do you see her?" she cried to Victor. "Blanc! We're here! Where are you?"

A dark shape wavered in the smoke. Saskia stood up, ducking to try to avoid the smoke, and ran toward it. "Blanc!" she screamed, the smoke searing her lungs. The shape turned toward her, the glint of a rifle muzzle flashing in the firelight.

"Nazari!" Blanc bolted forward, emerging out of the smoke. Her face was streaked with black soot and her hair was soaked with sweat. "Thank god," she gasped. "Where's Owen?"

"We spread out," Saskia said. "He's half a kilometer west of here."

"We've got to get to him." Blanc's eyes were wild with fear. "We've got to call off the mission."

"What?" Victor was at Saskia's side. "We can't! You have no idea—"

"*You* have no idea!" Blanc shouted. "The fire is out of control. Caird is dead."

"What?" Saskia whispered, the news hitting her like a punch.

"It's this damn—" Blanc kicked out the ground, the debris fluttering up around her. "It must be some sort of polymer foam; it's the most flammable material I've ever seen. There was probably a plant nearby—they put this stuff in furniture. The fire got out of hand immediately." She pulled a slim metal canister from where it had been strapped to her back. "This is the last of the fire suppressant."

"Are you serious?" Victor lunged forward, but Blanc jerked the canister away from his grasp.

"We had to," she said. "The fire just—" She shook her head, and Saskia realized she was crying, the tears bleeding into the droplets of sweat running down her face. "We've got to get out of here now."

"We *can't*," Saskia said, and she felt her own tears on the edges of her eyes. "Victor's right. You don't understand what this structure is capable of. We've got to get these samples back to ONI."

The fire was leaping across the excavation site, roaring like a monster. Banshees circled overhead, dropping down into the flames, lifting back up. *A rescue operation*, Saskia thought. Even the Covenant were getting the hell out.

"Give me the suppressant," she said.

"What?" shouted Victor, just as Blanc shrieked, "No!"

"I'll clear a path," Saskia said. "You go get the others. I'll lay the suppressant down thick. We only have a short way to run. Owen said the structure itself most likely can't be damaged by fire, so once we're in, we'll probably be fine."

"Are you insane?" Blanc screamed.

"There's a super-weapon under there," Saskia said, pointing her finger at the Covenant device rising up before the fast-encroaching wall of fire. "Or at least something that the Covenant will use as one. If we don't get to it first, the Covenant will. And if they do, the war is over. Humanity is over. ONI needs those samples so that we can fight back."

Blanc blinked. The firelight flashed over her wet skin.

"We saw what it was capable of," Saskia said. "If we wait until the fire clears, the Covenant will just move back in. We have to use the fire as cover to finish the mission."

Blanc stared at Saskia, clutching the fire suppressant to her chest. Saskia held out one hand. "Please," she rasped, and she didn't say the rest of what she was thinking: that this was the chance for her to prove once and for all that she could be trusted in a way her parents never could.

Slowly, Blanc held out the suppressant. Saskia took a deep breath. "Thank you."

And then Victor dove forward, grabbing the suppressant.

"Victor!" Saskia called.

"Let me do it," he said. "I can run faster than you. Go get the others. I'll lay the path."

"Victor, I can do it—"

"If you're going to do this," Blanc shouted, shoving herself in between them, "we have to do it now. That fire is almost to the structure."

Saskia looked out at the site. Covenant soldiers were drifting upward weightless out of the flames, their bodies climbing upward in a large beam of light. It was a Covenant craft, pulling them up with its gravity lift.

"Fine," she said. "But please just—be careful."

"I always am," Victor said. "Now go! I'll meet you at the rendezvous."

And then he was gone, vanishing into the flare of the fire.

Blanc looked at Saskia. "Tell me where to go," she said. "I'll help."

"That way," Saskia said, pointing to the left. "Evie and Dorian are that way. I'll get Owen."

And then she was running too.

CHAPTER NINETEEN

VICTOR

The heat almost reminded him of Brume-sur-Mer during the dry season, the same intense, baking swelter, an overpowering shimmer that soaked through his skin and seemed to roast the inside of his bones. When they didn't have school, he and Evie would wake up early and go down to the beach to shoot footage for his holo-films, the heat already settling in as they set up the models and tested the camera settings. By lunch, it would be too hot to stay outside, even with the salt breeze whipping off the ocean, and they would drive into town and escape into the coffee shop, where they would order frozen drinks and sit in the back corner, away from the blazing sun pouring through the windows.

He thought he had known heat then. He had chewed on ice and slept in the cool dark of his bedroom during the hottest part of the day, mid-afternoon, the cloudless sky bleached the color of bones. Nighttime wasn't much better, even with the sun down; the heat lingered, as if it were baked into the soil. But he could still remember running errands with his mother, taking the ferry into Port Moyne to visit the supply warehouse there in the hour before it closed for the day. The night's sticky swelter. The bustle of the city slowed down, as if it were trapped in molasses. A heat so endless it was like the rainy season couldn't come.

But he hadn't known heat. Not like this.

He made his way across the clearing, kicking aside that flammable white debris, trying to keep as low to the ground as he could. The smoke was thick as water, but if he got down, he could almost breathe normally. And so he crawled, the suppressant strapped to his back. He wanted to start at the entrance and work his way back. Try to beat the fire as best he could.

He peered up at the large machine the Covenant had placed above the Forerunner structure. Most of the remaining soldiers were using it as a fire shelter. What looked like a Phantom dropship was hovering overhead, Covenant soldiers rising up to its gravity beam and then into the craft's belly. Victor kept crawling. He couldn't watch this drama play out. He had to get to the dig entrance.

And it was right dead ahead.

He was pouring sweat, the dirt beneath his palms turning to mud with his touch, then caking and drying and flaking away just as fast. Sparks flew off the fire and dusted across his back, sharp stings of intense pain that he brushed aside. But he didn't regret taking Saskia's place. This was the sort of thing he had learned in his time in training, his time with Owen. Use your strengths. Saskia was smart, resourceful, and fearless: He knew that she would be of more use to ONI than himself. She didn't need to risk her life crawling through the fire.

So no, he didn't regret it. Not one bit.

He came to a base of the Covenant machine, looming over the hole. Up close he confirmed the suspicions he had when he first saw it: This machine was some kind of a scanning device, the Covenant's way of prying open the secrets of Forerunner technology without having direct access. The entrance to the structure yawned open, a dark, inviting hole, free from smoke and heat. Victor pulled the suppressant canister around and yelped when he touched the metal; he pulled his hand away and saw the dark angry burn on his palm. Good thing he could do this one-handed.

He activated the suppressant, tilted the canister down. The foam gushed out, hardening almost instantly in the sweltering air. He cursed, thumped the side of the canister. The suppressant stuck out from the spout like a piece of coral.

Victor heard a deep, thunderous groan. It was the Covenant's scanner, sinking down on its melting stand. Damn it, they would have to move fast. He reached down with his burned hand and broke off the solidified suppressant, screaming in pain. Smoke poured into his mouth, down his throat, into his lungs. He tossed the suppressant down and then got low, spraying practically into the dirt, crawling backward over the open space. He kept his gaze on the suppressant, building a path along the ground. His vision blurred. He shook his head. *Focus*. He was almost to the edge.

The smoke was falling around him, dark as a storm cloud. All he could smell was fire, all he could smell was *heat*, a scent like the strike of a match, burned flesh, like swooning beneath the glare of the sun. The fire roared with laughter, mocking him. His lungs felt tight. The world flickered.

He was almost there. Almost done.

The smoke was everywhere.

The canister dropped out of his hands, rolled over the white path of the suppressant. He watched it tumble toward the structure. As if it wanted to help.

He wasn't crawling backward anymore. He couldn't. It was as if the smoke had bound him to this place.

He couldn't breathe.

He couldn't feel anything but the Brume-sur-Mer sun. The heat of the beach. Home.

He knew if he closed his eyes it would be over.

He closed his eyes.

CHAPTER TWENTY

DORIAN

on't stop to think!" Owen roared, somehow louder than the fire raging around them. "It'll be better inside the structure, but we've got to act fast!"

Owen wasn't lying; the large, looming Covenant scanner was tilting precariously, threatening to collapse all over the entrance to the structure. There was a part of Dorian that wanted to turn around and run to the rendezvous point, where he would at least be able to breathe. But then he saw Evie and Saskia pounding their way to the shelter entrance and he knew he couldn't. Not the girls, and not Victor, who had laid a path and then vanished into the smoke. Dorian hoped he was lying in wait at the rendezvous, his role in the mission done.

So Dorian kept moving, trying to follow Blanc's instructions for running headlong into the fire: keep low, try not to breathe too much. He pushed forward into the smoke and heat, his feet pounding against the path of fire suppressant leading them straight into the structure.

"Go! Go! Go!" They were at the entrance of the hole, the Covenant scanner tilting precariously above them. Dorian could hear the internal groaning of its crumbling structure. Not good.

Dorian half boosted, half tossed Evie into the dig, then Saskia. Dorian took a deep breath as Owen grabbed him around the waist and then let go. He landed hard on the packed dirt below. The air was clearer down here, but just as hot. Dorian wiped away the sweat dripping into his eyes.

A loud and thunderous thump as Owen landed beside him. "You okay?" Owen asked. "Breathing fine?"

"Breathing as well as I can," Dorian said, and then he slipped into the structure itself.

The air changed: The temperature dropped, the world grew quiet. The roar of the fire couldn't make it through the stone walls. Dorian almost forgot about the conflagration raging overhead, and he wondered if there was something to Evie's theory that this building was used to rearrange molecules, if they were somehow in a different pocket of space than the fire outside.

But then he heard a scraping, grinding groan again: the scanner, threatening to topple. They had only minutes left before that thing came down.

"We've got to move fast!" Saskia shouted, shoving the coil of rope into his chest. "Like we talked about, remember?"

Like they talked about.

Saskia and Evie were already attacking the wall, positioning the construction laser Dorian had found stashed in a back room of the transport center, buried beneath a bunch of rubble. A lucky find, although he had no idea how well it was going to work on Forerunner stone. If anything could work, it'd be that laser.

Probably better than what he was going to be doing.

He looped the towing cable around the sculpture, shoving it down between the sculpture and the wall, pulling tight, locking it into place the way Uncle Max had shown him when he was a kid, helping out with the tourist boats. He locked the other end of the rope around the gravitic binder that powered the forearm-sized tension steel cutter and pulled.

Nothing happened.

Saskia and Evie fired up the laser, sending off sparks and tiny fragments of stone. Dorian dropped the cable and knelt in front of the sculpture, examining how it was connected to the entire room. It wasn't carved into the wall, just like Evie had said. She had remembered correctly. He could see where the sculpture ended and its display platform began. They were separate components, which told him it could be moved.

It was just too heavy.

"Are we getting it?" Evie shouted over the whine of the laser. "Where are you at, Dorian?"

"Working on it," he said.

A loud crash filtered down from above, Covenant metal on metal. Evie and Saskia both shrieked, and Dorian felt his whole body go rigid with fear, as he saw one of the scanner's legs begin to buckle. He picked up the cable again.

"We have to leave now," Owen said from the doorway. "That scanner is about to topple completely."

"We're almost done," Saskia called out.

Dorian felt a wave of hopelessness, the cable limp in his hand. "It's too heavy," he said. "The steel cutter isn't working like we thought it would. I can't get it."

"Well, you should have told me," Owen said, and Dorian scowled. But Owen was already reaching around the base of the sculpture. "On my count," he said as more debris crashed overhead, as the ground around the structure trembled.

"Got it!" shouted Evie, and Dorian saw her drop a large chunk of the wall into a satchel Saskia was holding.

"One," Owen said.

Dorian shoved aside his anger and hurt. None of that mattered right now.

"Two."

The ground shook again; something boomed above them.

"Three."

Dorian used the tension cutter's binder to pull with every ounce of his strength. At first, nothing happened, but then there was a snap and a long, horrible ripping sound, like iron being torn in half. And then Dorian was flying backward, the cable and cutter in his hands. He slammed into the far wall, and the world flickered in and out of his vision. Distantly, he heard screaming.

No, not screaming. Cheers.

He lifted his head. When his eyes focused, he found Owen standing with the sculpture in both hands. Long strands of what looked like seaweed tumbled out from the bottom of the statue. So it wasn't the weight that was keeping it moored, it had been connected to the wall after all. Just not with stone.

A crash up above.

"Go!" Owen yelled. Dorian dropped the cutter and cable, pushed himself away from the wall, and followed after Evie and Saskia as they sprinted out of the structure. It was like stepping into the engine of a starship. The heat was astonishing.

He crawled up the side of the hole, scrambling over the hot earth, his palms scorching with each touch. When he looked up, the sky was fire.

He forced himself to keep going.

Somehow, he made it to the surface. The fire raged around him, and the scanner had toppled, leaving all but a narrow path for him to escape into. He ducked through it and emerged on the other side, into the smoke. The fire suppressant was working; flames rose up on either side of the path, enough that Dorian was able to run through them, the heat singeing his skin. He spotted glimpses of Evie and Saskia up ahead through the smoke; he thought he heard Owen behind him but didn't dare turn around to check. He just ran, as hard as he could.

Someone screamed.

It came from up ahead, but Dorian couldn't see anything in the smoke. He tried to shout, but his voice was caught in his throat.

Another scream. This time, Dorian recognized the voice. It was Evie. And she was screaming for help.

He ran, gasping and choking in the thick, smoky air, his eyes watering. He passed the fire line, the suppressant path winding off sideways out of the clearing. Through smoke he saw Evie and Saskia, both kneeling.

"Evie!" he choked out, stumbling forward. Evie looked up at him, her face shining with sweat.

"It's Victor!" she screamed.

All of Dorian's blood froze in his veins. He stood dumbly on the path, the fire roaring behind him.

And then Owen was racing past him, skidding to a stop next to Saskia and Evie. That brought Dorian to his senses, and he pushed forward. In the bloody firelight, he saw Victor lying collapsed on the ground, his skin patchy with burns.

"He's still breathing," Saskia said, her voice brimming with tears. "But—"

"Dorian, take the statue." Owen shoved it at him, and Dorian wrapped his arms around it, staggering a little beneath its weight. Then Owen scooped up Victor and draped him over his shoulders.

"Let's get to the rendezvous," Owen said. "And then let's get off this world."

CHAPTER TWENTY-ONE

SASKIA

Saskia had forgotten what it was to be clean, to wear fresh clothes, and to eat food at a table, with cutlery and napkins. She had forgotten what it was to be safe.

But now they were safe, back at Tuomi Base, surrounded by UNSC troops. She, Evie, and Dorian shared a room on the edge of the facility, with beds instead of cots, and temperature controls, and comm systems that Evie used to talk with her dad.

And every morning so far, they heard from the med bay that Victor was still alive.

It was another comforting thought in that first day of relative normalcy after their extraction from Meridian. He was still alive. Nothing else about his condition was good: He was unconscious, packed away in a healing pod. They weren't allowed to visit him. Saskia had tried, that first morning. Strode right down to the medical wing and asked to see him. But the nurse at the station had just shaken his head sadly, told her, "He's under observation. No visitors."

"You don't understand," she said. "It should be *me* in there."

The nurse had frowned at that, his brow creasing. Saskia left before he called up a commanding officer.

She couldn't get that thought out of her head: that it was supposed to be her. That Victor was only encased in that healing pod because he had insisted on taking her place. She could have stopped him. She could have fought him for the suppressant canister. It made so much more sense for her to risk herself: He had a family, parents and sisters who would be racked with grief. She had no one.

Well, no one except for Local Team. But Victor had them too. Saskia was clearly the one to sacrifice if a sacrifice was called for.

And Saskia didn't even know if Victor's family were aware of his status. Evie and Dorian had both been allowed to contact their families, but they'd been informed that it was in violation of more than a dozen security regulations to share any information at all about their mission and its aftermath, and Saskia had no way of knowing what, if anything, had been sent to Victor's parents.

There were other things too, issues with ONI that Saskia didn't want to think about. Of course the samples they brought back with them on the extraction had been swept away for study and further development. This was what they wanted the samples *for*, after all. But what about the Forerunner structure in Annecy? What about Brume-sur-Mer? What about Meridian? After the extraction, the survivors had been rushed back to the base to recoup and debrief, but then there was only silence from Command.

Their strange experience in the Forerunner structure still haunted her, and Saskia worried that the Covenant had somehow gotten ahold of the technology with their scanning machine—if what happened in that one room could be weaponized against an entire world. The thought made her shudder.

After her failed attempt at visiting Victor, she had gone for a walk around the edge of the Tuomi Base buildings. The air was crisp with the first strains of autumn, without being frozen solid like the air in

Annecy. She mulled over what was wrong, trying to pin it down, and failing.

"Hey, Saskia! Wait up."

Saskia stopped, turned around. It was Dorian and Evie, walking side by side across the grass. Evie lifted her hand in a wave, and Saskia drifted over to them, the sweet-scented wind ruffling her loose hair.

"How you holding up?" Evie said.

"I'm fine. You?"

Evie hesitated. "I'm fine."

Dorian looked over at her. "C'mon, Evie. That's not what you told me."

Saskia was swallowed by a sudden swell of panic. "What? What's wrong?"

But Evie just shook her head. "Nothing's wrong, I just—"

"We wanted to talk to you about it." Dorian frowned. "Let's go a little farther out, though."

Saskia glanced back at the military buildings, blocky and silver, imposing in the sunlight. Then she nodded.

The three of them cut across the grass, not speaking. The wind picked up, whipping around flecks of golden dust.

"Have you heard anything about Victor?" Evie asked.

"I tried to see him, but they wouldn't let me."

Dorian snorted. "Something's up."

Saskia looked up at him. "What do you mean?"

He stopped, turned toward her. The military base glittered in the sunlight like some far-off jewel. "He almost died—might die—because ONI wanted that Forerunner artifact so badly. There's something going on that they're not telling us."

Saskia sighed. *More of this, then. Dorian and his paranoia, his distrust.* "Is this about Owen lying to us?"

"What?" Dorian shook his head. "No. I didn't even say anything about Owen."

"This is about ONI," Evie said quietly. "It's about Victor and the fact that they're keeping something from us about him."

"What? What could they be keeping from us?" Saskia asked, trying to ignore the doubt nagging in the back of her head.

"I think they're doing something to him. Not just keeping him alive, something more," Evie said quickly. "I think that's why they haven't told us anything. They're keeping us in the dark."

Saskia wrapped her arms around herself, looked out at the distant horizon. The sky was hazy with dust.

Something felt wrong. She couldn't deny that.

"We don't have proof of anything," Evie said. "It just—it feels strange, don't you think? Why won't they give us any answers?"

"Our friend is dying in a UNSC medical facility and they won't tell us anything about him," Dorian spat.

"We don't know if he's dying," Saskia whispered. "We're not on Meridian anymore, we're not running errands for ONI. For the first time in days we're finally safe—so can you two give this conspiracy nonsense a rest?"

Dorian didn't say anything. Neither did Evie. For a long time, they stood there without talking. Saskia rolled the idea around in her head. Finally, she spoke. "Okay, fine. What are you getting at exactly?"

"We're not sure," Evie said. "We're just tired of the secrets." She paused, her arms crossed, staring off into the distance. At first Saskia thought that was all she had. But then Evie continued. "Remember Orvo's training exercises? How it taught us to think past how things appeared on the surface?"

Saskia nodded.

"Well, I'm trying to think like *that* about this."

"Whatever's going on with Victor isn't simple medical treatment," Dorian said. "Remember those scientists who were asking about the Forerunner artifact on the holo feed? They're here, on base, and they've been visiting Victor and running tests. That means it's not just about his injuries in Annecy," He looked at Saskia, his eyes glittering. "Something else is wrong."

Saskia studied Dorian and Evie, their expressions downcast, and began to realize why this was weighing on them so much. If Victor's injuries weren't limited to what happened in that last operation, then it meant something else was wrong. And if something else was wrong, Victor might not be the only one affected.

What was it Owen had said after Brume-sur-Mer?

Civilian life will be hard for you now. You'll see.

Part of her knew exactly what he meant, the other part wished that she could forget the last three months entirely. Owen was right. Nothing would ever be the same.

Two days later, Captain Dellatorre wanted to meet with them.

Saskia expected it to be a debriefing of the entire mission, from Brume-sur-Mer to Annecy. They'd never actually done that since arriving at the base. But when she walked into the meeting room, she knew instantly she was wrong. While Owen was there, Farhi and Kielawa and the rest of the militia survivors weren't. But the doctors from the debriefing on Annecy were. What were their names again? Chapman? Salo? She couldn't remember the third. But all three wore grim expressions, medical comm pads blinking in their hands.

"Please," the captain said, not even bothering with her usual fake smile. "Have a seat."

He's dead, Saskia thought, sliding down at the table. She blinked back tears, tried not to scream.

One of the doctors—Dr. Salo by her name tag—tapped on her comm pad.

"What's going on?" Dorian demanded as he careened through the door.

Captain Dellatorre looked over at him calmly. "What have I told you about following protocol?"

Dorian scowled, but he stiffened his shoulders, threw up a salute.

"Thank you. Let's wait until we're all here."

Immediately, Evie strolled in after Dorian, her face pale, her eyes red. Saskia watched Owen as he watched Evie and Dorian take their seats. Did he know why they were here? His face was expressionless.

The captain cleared her throat. "I have some bad news," she began.

"Is Victor dead?" Saskia blurted, the guilt of the idea pulsing with her heartbeat.

"No." Captain Dellatorre paused. "Not yet."

"Not yet?" Owen leaned forward, his features dark with concern. So he hadn't known. The thought comforted Saskia. "Ma'am, what do you mean?"

The captain sighed. "Victor's injuries were severe but nothing that we haven't treated before—second- and third-degree burns, smoke inhalation. These are serious issues, yes, but easily remedied."

"So what's the problem?" Evie asked.

Captain Dellatorre looked down at her comm pad. "The problem," she said, "is that Victor is not responding to any of the treatments."

Saskia frowned. "What do you mean? How could they not be working?"

"That was what we were wondering." She nodded at Dr. Salo. Outside of a holo, it was clear her long hair was dark gray, not black, and she looked much more tired. "Dr. Salo has been handling Victor's case. Please, tell them what you found."

Dr. Salo looked out at the table. "We ran several tests, when the treatments were proving impotent," she said. "What we found was—it was unnerving."

Saskia felt a hollowness inside her chest. She dug her fingers into the chair.

"The reason Victor is not responding to treatments is because he appears to have some kind of medical anomaly. We cannot determine the source. It doesn't look like anything we've seen before."

"What?" Evie whispered. "What do you mean, you haven't seen anything like it? Like, it's a new kind of virus?"

"It's not a virus at all," Dr. Salo said. "It's not bacterial either. It seems genetic in some way, but his previous medical files all show the same tests coming back normal. Regardless, it doesn't seem to be acting like a typical genetic condition. We simply"—she held out her hands—"don't know."

"So what's going to happen to him? Is he going to die?" Saskia asked.

"We're keeping him alive for now," Captain Dellatorre said.

For now? Saskia looked over at Evie and Dorian, thinking back on that strange conversation in the field. Evie was pale, her eyes wide, and Dorian looked furious—he had the air of someone who had just had his worst suspicions proven right.

"However, there is more."

Saskia turned back to the doctor, her breath caught in her throat.

"We have theorized that Victor's complication came from exposure to the Forerunner artifacts. There are certain . . . symmetries in the samples we've taken from him and samples that the Forerunner team is working with. I'm afraid the connection is undeniable."

"Oh no," Saskia whispered, the realization crawling over her like a mist.

"As you'll recall, we took blood samples from all of you after you returned from Meridian. We wanted to test you—all five of you, including Spartan-B096." Dr. Salo nodded at Dr. Chapman, who tapped on his comm pad. "We have the results now."

Saskia felt numb. She flashed back to the blood test when they'd gotten off-world—she thought it was standard, that they were just making sure she wasn't sick. Captain Dellatorre sat with her hands folded in her lap, looking down at her comm pad. Did she and the rest of ONI know this was a possibility? Had they sent them into that structure with the understanding that this would happen?

"What is it?" Dorian demanded. "What's the result? You can say it in front of all of us; we don't have secrets." He shot a glare at Owen when he said this. Owen didn't react.

"Ms. Rousseau," Dr. Faraday said. "I'm afraid your sample is positive."

Evie gasped, let out a sob. Saskia reached across the table, grabbed Evie's hand. Dorian threw his arm around her shoulder. Saskia knew she didn't need to hear the rest of the samples. They would all be positive.

Still, she squeezed Evie's hand as tight as she could while the results were read.

Dorian: Positive.

Saskia: Positive.

"Spartan-B096," Dr. Faraday said. "You're negative."

Saskia whipped her head around. Owen's usual stoic expression flashed away, just for a second. He seemed—shocked. And perhaps a little guilty.

"So your theory was correct," the captain said.

"Theory?" Saskia looked over at her. "What theory? You said you'd never seen this before!"

Dr. Salo blushed. "We theorized that Spartan-B096 might not be affected, due to the treatments he received as a child, during the SPARTAN-III augmentation process."

Saskia sat up, her heart pounding.

"At this point, I need to note that what you're hearing is classified and well beyond your scope of clearance," the captain said, and Saskia felt a surge of rage.

I'm just tired of the secrets, Evie had said, and Saskia, in this moment, was too.

But Captain Dellatorre continued. "However, for the sake of the situation, it warrants an explanation. I'll tell you as much as I'm able." She took a deep breath. "All Spartan-IIIs have their genetic code modified as part of their treatment. Somehow, that genetic modification inoculated B096 against the aftereffects of exposure to the artifact."

"So where does that leave us?" Evie asked. "What good does it do us that Owen is immune? What good does it do Victor?"

Dr. Salo looked over at Captain Dellatorre. There was something in Dr. Salo's expression that made Saskia want to look away.

Captain Dellatorre leaned forward, her hands folded in front of her. She seemed like a kind but strict teacher, someone with bad news who still wants the best for you.

"This gives us," she said, "an opportunity."

"What?" shouted Dorian. "What the hell is that supposed to mean?"

"Dorian," Owen said in a low voice. "Enough."

"Don't tell me what's enough!" Dorian yelled, standing. "Our friend is dying, and we've got the same thing. You all don't give a damn about us—"

"If you would follow protocol and let me finish," the captain said, "then you would know that I'm trying to save Victor's life. You of all people, Mr. Nguyen, should appreciate this. It was your idea, after all, to procure the artifact from Brume-sur-Mer in the first place. Had you followed protocol then, we might be in a different situation now. There's a solution to this problem, but it's going to take you listening for once instead of running your mouth. Do you understand that, Mr. Nguyen?"

A heavy silence moved through the room. Dorian stared at her. For a moment, Saskia thought he was going to stalk out of the room and straight into a dishonorable discharge—if that was even possible given their paramilitary status. But then his shoulders slumped and his expression softened. "Really? There's a way—"

"Yes. We're giving Victor and all of you an opportunity to *survive*."

More silence. Saskia felt the weight of her fear and her doubts pressing down on her. Something had felt off ever since they arrived back at the base. She was starting to understand why.

"Captain," Owen said. "Is there a treatment?"

"Not directly, no. We've never seen this anomaly before. But given what we know so far, all four of you will likely benefit from a new program we've been developing. It is an experimental procedure, somewhat similar to the procedure Spartan-B096 went through. However, it's designed for older subjects."

A chill raced through Saskia's body. She thought of Owen explaining how he'd come to be, the way he'd skirted around the reality of the treatments he'd been given.

"We are looking to develop the next wave of Spartans," the captain said. "Not children who have been trained and modified, but adults. We have already begun to administer the procedure to Victor, and so far he seems to be responding favorably to the treatment. It was our one shot at saving him. Now we'd like to save you as well."

"You've already started the program on Victor?" Evie asked. "Do his parents know?"

"Of course." Captain Dellatorre laughed a little, shook her head. "You all really think we're boogeymen, don't you? They granted us permission. They want their son to survive."

Dorian scoffed. "Is there a guarantee it will do that?"

"He's going to die if we don't do anything," the captain said. "And while the three of you are healthy now, there's no reason to think you will stay that way. One injury, one sickness . . . it could kill you."

Saskia dug her nails into the skin of her arms, fear surging up inside her.

"But if it works," Captain Dellatorre said, "not only will it stem the complications you've incurred by your contact to the Forerunner artifacts, but you will be different. You will be stronger. Faster. Better in every way." She smiled at Owen. "Just like him. And you'll be helping to usher in a new age of Spartans to lead us in the fight against the Covenant. You can help ensure that what happened on Meridian doesn't happen anywhere else. You've seen it yourselves these past few months: Spartans are our best hope at stopping this enemy. With this procedure, you can protect your families. You can help ensure that what has happened on Meridian doesn't happen anywhere else." She took a deep breath. "But I won't sugarcoat it: As dangerous as the procedure to become a Spartan is, it's not nearly as dangerous as actually being one. I'm sorry this happened to the four of you, I truly am—but these are the cards you've been dealt."

"May I say something, Captain?" Dorian's voice cut through the thick quiet. Saskia couldn't tell if he was feigning respect, or if he was really serious this time.

Captain Dellatore nodded.

"You have us here, isolated from our families, in a desperate situation with no apparent alternatives, and you expect us to feel like this is our decision?"

Captain Dellatorre lifted her chin, considering him. "Do you remember what I told you before you agreed to sign on, Mr. Nguyen?"

A pause. "You told me I wasn't a child."

"You're not, Mr. Nguyen. And the UNSC has been telling that to people your age for the last twenty-five years. They told it to me when I was your age, and they told it to my predecessor before me. This is what it is to go to war for our right to exist. If you want to see future generations, then you need to think very hard about what the right step forward is. I understand you've lost people on Meridian. There are millions of others who have lost people just like you have and billions more who will if we don't stop this enemy. You're not a child, Mr. Nguyen, and you can't afford to continue to think like one."

Dorian stared at the wall behind the captain, his jaw tightening.

She stood up, gathered her comm pad. "Take a day to think it over. But I will need your answer by 1700 tomorrow."

"I can't believe Victor's parents agreed to it," Dorian said, his footsteps echoing off the walls. "It's . . . it's a life debt to ONI. Have you read the papers? Just when we thought we were getting out of this, we're enlisting for life."

"Victor's parents were probably desperate," Evie said quietly. "Like we all are. Their son can live, can become a hero for the UNSC—something he already wanted."

Dorian slammed his fist against the wall. "No, I mean I literally can't believe it. Do you think they *really* got his parents' permission? What if they're just doing it?"

"Oh, calm down. Yeah, they haven't been entirely honest with us, but they also had no way of knowing what would happen inside the structure. I mean, we're far from the perfect candidates to become Spartans. You can barely follow orders, and I'm not some expert marksman. None of us even wanted to join the military before this happened. And have you seen the other candidates? Their achievements are—" She waved her hands around. "Honestly, we're lucky they're even agreeing to give us this opportunity!"

Saskia lagged behind Dorian and Evie, only half listening to their exchange. It was the next day, and she had only five hours to decide if she wanted to go through with the treatment. All night she had lain awake, thinking back to her conversation with Owen, then imagining some alien creature growing inside her, crawling up the walls of her blood cells, changing her somehow.

A new procedure, she thought as Dorian's and Evie's voices drifted around her. Not the exact same as what Owen went through. Perhaps it was easier, though the captain had made it clear it wasn't without risk. If it was designed for adults, there was no way ONI could indoctrinate her or the others the way Owen had been. Even though she had to admit that his indoctrination was the only reason she was alive—she just didn't want it happening to her. Perhaps that was selfish. But it was also a comfort.

No, her concerns were more that the procedure was *new*. Untested. Potentially unsafe. And there was no guarantee that it would stop the genetic alterations in their system.

No guarantee they would survive the genetic alterations without treatment either.

She swiped through all the paperwork ONI had given her—waivers of liability, descriptions of what would happen to her. The paperwork made her feel comforted too. It was a show of respect. They were letting her make the choice.

Her thoughts kept swinging back and forth, even as they approached the medical wing. The nurse at the entrance glanced up at them, gave them a kind smile.

"I was told you'd be stopping by," she said. "Please, we need to confirm your identities." She gestured at the hand scanner fixed on the table. Saskia pressed her palm to the glass. A swoop of heat and then the door clicked open.

"Third door on the left," the nurse said.

Saskia waited for the others, and then they went into the corridor together. The lights were bright but sallow, the air tinged with a chemical scent that burned the back of Saskia's throat.

"Third door on the left," Dorian said when they arrived at it. He pushed it open. The air inside was unmoving, almost stale, that medicinal scent so strong as to be overpowering. The pod clicked and hummed and hissed, and as they approached, the lights flickered on inside it, revealing Victor, naked save for a strip of cloth across his waist and the wires crawling over his body, hooking him up to the machinery.

Evie let out a whimper, pressed her hand to her mouth. Saskia moved closer to her. Victor's skin was splotchy and red from the burns, and his face was drawn, his unburned skin ashy, almost gray. If it weren't for the rise and fall of his chest, he would have looked dead.

They stared at him for a long time. There was no sound but the pod equipment and an occasional sniffle from Evie. Saskia couldn't tear her eyes away from Victor, looking so lifeless and worn out in the midst of all that life-saving technology that just . . . wouldn't work.

And then she thought of Owen, healthy, strong. Not dying in a gray shriveled heap in a hospital wing.

And then she thought of herself. What would it be that would activate the anomaly? How serious an injury would she have to sustain before her body refused all treatment? A broken leg? A paper cut?

How long before she was lying in a healing pod, not healing at all?

"I can see why his parents agreed to the treatment," Evie said suddenly, in a quiet voice. "Anything is better than this."

Dorian kept staring at Victor. "I think you're right. Still." His frown deepened, turned into a scowl. "This would never have happened if they hadn't sent him to Annecy."

"But it *did* happen," Evie said. "And it was Victor. He wanted to go—he wanted to fight to stop the Covenant. He wanted to fight for Meridian. His parents signed the waivers, but what do you think he would say? Would he agree to the procedure?"

Dorian didn't respond. They all knew the answer.

Saskia drifted up to the healing pod, placed her hand against the glass. It was warm to the touch, like a human body. When she dropped her hand away, her fingerprints remained like ghosts.

Looking at Victor was like cutting herself with a piece of glass. It was a pain that would scar. Because it should have been her drifting in that pod, floating toward an unknowable death.

"The captain was right. We aren't children anymore," she whispered, watching her reflection in the glass. "This is about ONI being resourceful. They have a chance to save us and develop their new program—of course they're going to take it. My parents were the same way. Not cruel. Not totally benevolent either. Just . . . in between. They did what they needed to survive. I guess that's the cost of this war." She lifted her gaze until she saw Dorian and Evie behind her in the reflection.

"And I don't want to die," she said. "Not like this."

She turned around, trembling. Evie and Dorian stared at her.

"Are you saying—"

I lost my family, and ONI gave me a new one.

"At least we know we'll be helping save humanity," she said. "Regardless of what happens."

Evie and Dorian looked at each other.

"What do we have to lose?" she said. "Our lives?" She gestured at Victor. "I'm willing to at least try."

Evie stepped forward, pulled Saskia into an embrace. "Me too," she whispered.

Saskia felt the tears then, a hot flood that she wiped furiously away, certain Dorian would make fun of her. She looked up at him, but his face was twisted up too, and she realized there were tears in his eyes.

"I'm not letting you two do this alone," he said.

And then he threw his arms around both of them, bringing them in for an embrace. Saskia tried not to think about the future. It was nothing like the future she had ever imagined for herself.

But at least in this future, she had a family.

ABOUT THE AUTHOR

Lightbox Shop Photography

CASSANDRA ROSE CLARKE's work has been nominated for the Philip K. Dick Award, the *Romantic Times* Reviewer's Choice Award, the Pushcart Prize, and YALSA's Best Fiction for Young Adults. She grew up in south Texas and currently lives in a suburb of Houston, where she writes and serves as the associate director for Writespace, a literary arts nonprofit. She holds an MA in creative writing from The University of Texas at Austin, and in 2010 she attended the Clarion West Writer's Workshop in Seattle.

DIVE DEEPER INTO THE HALO UNIVERSE!

Explore the first book in the **HALO: BATTLE BORN** series and brush up on Spartan protocol in the first ever **OFFICIAL SPARTAN FIELD MANUAL**!